OWEN OLIVER

Also by Lena Kennedy

AUTUMN ALLEY
DANDELION SEED
DOWN OUR STREET
EVE'S APPLES
LADY PENELOPE
LILY, MY LOVELY
LIZZIE
MAGGIE
NELLY KELLY
SUSAN

Owen Oliver

by

LENA KENNEDY

GUILD PUBLISHING
LONDON · NEW YORK · SYDNEY · TORONTO

This edition published 1990 by
Guild Publishing
by arrangement with Macdonald & Co Ltd.
First reprint 1991

CN 2273

Printed in England by Clays Ltd, St Ives plc

CHAPTER ONE

Good-bye, London

Owen Oliver sat in his bare attic with his head in his hands thinking gloomily about his predicament. Outside the sooty window all he could see were London chimney pots. Immediately around him were the bare necessities he needed for living – a few books, a low bed in the corner and a plain wooden table which served as both desk and diner.

Twiddling his long quill pen around in its ornate green inkstand, he was reminded of his father. This quill was a relic of more prosperous times and it had belonged to his late father before he was sent off to the debtors' prison.

Today Owen was feeling very lonely as his mind wandered to thoughts of his lost love, a sweet, high-bred and very pure young lady. But how cruel she had been! He had been such a fool to aim so high! He had loved her desperately. Running his fingers nervously through his brown curls, he picked up the sheet of perfumed paper which lay before him. He had read it so many times but it hurt him anew as he read it again: 'I never want to see or hear of you again.'

Screwing the paper up in his hand he threw it violently on to the floor. Tears rushed to his dark blue eyes as he looked despairingly about the gloomy room, at the dirty grey walls, the smoke-blackened beams over his head and the cheerless fireless grate. It was so depressing, spelling of nothing but poverty.

He suddenly felt very claustrophobic and had an overpowering urge to get out, away from his grim surroundings. He could escape from his attic room but he was unable to get away from that whispering voice in his head which taunted him constantly.

'You,' it said. 'You are nothing, a nobody, just like your initials.'

Grabbing his hat from behind the door, Owen placed it on his head and then wriggled into a tight, faded jacket. Within seconds, he was running down the stairs and out into the crowded streets outside.

It was Saturday afternoon and a huge crowd of people milled towards London Bridge. Like a leaf in the breeze, Owen let himself be carried along by them. In his confused, depressed state of mind he was hardly aware of the jangle of unknown voices, the jostling fat buttocks of women pushing against him, or large bonnets and huge bundles which obscured his vision as the local population went home from the market or fought to get to the wrestling match on the other side of the bridge. Everyone was determined to get across that river and they pushed and shoved and trampled on each other in their effort to do so.

Owen had not got very far. In fact he had only just reached the bottom of the slope which led up to the bridge when he suddenly had to stop and cling to the railings. A gargoyle grinned down at him with a hideous expression. Owen was breathless and realised that he was now panting with fear. For in fact crowds made him nervous. They made him feel as claustrophobic as he had been in his lodgings. The panic he experienced always took him back to his childhood, with memories of dark cupboards and screeching, quarrelling parents.

The two-way traffic on the narrow road was causing havoc. Fighting for space to move were wagons loaded with farm produce, stage coaches with high roofs, and horse-drawn buses which competed with coster barrows and gentlemen on horse-back. Whips cracked, wheels collided, drivers swore loudly while the women on the pavements giggled and screamed as horses reared up in terror. It seemed that all sign of sanity had disappeared on that Saturday afternoon on London Bridge.

Owen held on tightly to the railings and looked down into the river, at the swirling rubbish floating on the surface of the foaming water churned up by the mail boats. Suddenly the pressure of the crowd loosened its hold and Owen was on the move . He allowed himself to be carried along again, like that rubbish under the bridge.

'Keep calm,' he told himself repeatedly. 'Don't panic. Eventually you will get out at the other end.'

He was almost half-way over when his passage was blocked by a huge dray, full of barrels and pulled by two dapple-grey shire horses. It was stationary and the big muscular driver was holding a heated argument with a bucolic gentleman on horseback.

'Git over!' the driver roared. 'Git that bleedin' old nag on its way afor it drops dead on yer!'

Recognising the voice, Owen looked up to see the rugged face of an old acquaintance, Jed, looking down at him. Jed saw him at the same time and leaned down to give Owen a poke in the ribs with his long whip. 'Hey there, lad,' he called in a throaty voice, 'What are you doing down there? Get up on the cart. It's safer among them barrels than with those dratted maniacs down there!'

With a sigh of relief, Owen climbed up onto the cart and sank down between the barrels of wine. As he closed his eyes in relief, he was aware of how weak he had become. But whether it was fear or the fact that he had not eaten much food recently, he did not know. How foolish he was to get so nervous! Surely it was time he learned to control these feelings!

The old wagon rumbled on over the cobbles with Jed swearing under his breath and cracking his whip until they were at last over the bridge. Now the traffic was slowly levelling out and the crowd of pedestrians dispersed in various directions.

'How far yer going, mate?' called the carter. 'You'd better come on up to this end and we can have a chat. It never ought to be allowed, having all these folk on the bridge. It's going to collapse one day, mark my words, and drop the whole blooming lot in the river.'

Owen moved up to the end of the wagon and seated himself on a barrel. He was beginning to feel much better as a fresh breeze blew across the fields at Greenwich.

'It was rather overcrowded,' he agreed quietly.

'Seen it worse,' replied Jed. 'Takes me nigh on an hour to come over some days. It didn't ought to be allowed, I say. You're off to the fair, no doubt?' he queried.

'No, sir,' replied Owen. 'Just taking a breath of fresh air.'

'Well, that's free and it's all we'll be able to afford soon. Look at me – working overtime when I should be home with the wife and children,' he complained.

Jed hardly paused for breath as he kept up his patter while the strong grey cart-horses pulled the wagon up the steep hill.

Owen leaned back. He felt warm and comfortable sitting in his seat just behind Jed's broad back and in the wagon which smelled so sweetly of wine. Jed was just like a ship's captain, a husky soul, so fearless and brave on that high seat. It was strange how these earthy folk soothed and calmed Owen. With them he almost felt secure and happy. What could be their secret?

'I've got some deliveries to make at the White Hart,' Jed continued to talk in his slow voice. 'Then it's back down the road for me, lad, to me little old house in Woolwich. You coming all the way with me?'

'No, thank you, I'll get off at the top of the hill, if you don't mind,' replied Owen.

'Well, don't get lost,' warned Jed. 'It's not safe up here after dark, what with footpads and gawd knows what evils.'

Owen slipped quickly down from the cart and said good-bye to Jed as the old wagon lumbered on.

For a while, Owen Oliver stood still looking down at the big city of London lying down in the valley. He could see church spires, it seemed, everywhere, and behind the banked-up storm clouds, the sun cast red and grey shadows across the scene. Yes, the world itself was really beautiful, he thought, watching how a breeze rustled the tree tops, and the setting sun turn the tips of the leaves to gold. Owen sighed. He was surrounded by so much beauty and he wanted so much to express it in words or pictures. But he always failed. Other people distracted him, brought out his nervousness, and caused him to stammer. Invariably he would find himself withdrawing into glum silence.

In his mind's eye there appeared again, his lost love, with her soft fair hair under the little bonnets, and that unforgettable, demure expression as she passed him the *billet doux* she had pulled from the fur muff when she came to the bookshop where he worked.

Owen had been instantly smitten and poured out his heart to

her in pages of passionate verse. And then she had mocked
him, read his poetry out loud to her giggling companions.

Now he wished he had not crept into the garden unan-
nounced! A true gentleman would have known how to retire
gracefully, but he, fool that he was, had screamed and shouted,
danced and gibbered like a monkey. Yes, it was quite obvious
to everyone that he was not well-bred. So why did he bother?
He was as poor as a church mouse. Why could he not be
simple, hard-working and happy like the carter?

On top of that lonely hill, Owen Oliver commiserated with
himself as the chill evening air made him shiver. The sun, a
great ball of red fire, had now begun to disappear over the
horizon. Soon it would be night. He had better return to
London.

So back to the noise and violence of the big city at night
Owen turned. Automatically he headed for a footpath and
walked in the direction of the city. Soon the moon was up,
casting its silver light on the long figure crossing the rough
heath.

The rutted path seemed endless as it wound its way over
heathland. Owen had lost all sense of direction. He was not at
all sure where he was going. The fingers of bracken glittered in
the moonlight and strange shadows were cast across his path.
Ahead there seemed to be a grey mist and a vast expanse of
blackness.

Owen felt as though he were walking to the edge of the
world. Breathing deeply, he filled his lungs with cool sweet air
and swung his long thin arms energetically. His spirits were
suddenly surprisingly higher. Here I am, he thought, a nobody
going nowhere.

Sometimes he jumped a ditch, sometimes he climbed a gate.
Rabbits scattered ahead of him, owls hooted in the trees.
Driven by some uncontrollable force, he went on and on.

The moon had begun to wane, and a wet mist penetrated his
coat. As his legs began to feel numb, his eyes ached and sanity
began to return. What a fool he was to walk so far! Owen
pulled his jacket collar up about his ears as far as he could and
shivered. Around him it looked very creepy. He could just
make out thick woods and a vast misty plain. Perhaps he ought
to turn back. He slowly came to a halt and stood with hands in
his pockets wondering what to do, when suddenly a black and

white bull terrier came bounding towards him. It did not seem very friendly as it growled and bared its teeth. Owen was afraid of dogs and his knees went weak.

Suddenly a gruff voice from the hedge called, 'Come back, Old Dawg, come back I say.'

Then there was much grunting and swearing as a huge figure rose from the wayside. The man towered over Owen, and he seemed to be as wide as he was high, and virtually shapeless, bundled up with thick clothes. Around his neck was wound a long woollen scarf, and a heavy top coat was hitched about his shoulders. Although his voice was gruff, it was not unpleasant. He puffed for breath as he spoke. 'Don't let that little tyke worry you. He's only guarding me. I was having a little kip, though I didn't mean to sleep so long.'

The man looked up at the sky. 'It must be getting nigh dawn,' he said.

Owen gazed at the fellow with apprehension as he watched him reach out for the thick nobbly stick, but he relaxed when he said, 'Coming my way lad?'

Owen eyed the dog warily. 'I was thinking of turning back here,' he said.

The man snorted. 'Turn back?' he cried. 'Why, it's bloody miles to the road. Where are you heading for, then?'

'Nowhere in particular,' Owen replied lamely.

Two deep brown eyes surveyed him shrewdly. Then the man coughed loudly and spat into the hedge. 'You're on the road, then?' he stated.

Owen nodded. He could not think of anything to say.

'Well then,' said the huge man, 'you'd better come along with me, 'cause we knows the way, don't we, Old Dawg?'

So the man's burly shape rolled on, with the dog skipping and jumping beside him. Owen tagged along behind.

The pace was brisk because it was now all downhill. Owen's new acquaintance sang sea shanties and occasionally broke into conversation. 'Knows this path like me own backside,' he boasted. 'I'd like a sovereign for the times I walked it – drunk and sober.'

Owen was still a little afraid. He said nothing and just listened.

'We've been down to Bexley to do a bit of ratting,' the man explained. 'See that there Old Dawg? He can kill seven rats at one go. Champion, he is. He's won me a packet tonight. That's how I got a drink too many and missed the wagon. But it doesn't matter. I walk home more often than I ride on Saturday nights,' he chuckled.

The man turned and gave the glum-looking Owen a shrewd glance.

'On the way to Dover, I suppose, are you? Most gents that come this way are going to find better prospects abroad, they say. Baloney, says I. There ain't no place like England. And as for Kent, why, Kent's the best place in the whole world.

'Are we in Kent then?' ventured Owen timidly.

The man nodded. 'Where I met you it was the border. From now on it's the Weald all the way down to Rochester. If you are wise, you will rest up in Rochester and wait for a hitch down to Dover, because it's a bloody long road otherwise.' He seemed to have convinced himself that Owen was heading for Dover and Owen was too tired to disillusion him.

Through muddy ploughed fields they trod, and on through apple orchards where the trees stood like lines of soldiers. Daylight came slowly, pink and silver intermixed. A cold wind had blown up and the birds were beginning to rustle in their nests and get ready to greet the day with a song.

'Come on, lad,' said Owen's companion, 'get a move on. We'll just get down there at daybreak in time for refreshment with the shepherds.'

Once down the hill the land flattened out into low-lying meadows washed by the morning dew. Now a pale sun peeped over the horizon. The air was suddenly filled with the sound of bleating sheep and barking dogs. The bull terrier went wild with excitement and dashed ahead as fast as his four legs could carry him.

'Tired, boy?' The man asked, as he saw Owen trudging along with his eyes half shut. 'We'll be down there soon and we'll get a nice hot brew.' He rubbed his large hands in anticipation.

Soon they came to a large barn. The sound of sheep bleating in the pens inside was almost deafening, while outside the barn, seated around a bucket fire, were half-a-dozen shepherds, the long crooks of their trade beside them.

'Howde, lads!' roared the big man.

'Howde, Tom!' they all cried back in unison.

Owen crouched beside the fire, scrutinising the shepherds' wrinkled faces, as they slurped down a hot beverage from tin mugs. A young lad produced two mugs for Tom and Owen and one of the old men filled them with the hot milky liquid.

Owen drank it gratefully. It was very satisfying, and suffused him with warmth right down to his toes. It was hot milk spiked with something delicious. He felt so drowsy, he nodded in the heat of the fire until a hefty poke in the ribs from Tom suggested that he go into the barn and take a nap before he fell into the fire itself.

Owen went to the barn and crept into the warm sweet-smelling hay. Within seconds he was asleep.

An hour later a large boot nudged him. 'Get moving lad.' It was Tom.

The young lambs were calling plaintively for their mothers. Owen yawned. He felt wonderfully relaxed and just wanted to remain snuggled down in the sweet warm hay.

'Hi, there,' growled Tom. 'Come on, let's hit the road.'

When Owen finally pulled himself up and staggered into the bright sunshine, Tom was engaged in a long conversation with one of the old shepherds whose accent was as thick and rich as country butter.

'Roit,' he was saying, 'Be orf naw then, oi be getting a bit low on the hard stuff, Taamy lad.'

'See you in town on market day, old son,' replied Tom, giving the old man a thump on the back. 'A nice drop o' the ol' Jamacy, how's that?'

So it had been rum that had spiced the morning brew thought Owen. Rum presumably provided by this amiable giant, too.

Tom whistled to Old Dawg, who came bounding over the fields, and the threesome set off once more over the hills and dales. As they jumped wide dykes full of water, and negotiated the wooden stiles, Owen's jovial companion talked, sang and whistled.

'Look down there,' Tom said suddenly. 'That, mate, is the old Thames.'

Owen thought he could have been talking about a personal friend. He gazed down at the long silver strip that wound over the green marshland. 'It is a magnificent view,' he said mildly.

'Why, that's the best damned sight in the world,' shouted

Tom. 'How many deep sea sailors would give anything to see the old Thames and home port?' For the first time he looked rather aggressively at Owen. 'Don't suppose you ever went to sea, sonny. It don't look as if you got enough guts in yer.'

Owen felt downcast. 'No,' he said. 'I never did much with my life, and what I have done has not been of my own choice.'

The serious brown eyes under the wide slouch hat immediately became sympathetic. Tom placed a gentle arm about Owen's shoulders. 'Take no notice of me, lad,' he said. 'I'm a rough ol' fella but I do know what you mean – little kids slaving in mines, honest men rotting in the debtors' prison. That's why I love the country life, and the things that God provided, not man.'

Owen was curiously comforted by this boisterous confident character.

Soon they approached a little hamlet where field workers hailed them, and children came out to run and laugh beside them.

'The next cottage we come to is my home,' Tom informed Owen. 'You'd better come and have a bite of breakfast with me. Then I'll put you on the right road for Rochester.'

Owen was about to confess that he intended to return to London but Tom had forged ahead and was waving one great arm at a lady who stood in front of the most picturesque cottage Owen had ever seen. It had low eaves, a tall brick chimney, and a tiny porch hung with honeysuckle. At the gate stood a tiny lady whose hair was held neatly in place by a small lace cap with frilled edges which fell about a small waxen face. The bright blue eyes stared out sharply at the two men. Her black dress curved out from a wasp waist and a wide lace collar covered her neck and shoulders.

'It's me, Ma,' said Tom. 'Go on, Old Dawg,' he muttered, 'Go tell her we's home.'

The terrier sped off towards the gate, yelping a loud welcome. Reaching the woman, he suddenly put his tail between his legs and slunk off towards the back of the cottage.

'It don't look so good,' muttered Tom.

The lady stood perfectly still, her face stern and unsmiling. Her hands in their lace mittens were crossed passively on her white apron.

'What's yer name, boy?' whispered Tom.

'Owen Oliver,' Owen replied.

'Hello, Ma,' said Tom brightly as they drew close. 'Here's me friend Olly come to see yer.'

The woman did not smile or even move a muscle except her lips. 'You have been out all night,' she said accusingly.

'I know, Ma, couldn't help it,' Tom shouted straight into her ear.

Owen assumed that the lady was stone deaf. 'Meet me friend Olly,' he said. 'Walking to Dover, he is.'

'Who?' his mother demanded, casting a sharp glance at Owen.

'His name is Olly. He's down on his luck. On the road, he was, Ma.' From that moment Owen was always called Olly by his new friend.

'Don't know no Ossies.' Tom's mother grumbled. 'Where does he come from?'

'From London, Ma,' Tom proclaimed loudly.

There was a glint in those stony eyes at the mention of the capital city.

'All right,' she said, 'better come in and have some breakfast. I'll deal with you later, young Tom.'

With sly nudges and sniggers, Tom edged Owen into the cottage. Owen realised that he was being used as an excuse for Tom's night out.

Soon he was sitting in front of a table loaded with hot milky porridge, bacon and eggs and freshly baked bread. What a feast! Such a feast for an empty stomach!

Neat and precise, Tom's mother sat at the table. A stern light appeared in her eyes every time she looked at her errant son. 'Eat hearty, Ossie,' she told him. 'You look undernourished, boy. Still, I know times can be hard up in London and good food is not easy to come by.'

'We are Londoners, you know,' said Tom proudly.

''Tis now a very dirty town by all accounts,' said his mother. 'I've never regretted leaving it behind.'

'It is a very crowded city, ma'am,' said Owen politely.

'You are a very well-spoken lad. Why have you left home?' the old lady asked.

'My parents are dead, ma'am, and for a long time I have earned my own living.'

In spite of her deafness, Tom's mother was well able to

converse, her keen eyes watching every movement of Owen's lips. But each time her son addressed her, he leaned forward and shouted in her ear, as he did now. 'Shall I tell him, Ma?'

A strange, secretive smile crossed her tight lips as she nodded assent. Tom told Owen of how he and his mother had also walked from London many years before. 'Me Pa was injured in the seamen's hospital in Chatham and me two brothers were missing at sea. We came to get news of them, but it was no good. My brothers' ship was lost and Pa only lived a few days.

'We had run out of money, so we started to walk back. I was only a lad, just ten year old, wasn't I, Ma?' Tom shouted in her ear.

Tom's mother patted her son's hand indulgently as if giving him permission to proceed.

As he watched them, Owen was acutely aware of the warm bond of affection that existed between this tiny mother and her big childish son. 'So we got lost,' Tom continued. 'We were ragged and starving, and didn't know where we were. Then one stormy night a curate came riding by and picked us up. We've not looked back since.'

Now Tom's mother picked up the story, and described to Owen how ill she had been but how she had recovered and subsequently taken a domestic post in the curate's household. It was, she said, a post she still held.

'So you see, Olly,' said Tom, 'we know all about being on the road.'

Owen smiled sheepishly. He was feeling very warm and relaxed with these two kind people, though deep down he did feel a little shifty. Tom and his mother seemed to believe that he was a homeless lad, and had been so spontaneous in their desire to feed and sustain him. And, of course, that was not the case at all. He wanted to tell them the truth, to be frank and open with them, but his confounded nervousness prevented him from doing so.

'There's no need to hurry away, Olly,' said Tom. 'Ma likes you, and anyway, it's Sunday. Stay a while, come for a walk around the village with me.'

'Why not?' chirped Tom's mother. 'It will keep Tom out of mischief, the company of a nice lad like you.'

Owen shook his head. 'But I can't accept your hospitality. I'm

Owen Oliver

a very poor lad and am unable to repay you,' he protested.

'Bosh!' declared the old lady. 'Take him away with you, Tom, by all means, but there are a few chores to do before you go gallivanting.'

So Owen helped Tom collect wood from the forest behind the cottage and stack it against the side wall. They pulled up large green cabbages and onions, and collected the eggs from the hens.

With the chores done, the two men washed under the pump in the yard before setting off for Tom's favourite tavern out in the marsh.

The Lobster Inn was a veritable smugglers' retreat. Farm labourers, fishermen and sailors home from sea all congregated there under the low ceilings and chatted and enjoyed the strong cider the innkeeper offered. When Tom and Owen arrived, the other men were playing a popular game called Rings, in which each player threw a ring at a bullock's head on the wall. Tom joined in immediately and laughed, shouted and swore with vigour. But Owen sat by the wall, mute as always.

'Who's the odd fella?' a sailor asked.

'He's a pal of mine,' replied Tom aggressively. 'He's down on his luck and walking to Dover.'

From then on it was drink-up-mate-and-have-another, but two half pints was all Owen could manage. He longed to be able to get up and shout and join in with the rest of them but it was impossible. He just sat tongue-tied and stiff. He felt very pathetic.

'We'll have a little kip in the orchard,' Tom said. 'We'll wait until the old lady goes to church. That way she won't smell the booze.'

Owen sat in the long grass with his back against a gnarled old apple tree while Tom stretched out nearby. He slept with his mouth wide open and snoring like an old badger. Owen wondered what he should do. Perhaps he ought to creep away, he thought. This was all fine while it lasted but he was accepting Tom's friendship under false pretences. But the peace and beauty all around held him; he could not make himself go.

At seven o'clock that evening, Owen stood in the front row of an old Norman church. Tom was looking very spruce in his black Sunday suit and stiff collar, and next to him stood his little mother in her blue bonnet covered with flowers. Mother and son shared a hymn book and sang all those God-fearing hymns in strong voices.

After the service Owen was introduced to the curate. He was a young man, their old benefactor having passed on some time ago. Then the three of them went home to a large supper of cold meat and pickles. By ten o'clock Owen was in the attic in a comfortable bed which smelled of lavender. And London seemed a long long way away.

CHAPTER TWO

Rural Comforts

Owen was woken by the lusty crowing of the young cockerel and the clucking of the hens. It was just dawn. He lay in his warm bed wondering what he was going to do. It was Monday and if he was not in the shop by nine o'clock he would probably lose his post. And such steady positions were not easy to get. Despite such thoughts, he continued to feel very relaxed. He lay back with his arms behind his head, enjoying the quiet atmosphere of the small neat attic with its clean patchwork bedspread and pretty curtains. It was all so different from the bare garret he had left behind.

'Time to get up, Olly!' Tom's gruff voice called from the bottom of the stairs. 'I have to be out early this morning.'

When Owen went downstairs, he found Tom, clad in his farm boots and woollen jersey, clumping in and out, bringing in wood and buckets of clean water, while Tom's little mother stood over a pot on the stove stirring the hot bubbling porridge.

The smell of the appetising hot meal was very welcoming and Owen managed to devour two bowls of porridge and three slices of bread and jam. On the table were two packages containing sandwiches.

'There's a bite for you to eat on your way, lad,' said Ma. ''Tis a pity you're leaving us.'

'I don't see why he don't stay,' grumbled Tom. 'A clever boy that can no doubt read and write. What's he want to go wandering for?'

'There might be a job for him with Uncle Dobbs,' suggested Ma.

14

'Good idea,' cried Tom, 'always in a muddle, is Old Dobbs. I don't know how he holds that office together.'

As they discussed their plans, Owen felt that he had no will of his own. When he got up to go, Tom's mother produced a long scarf to wrap around his neck. It was identical to the grubby one Tom wore. Ma reached up on tip toes and wound it tightly about Owen's neck until he felt himself in danger of being throttled.

'Got to keep warm these chilling mornings,' she said. Then, with his packet of sandwiches under his arm, Owen found himself on the road once more. Beside him strode Tom in his great coat and slouch hat. 'Step it out, boy,' Tom said. 'I have to be at work by seven o'clock.'

About a half mile down the road they came across a wagon which was partly loaded with sacks of cabbages. It was a ramshackle affair, really just a cart, and driven by a very old man. Tom and Owen jumped in among the sacks and the old horse plodded along down the hill over the river bridge and into the town where the early morning streets were almost deserted. Here and there were a few sailors prowling back after a night ashore, a milk cart and stray cats, and several ragged homeless children who sat by the wayside ready to beg when the workers came pouring into town.

The town was built high on a hill, and seemed to be made up of rows of slate-roofed houses which huddled together almost to the banks of the Medway. All around, the air was fresh and salty, and gulls swooped down over the quayside as Owen and Tom went through the big dock gates. Carried along by Tom's forceful personality, Owen made no protest as his day was planned for him amid the hustle and bustle of dockland where, in the long reach of the river, ships of all nationalities lay anchored.

'Now boy,' Tom said. 'You get up there on that wall. You'll get a good view down river, and you will see me over there,' he said proudly. 'I'm in charge of that scaffold.'

Owen cast his eyes over the lines of funnels and tall masts which decorated the sky line. 'Now Olly,' said Tom in a paternal tone of voice, 'hang about, don't get in no trouble and I'll be with you midday to catch old Dobbs before he gets into The Sun and gets too boozed.' He slapped Owen on the back and then his wide ungainly figure stomped out of sight.

Now is your chance, Owen told himself. Make a run for it, otherwise you will never get away. But again he could not. Instead he idled his time away on the river wall, staring down at the untidy straggle of houses, and then away to the wide sweep of the river. He ate his sandwiches, threw bread to the hungry gulls and lolled lazily in the sun. He could just make out Tom's huge shape sweating and straining at the pulley to haul the sacks of sand up from the ship's hold. These sacks were then passed along a line of men to carry them down to the gangplank.

Owen was possessed by a warm, well-fed feeling, a sensation that had not been with him for a long time. He felt almost happy.

At midday, as promised, Tom appeared. He was covered with dust and his face was red and glowing with perspiration. His black hair blew in the breeze and his fine bulging muscles rippled as he walked along with the swaying gait of a sailor. 'Wakey! Wakey! Olly!' he shouted. Obediently Owen got down from the wall, put on his hat and followed Tom down the winding street to a little tavern which faced the pier.

'Old Dobbs is bound to be three sheets to the wind already,' explained Tom, 'but he ain't a bad old boy.'

Owen listened politely and said little. He was stunned into a deeper silence by the sight of Uncle Dobbs whom they found sitting in the small private bar, his huge tummy resting on his knees and his high-domed head lolling pathetically sideways as if he had a permanent crick in his neck. The last remaining lock of hair on his otherwise bald dome was combed into an extraordinary curl and plastered down on his forehead. His bulbous nose seemed to be a range of colours, from pink to deep mauve. He sat looking very content, perched on his long narrow seat, a large tankard of cider in his hand.

'Hello, Dobbie!' roared Tom in a tone that echoed around the ancient timbers of the inn.

Dobbie's hand fumbled in an elaborate waistcoat pocket and pulled out a pair of spectacles on a long cord. He placed them on the end of his colourful nose and peered at his visitors.

'I've brought a friend to see you,' shouted Tom.

Dobbie's bleary eyes viewed Owen from head to toe and then back to Tom. 'You brought anything?' he whispered hoarsely.

Tom bent over and whispered loudly into his ear. 'No, it's too risky now. Maybe tonight.'

Dobbie nodded; picking up his tankard of cider, he drained it. Then slowly and ponderously he rose. 'Come over to the office,' he said.

Uncle Dobbs' office was directly across from the tavern. It looked rather derelict. The brass plate on the door carried the inscription: Browne & Dobbs. Shipping Agents.

Inside, the office smelled of dust, alcohol and old parchments. Breathlessly Uncle Dobbs sank into a large chair and produced a bottle of cider. He slowly filled his glass, and then relaxed a moment. Owen stared about him at the untidy, paper-strewn desk, the half-open drawers, and the papers all over the floor. The high shelves were loaded with ledgers all covered in cobwebs.

'He likes his liquor,' whispered Tom.

'Well,' Dobbs finally said. 'What can I do for you, young Tom?'

'This is me second cousin, Owen,' lied Tom. 'He wants a job. He's a smart boy. He can read and write and draw pictures.'

Owen smiled in amusement at this glowing description.

'What's his name?' asked Dobbs suspiciously.

'Oliver,' ventured Owen quietly.

'Don't know no relative of that name,' said Dobbs.

'He's from London,' roared Tom.

'No wonder,' sniffed Dobbs. 'Never mixed with that lot. None of them could read or write. All rogues and thieves, they were.'

Owen suddenly felt alarmed but Tom gave him a little wink. 'Lives in the cottage with me Ma, he does,' he continued. 'She thinks a lot of young Owen, she does.'

Dobbs squinted at Tom with his piggy little eyes encased in fat. Then he looked at Owen. 'Know anything about shipping?' he asked.

'No,' replied Owen, 'but I am trained in accounts and warehousing. I started to study law but was forced to give it up.'

'Money matters, eh?' grunted Dobbs. 'Been to a good school, then.' He seemed to be talking to himself more than addressing Owen. 'Go over there, lad, and see if you can restore order. I'll tell you tonight if you've got the job.'

Owen hesitated but Tom snatched off his hat and hung it behind the door as he pushed Owen down into a seat at the muddled desk.

Dobbs rose slowly once more. 'I'll go and finish my dinner,' he said. 'You coming, young Tom?'

Once he was alone, Owen began to sort out the mess on the desk. It did not take long for him to realise that the papers were all cargo manifestos with a name for each vessel. In no time, he had systematised it, listing, filing and numbering every page before stacking them tidily in the drawers.

After a couple of hours, the office had become very stuffy but try as he might he could not open the window. It had clearly remained closed for far too many years. Absorbed in creating order out of chaos, Owen found that time passed quickly.

In the late afternoon, Dobbs returned in a very befuddled state. 'Good boy,' he said, patting Owen's head as if he were a pet dog. Then he sat down in the corner and dozed off to sleep. Owen kept working.

After the sun had gone down, Tom arrived back from work. He looked very tired and he was covered with a white chalky dust.

Dobbs stirred, stretched and yawned, and Tom heaved him up.

'Lock up, boy,' Tom said to Owen. 'We'd better get this old sod home.'

Between them Owen and Tom escorted Dobbs back up the hill. As he stumbled along he hummed sea songs and ditties. At the top of the hill was a low, half-timbered house. The black door had a lion's head knocker made of brass. This was clean and brightly polished.

The two men pushed old Dobbs up the path and propped him up against the front door. Tom gave a terrific rat tat on the brass knocker, then cried: 'Come on, Owen, run like hell!'

Chuckling loudly, they fled down the hill, with Tom shouting with glee like a schoolboy. 'Mustn't let her catch us,' he said. 'Proper old dragon she is.'

Once they were well away, he put an affectionate arm about Owen's shoulders. 'Good lad,' he said. 'You've got a start with old Dobbs. It'll be all right now. He's on his way out.'

Owen thought Tom was rather callous towards Dobbs, especially as it seemed that it was he who supplied the booze that was killing the man. But he was enjoying the company of the energetic Tom too much to worry about his sense of morality.

He was surprised to learn that Tom was only twenty-five years old. His heavy build and gruff voice made him seem older. 'We better step lively if we're going to catch the wagon home,' Tom warned, his long legs striding forward.

They found the wagon at the crossroads outside another tavern. A crowd of men stood in the doorway swilling down frothy pints of ale. Owen declined to enter, preferring instead to sit by the river and watch the sun go down on the estuary. Tom had a pint before they both climbed back on board the cart. Other men climbed up with them, and as the old nag clip-clopped through the country lanes, all except Owen passed a bottle around and sang folk songs with rural vigour.

As they neared the cottage, Old Dawg ran out yelping in greeting. The lamp had been lit, the front door was open and a smell of honeysuckle filled the air. They found Tom's mother sitting by the fire, knitting. The table was laid and on the stove was a delicious steaming stew ready to be served to the two hungry youths.

After the meal they sat around and talked. Ma loved to be told the events of the day. 'Well, I'm so glad you're going to stay with us, Owen,' she said sweetly.

Owen yawned sleepily. It had been a lively, invigorating day, and he was exhausted. It was not long before he was curled up in his warm, sweet-smelling bed.

Arriving at the office the second day, Owen and Tom found old Dobbs was already there and comparatively sober. Tom opened the shutters and lit the smoky fire.

Old Dobbs, whose head was as shiny and polished as a full moon, wheezed himself slowly down into his chair.

Tom leant down and shouted in his ear. 'Me Ma wants to know if Owen has got the job, then.'

Out came the little spectacles. Old Dobbs peered at Owen once more. 'He is very young,' he muttered, 'for such a respon-sible post.'

'He's eighteen,' roared Tom. 'He just looks younger because he's so skinny. He's been half-starved, poor sod.'

Dobbs stuttered, fussed and fretted. He filled up his glass

with cider and took a long drink.

'Oh well,' he said, 'as long as he can read and write, he'll soon learn. I'll give him four pounds a month.'

'That's no good,' roared Tom. 'Me Ma says he's got to get eight. He pays a pound a week for his keep.'

Dobbs sighed. 'Oh well, if she says so. All right, two pounds a week.'

In his most recent position, Owen had only earned one pound a week to cover his food, clothes and rent, so he was delighted.

Within weeks he had settled down to running Dobbs' office very efficiently, and the sea captains and insurance brokers who called in clearly approved of this polite capable youth whose keen dark blue eyes greeted them so seriously and attended to their wants without any fuss. The lad was so different from that boozy, belligerent old Dobbs.

Tom often breezed in and out, sometimes bringing along in his back pocket a bottle of old Jamacy for Dobbs. 'Like's a drop of the hard stuff, he does,' Tom explained. 'It makes a change from all that cider he gobbles.'

But where and how Tom got the rum was a complete mystery to Owen.

The worst part of his job was hoisting the old man up the hill with Tom each night, knocking on the door of his grand house and then dashing off. It was always the same. Sometimes a shrill female voice came winging after them but they never stopped to answer.

Owen once asked Tom whose voice it was.

'It's the old dragon,' Tom said. 'And gawd help us if she ever catches us.' That was all he would say.

The journey home always required visits to several taverns on the way and Owen usually waited outside with the old nag.

'Got a queasy tummy there, lad,' remarked Tom when Owen had been sick after an excess of ale. 'Not enough grub gorn in there.'

On the whole, Owen's had turned into a very happy life. Tom's old mother fed him well and was kind and looked after his welfare. In the week he worked at Dobb's office and weekends were spent out on the marsh with Tom, Old Dawg and a shot gun. Even Owen got caught up in the excitement of seeing a flock of wild geese flushed out by Old Dawg and hearing the loud pop of the gun before the thud as a dead bird hit the ground. But all the same, he was not overly keen on these blood sports, for his sympathies tended to be with the slain birds. He was always saddened by the sight of a long graceful neck oozing blood, and ruffled and torn plumage. He never told Tom how he felt but he always refused to handle the gun.

Some summer evenings were spent in the old quarry, a great gulf in the land where tons of chalk had been removed. Now bright clumps of yellow gorse broke up a carpet of daisies where nature repaired the wounds on the land. All around, the tall mauve willow herb sent its fluffy seeds floating out gracefully into the breeze. Owen loved this spot. It was so peaceful. It made him feel as if the world had been left behind.

This day, however, Owen's peace was disturbed by Tom and Old Dawg. Tom had brought a ferret with him which he put in the maze of rabbit warrens in the quarry. Within minutes out came the panic-stricken rabbits, to face Tom's gun and old Dawg's sharp teeth.

Owen lay with his face pressed to the grass and his fingers in his ears so as not to hear the cries. One by one, the dead rabbits were slung down on the grass beside him, their hind legs tied up with string. Old Dawg lay resting on one side, tongue hanging out and panting excitedly.

'You *are* sqeamish, boy,' Tom mocked. 'You can't stand the sight of blood, then?'

'I don't hold with unnecessary killing,' said Owen quietly.

'Not necessary?' shouted Tom. 'Why, boy, what are you saying? That's food, good food,' he said, pointing to the rabbits. 'In town you can starve but out here nature provides.'

'I do realise that, Tom,' replied Owen, 'and I wish I could agree with you.'

'Listen, boy,' Tom continued in the same dogmatic tone, 'I have been a wandering half-starved waif but I learned how to survive the hard way. Now it's time you did.'

There was no reply from Owen. He could never raise enough courage to argue with Tom.

In spite of such incidents, these were happy, invigorating days. Some Sundays they borrowed a boat to fish off-shore, returning with the hold full of mackerel which Tom distributed generously among his friends and neighbours.

On all the good food, Owen filled out. His skin glowed with a healthy tan, he smiled more often and was even, on occasion, heard to whistle a jolly tune. He bought a Sunday suit with his earnings and regularly attended church with Tom and his mother.

During the long evenings, the two men roamed the orchards, passing miles and miles of apple trees, munching the crisp fruit and picking up the windfalls for Ma's fruit pies. They often had intimate conversations, almost as immature boys might.

'Have you ever had a sweetheart, Tom?' asked Owen.

'Me?' Tom laughed loudly but then looked shy. 'The old lady is my sweetheart,' he said. 'What do I want with women?'

'I was in love once,' confided Owen. 'She was sweet and fair but an awful snob.'

Tom nodded sagely. 'The worst kind, they are, nice and soft until they hook you, and then, God help you, 'cause the devil don't.'

Owen had a dreamy look. 'I made such a fool of myself,' he confessed.

Tom slapped him on the back. 'Now, stop worrying about it, Olly,' he said. 'They soon get over it.'

'Are you talking from experience, Tom?'

'Not me, boy,' chuckled Tom. 'I have seen too many of them girls down at the dockside. All kissing and cuddling, they are, then, as soon as the ship sails, they're down at the tavern with goo-goo eyes for some other poor sod.'

Owen smiled. It was apparent that Tom only knew two kinds of women: his loving mother and the sailor's floosie.

Gradually Tom and Owen became very good pals. Owen had never known such generous companionship before. But their interests were so different. On Saturday they went to Bexley. Tom wanted to see some cock-fighting in one inn and ratting in another. The smell of blood and the cruel jagged spurs that the cockerels wore to stab each other to death sickened Owen. And the raucous voices of the crowds and the loud barking dogs confused and frightened him.

But it was during a long ratting session that Owen drew his first set of cartoons. He had moved to a quiet corner and with his sketch book on his knee he began to draw, to capture the scene around him – the crowd of men and women, blousy, drunk, delirious and excited. They all appeared at the end of Owen's charcoal. Caught up in his creation, he was oblivious to the noise in the hot, sweaty room.

When Tom came to say he was ready to move, Owen closed his sketch book with a sigh of deep satisfaction. It had been a most rewarding afternoon. He and Tom hiked back over the Weald that night and happily shared a liquid breakfast with the shepherds. Invigorated by his drawing, Owen felt wonderful. He was becoming fit and healthy in his new rural existence.

CHAPTER THREE

The Waif

Summer slipped into a gloriously mellow autumn which in turn drifted towards winter. A wild wind blew up over the marshland, but in the cottage it remained warm and comfortable. Tom's mother was as vigorous as ever, combining her motherly duties in taking care of Tom and Owen with her duties at the curate's house. Owen adored her. On chilly mornings there was nothing more wonderful than to rise to a glowing fire and a bowl of hot porridge on the table. Ma was someone he would remember for the rest of his life.

Travelling into town early in the morning with Tom still had its hazards. Now that it was cold, the two young men would sit perched in the back of the old cart all muffled up in thick overcoats. They had long ear flaps attached to their caps to prevent the frost getting to their ears. Cold ears, according to Tom's Ma, could be very dangerous.

Recently the old cabbage cart had been moving more swiftly than usual. The old driver, Bentley, was confined to his bed with bronchitis, so his son Billy was driving the cart instead. Every morning he would whip up the old nag and yell into the air, his breath a hazy cloud in the frosty air. Silver drops covered the frost-stiffened hedges and glittered like diamonds. Early in the morning there was a lovely peaceful stillness in the air but this did not prevent them from becoming cold and raw-skinned during the daily journey into town.

Owen rarely said a word and sat silently while Tom joked with young Billy all the way. Young Billy was quite a reckless driver and ended the journey with a long fierce gallop to bring them into the market place.

Owen rather dreaded Monday mornings as they clip-clopped past the market square, for he hated to witness the sordid hiring fair that was in progress on that day each week. A hundred or more ragged children crowded together in the cold square, shivering in their garments, pallid faces above under-nourished bodies. There might be a whimpering babe in its young mother's arms, a stupid girl clutching a rag doll, shoeless boys in ragged breeches – all human fodder waiting in that bitter wind for the master who would hire them for a week's work out in the frozen fields or in the gloomy factories.

Once hired, these children became slaves, working twelve to fourteen hours a day. The law had been amended recently but the age of nine was still considered quite a reasonable one for employment. At least children under the age of eight were reprieved.

The sight of these exhausted youngsters sickened the sensitive Owen, while Tom would simply mutter: 'Poor little bastards.'

The more Owen brooded over this sight, the more he was horrified. Not even in London had he seen such terrible cruelty. Why, these children were being treated worse than dogs.

Hard-faced policemen, or Peelers, stood nearby with their truncheons in hand, ready to wade in and keep order, while the drunken men boozing in the ever-open tavern waited for the farmer or factory owner to collect their slaves for a payment that would buy them more booze.

'Surely something can be done to prevent this atrocity,' Owen exclaimed to Tom one day.

'No, lad,' said Tom, cynically. 'We can't interfere. They've got the law on their side.'

But each time they passed the spot, Owen dreaded what he might see. And he found that each evening he was compelled to capture the scene on paper. Every evening he would do so.

One morning the lane was very misty so the old horse had slowed down and as a result they had reached the square slightly later. The ragged children – boys and girls – had already been hired and were now being marched off in a long crocodile of shuffling feet and shivering bodies, watched over by a huge fellow with a big stick. Bitter anguish tore at Owen's heart as he watched them pass.

One little head caught his attention, as it seemed to shine out from that miserable scene. It was a silver-gold mane of hair, so long and shiny that it cascaded like a waterfall down a small back and framed the pinched white face of the little girl.

Owen's quick artist's eye caught and held that glint of silvery gold. Suddenly the small shape dashed from the line and headed away swiftly up the lane. With a quick swoop, the man was down on her, brutally wielding his heavy stick, producing shrill screams of terror from the child. She fought bravely and kicked out fiercely but the man held her long golden mane and viciously hauled her backwards. As he did so, a huge shape descended upon him and there was a sudden scuffle as Tom landed a hefty straight left blow to the jaw of the minder, who dropped to the ground and lay still.

Released, the child ran straight into Owen's arms and clung frantically to him, her heart beating fast in terror.

Owen put his arms about her and rocked her comfortingly to and fro, his own hot tears falling on her silvery hair. He was completely oblivious of the rumpus that was going on around him, as young Billy now went to help fight off the toughs who had begun to attack Tom. More men poured from the tavern to help their comrade, and then the Peelers joined in to try and restore order.

Children were running hither and thither but the old nag stood as placid as ever. Owen climbed back up into the cart, with the little girl wrapped in his coat. He sat down beside her and with his arm about her he whispered: 'No one is going to hurt you anymore.'

Eventually order was restored. Tom managed to emerge from the fray and climb up on the cart, while Billy made rude noises with his lips at the Peelers as they rattled away.

It was only when they reached the office that Tom noticed the little bundle tucked up amongst the cabbages. 'Crikey, Olly!' he hollered. 'What have you got there?'

The child had gone to sleep with her two thin legs sticking out from beneath Owen's overcoat. Thick gold lashes fringed her closed eyes.

'Pretty little kid, ain't she?' remarked Tom. 'But you can't keep her, Olly. Give her a good feed and turn her loose. These town folk are mighty funny, and it don't do to interfere in their rotten ways,' he advised.

Owen's intelligent eyes flickered defiantly. 'I'll take her to the office,' he said quietly. 'Then I'll find out where she comes from.'

'Well, please yourself, lad,' replied Tom. 'But don't say I didn't warn you.'

Owen picked up the girl and carried her into Dobbs' office. Setting her down, he lit the fire, and she sat staring at the flames, half asleep. Every now and then a dry cough wracked her thin body until Owen poured a glass of wine and held it to her blue lips. Then he found some ginger biscuits which she devoured greedily. Not one word was spoken. The child just crouched by the fire and allowed the heat of the flames to warm her thin body until she curled up inside Owen's coat and slept like a kitten.

Owen got on quietly with his tasks. Old Dobbs would not arrive until midday, and that would only happen if he was able to get past the Sun Inn. If he did not turn up at the office, Owen would go and find Dobbs after lunch and bring him back for his afternoon nap.

All the business was left to Owen these days. He had quickly learned the ropes: logs to decipher, cargoes to manifest, insurance claims to deal with. He had proved himself to be very capable.

But at the moment, the problem uppermost in his mind was what to do with this little girl. He would let her sleep now, and when she awoke, she could decide for herself. Owen put on his jacket, made up the fire and then went over the road to collect old Dobbs.

Dobbs was extremely drunk and belligerent, having got involved in a heated argument with a dogmatic sea captain on a point of sea law. It was some time before Owen could dislodge the old master from his comfortable corner, but at last he had winkled him out and slowly guided him along.

'Whippersnapper!' declared Dobbs. 'Think they know it all, they do. Why, I been cabin boy to purser – they can't tell me.'

As Dobbs muttered and mumbled, Owen escorted him over to the office, wondering how to explain the presence of the child asleep by the fire. But as Owen lowered the grunting and gasping Dobbs into his chair, he let out a cry of dismay. His coat lay on the floor empty. The child had gone.

Owen ran around the office searching for her and then dashed out of the door to look down the street.

But there was no sign of her.

'What's that doing there?' asked old Dobbs, staring blearily at the coat. 'Brought a stray dog in, didn't yer?' he grumbled. 'I don't like dogs. They get fleas. Get him out!' he ordered as he dozed off.

Owen felt very upset at the disappearance of the girl. For some reason, she had seemed very important to him. Now he felt impatient and depressed. It had been quite a day.

And now Tom was late. He had gone straight from work at the docks back to the tavern to finish his argument with the minder of the slave children. With no Tom, it meant that Owen had to stagger up the hill with old Dobbs alone, the whole weight of that obese body bearing down on his thin arm. Drunk and befuddled, old Dobbs grumbled non-stop.

'Don't thee get so cocky, boy,' he moaned. 'Business ain't yours yet, bringing in lousy mongrels.'

Owen could not be bothered to explain the situation to Dobbs. He was quite fed up with him. This time he dragged him up the road, propped him against his front door, banged on the knocker and fled hastily down the path. He was not looking where he was going and crashed into someone coming up the path behind him. He collapsed into a flurry of petticoats and wide ribbons.

'I do beg your pardon,' Owen gasped at the shocked brown eyes staring up at him. He got to his feet and helped up the young lady who lay in his path, her red rosy mouth open wide. Continuing to apologise profusely, Owen dusted the young lady down and handed her the little beaded bag which had gone flying to the other side of the path.

'Oh dear,' she gasped. 'You must be Owen.'

Just as Owen was about to bow and introduce himself properly, the front door of the house opened and a shrill shriek rang out: 'Katy, Katy! What are you doing down there?'

To Owen's disappointment, the young woman turned on her heel and fled into the house.

Ten minutes later Owen was waiting outside the tavern for Tom. His coat collar was turned up and his hands were plunged deep into his pockets. Poor Owen, he felt very dejected and wanted nothing but to flee back to London. The old nag pulling the cart pawed the ground impatiently while Tom stood outside ranting and raving and waving a hammy fist under the nose of a stout and seedy man.

Young Billy stood in the opposite corner with one eye on the Peeler as he tried to persuade Tom to give up his argument and start for home.

At last they were all aboard the cart. Several other old men were going the same way and had joined them in the cart and they and Tom shouted drunkenly all the way home.

It was dark and damp by the time they reached their destination. With a wet mist penetrating his clothes, Owen was relieved to see the dim lights of Honeysuckle Cottage.

Tom's mother was very displeased with both Tom and Owen. She had cooked a good roast and now it was so late it had surely spoiled, she said. Fortunately it had not and after the men had washed and devoured the splendid meal, the atmosphere lightened. Soon Owen was telling Ma about the tiny golden-haired child, of how she had coughed so badly and had eventually fled from him.

Ma was sympathetic but wary. 'Just as well, lad,' she said. 'It's best not to get involved with those town folk. The child was probably consumptive, and you have to be very careful about that, it's very catching, it is.'

Ma's remark caused Owen to lapse into gloomy silence while Tom would not let the subject go. He cackled and giggled. 'Nice little kid, she was, but too young for you, Owen. Ha! Old Dobbs thought it were a dog.'

Ma's glinty eyes surveyed Owen's face shrewdly. Then she reached out and slapped Tom hard across the face. 'Go to bed!' she ordered. 'You're upsetting the boy.'

White with shock, Tom obeyed. He went off blubbering like a lamb. It had been quite a day and he had had enough.

The following Saturday morning, eager to be out and about on his day off, Owen went to wake Tom in his room, a kind of outhouse attached to the cottage with a door leading straight into the garden. Inside this room, Tom kept a strange collection of objects – large shells, lame birds in cages which he nursed and set free, and old shotguns, swords, bottles and barrels. A large Spanish hat and an old fishing net hung on the wall, and piles of old broadsheets, which he could not read but liked to look at, lay by the narrow cot bed.

'Take him a cup of tea,' Ma said to Owen. 'I never enter that pigsty in the early morning.'

Owen took Tom a large mug of tea and sat on the bed while Tom pulled on his farm boots. 'Going out?' he asked Tom.

'Yes,' replied Tom. 'I am going to fill old Bentley's cellar with coal. I do it a couple of times in the winter. He's got a bad chest and has to keep warm.'

'Shall I come with you? offered Owen.

'If you want to, lad.' replied Tom.

So with the empty coal sacks over their shoulders, the men trudged out across the muddy marshland. Thick clay clung to their boots and hindered their progress until at last they reached the railway line. It was newly built and just a single track which wound its way over the marshland to service factories and cement manufacturers. There was one lone signal box and, beside it, a vast mountain of coal.

'Now stand easy, lad,' ordered Tom. 'Keep your eye on that box. The signalman has gone home to dinner, and there's no train due until this afternoon.'

Owen did as he was told while Tom energetically and quickly filled the big sacks with coal. He swung one over his shoulder and pointed to the other one for Owen to pick up. 'Come on lad,' he said, 'that's all.'

Weighed down by the heavy sack, Owen walked beside Tom across the marsh in the direction of home. He kept thinking to himself that the coal surely must belong to the railway. If so, then Tom was actually stealing. And if that was so, then he himself was an accessory to the crime.

But Tom seemed quite unconcerned about what he had done. He whistled loudly and cheerfully as he marched along.

At Bentley's cottage, the sacks were emptied into a home-made bunker, and then they went off to the Lobster Tavern in the middle of the marsh to play Rings and drink cider.

Owen was astonished but he did not dare ask if they had committed a crime. He was too afraid of the answer he might be given.

After luncheon, Tom was still bursting with energetic fervour, and he persuaded Owen to walk with Old Dawg to a remote tavern seven miles from town where a ratting session was in progress.

A large noisy crowd had gathered in a barn beside the tavern. Above the shouts of the audience could be heard the squeals of injured rats and the yapping of dogs. Within minutes, Tom was shouting with the best of them, swearing, laying down bets on Old Dawg, and swigging from the jugs which were being passed around.

The excitement was quite intense as each dog leaped forward to devour the rat springing from the trap. It was a lewd sickening sport; dogs fought, men argued and money changed hands.

Owen sat up on the ladder leading to the hay loft, his sketch-book on his knee. From there he sketched the sweaty faces, the wide open mouths, and the mean cruel eyes, of the old, the young. The men were packed tightly in together – farm labourers, landlords and servants. One by one, Owen drew them; it was the only way he could tolerate the scene.

It was almost dark when the event ended, and then there was the general exodus from the barn to the adjacent inn, which was called the Rat's Castle. There, of course, Tom, that big amiable giant, bought drinks for everyone. He was enjoying himself enormously, and he was clearly on his way to becoming hopelessly drunk.

In this particular inn was a woman called Fanny who seemed to like Tom. Owen noticed because it was not often that a woman was seen in Tom's company. Fanny was tall and slim and she had black hair which hung in a mass of black unruly curls. She had a lined, haggard face and around her shoulders lay a ragged shawl. She moved in and out among all the men with great familiarity.

Watching her, Owen thought there was something sad about those red puffy cheeks and large soulful eyes. Fanny wore an old blue cotton dress which clung to her figure and she had a fluid willowy way of walking. From his quiet corner, Owen watched the way Fanny cadged drinks, and his attentive eyes did not miss the sight of Tom slipping her some money.

Then Fanny stood by the rickety old piano and she sang, in a coarse, untuneful voice, a dreadfully vulgar song. Tom larked about with her and danced and sang, but he made no attempt to introduce her to Owen. He and Fanny together put on quite a performance which ended with Tom drinking a yard of ale from a container shaped like a trumpet.

A black mist had descended over the marshland when they finally left the inn. Tom was paralytically drunk and staggered out with Fanny clinging to his arm and Old Dawg tagging along behind. Watching by the door, Owen felt very embarrassed, as he saw them head for the barn. He did not know what to do or where to go.

Suddenly, with a lot of cursing and swearing, Tom flung Fanny away from him. She over-balanced and landed upside down in the ditch with her ragged petticoats flying up around her bare backside.

'Boy!' Tom called out to Owen. 'Where are you?'

Owen went forward to guide him.

'Let's kip in the barn till I sober up,' Tom slurred. He stumbled in and pitched forward on to the hay, with Old Dawg settled beside him.

Owen found himself a warm corner and put his head on his sketch-book. In no time at all he was asleep.

It was close to dawn when he woke to find something warm and soft beside him. He noticed the smell first, a warm, animal smell, and he thought it was Old Dawg. Owen put out a hand to pat the dog but suddenly came into contact with bare human flesh. He had touched a bare leg, for lying in the straw beside him was Fanny, her mouth open and snoring loudly and her legs wide apart. Owen edged carefully away but Fanny immediately woke up.

'Come on, lad,' she urged in a soft whisper. 'Be friendly, I won't charge you.'

With a startled yell, Owen leaped up and shot out of the straw as if it were on fire. Now Old Dawg woke up and barked so loudly that Tom was also woken. 'Get out, you slut,' he roared. 'Keep away from that boy!'

Fanny pulled herself to her feet and swaggered out, revealing her yellow teeth in a wide grin.

Tom got up and lumbered out too. 'Come on, lad, we best get moving.'

Soon Tom and Owen were heading over the Weald in the fresh morning air. Old Dawg scampered beside them. Tom had pushed his hands deep into his overcoat pockets and had nothing to say as they crested the steep hill and went on down to the riverside. Finally he spoke in a gruff voice: 'Nothing happened, did it, lad? With old Fan, I mean?'

Owen shivered at the thought but shook his head.

'Good,' cried Tom, giving him a resounding slap on the back. Then he began to laugh heartily. 'Oh, I was really worried,' he said. 'I thought I might have to get you doctored, boy. Poxed up to the eyebrows, is old Fan.'

Owen was astonished to think that there could be such vice and contamination amid this peaceful rural scene.

'She was not a bad little girl one time, Fanny,' explained Tom. 'My mate brought her from Maidstone but he went down at sea, and left her hanging about the dockyard. It's been a few years now. She's good company, I always treat her, but sleep with her? No thanks!'

The rooster was crowing as they reached home.

'Take it easy now,' said Tom. 'I'll go in my window and open the back door for you. Quiet now.' Stealthily, he crept down the garden path. All was quiet except for a rustle in the honeysuckle as the blue tits moved in their nests, frightened by Tom's massive presence.

Carefully and quietly Tom unlatched the window and placed two hands on the sill ready to vault inside.

But suddenly there was a loud whack! Ma's heavy copper stick came down on Tom's knuckles with a tremendous force and then her irate face appeared at the window. 'Get them there chickens fed afore you come in here!' she yelled. 'You've been out again all night, Tom, encouraging that boy in your wicked ways.' Whack! Another blow fell, this time across Tom's thick shoulders.

Tom ducked before he could be caught again. Then he turned and fled to the chicken house, with Owen sidling along behind.

'Come here!' Ma called to Owen. 'Get yourself off to bed, boy. A growing lad needs his sleep. I shall expect to see you at evensong tonight. The vicar's got a special service.'

So it was that after dinner that evening, Tom and Owen stood next to Ma in their Sunday suits, with their faces well scrubbed, in the ancient Norman church. The songs of praise were loud and tuneful, rising up to ring around the ancient oak beams. The candles flickered and the setting sun came through the stained glass windows casting a red glint on the hair of the choir boys as they belted out their parts.

But such an idyllic scene could not erase from Owen's

mind's eye the sight of those maltreated slave children. Over and over again he thought about the contradictions of life, and how these God-fearing people, for example, could allow such atrocities to prevail in their midst.

At the after-service supper table, Owen's sketches were produced for the benefit of the vicar and his guests. With the aid of a magnifying glass, Ma pointed out the people she could recognise.

'Why, that's old Seth! Just look at him, the drooling old scoundrel,' she chuckled.

'That's old farmer Bryce, him with the long nose,' joined in Tom.

'They are extremely good,' said the vicar. 'Don't you agree, sir?' He turned to the guest on his right, a learned colleague from the university.

'I certainly do,' replied this portly, well-spoken fellow. 'In fact, I would like permission to borrow the sketchbook if I may?'

Owen consented quietly. 'I can always do some more,' he said.

'It must be a very stimulating hobby,' continued the man. 'I believe you have great talent, young man, and I may be able to make some contacts for you.'

So it was that Owen took his first step to fame on that Sunday evening after he had been saved from the clutches of Fanny.

Christmas came, and it was a merry time in the village. Owen had not experienced such a happy time since his early childhood when his mother was alive. Tom managed to be fairly well behaved and attended all the church festivities with an uncharacteristic punctuality. Much of his leisure time during this period was spent with a beautiful white bird that he had picked up for dead on the marshes. It had a broken wing and was frozen stiff. It was in a bad way when he found it but with love and care it took only a few days before it was hopping about in its cage.

When the mysterious bird was fully fit, Tom invited in the other villagers to visit the bird to discuss its heritage and its reason for flying over the marshes in mid-winter. No one could tell him what it was.

On Christmas Day they ate a magnificent dinner of turkey and plum pudding, and then on Boxing Day they were guests of the vicar at a cold supper which included several of the more influential villagers.

Tom got quite excited on the homemade wine and went around kissing everyone under the mistletoe. When he tried to kiss the tiny wife of the doctor, he missed her and kissed the sour-faced doctor instead.

As always, feeling unsociable, Owen sat in the corner with his sketch-book, recording the scene for posterity.

The day after Boxing Day some unexpected visitors came to Honeysuckle Cottage – three young ladies and their mother. They arrived in a carriage, all wrapped up in fur, like little bunnies – bonnets, capes, gloves and fur-trimmed boots.

Owen stood in the small hallway, wondering how on earth they were all going to cram into the small cottage, while Ma, flushed and excited, trotted down to the gate to meet them.

'I'm off,' muttered Tom. 'It's them.' With that, he disappeared out of the back door.

Owen bowed and stood courteously to one side as the women all bustled inside, chattering and giggling, bringing with them a strong waft of lavender.

Honeysuckle Cottage rarely had guests of this kind. Owen stared, transfixed, as the ladies divested themselves of their wraps, hanging them on Owen as if he were a hall-stand. Then the wide crinolines pushed through the narrow opening into the parlour until it seemed to be overflowing with chattering women.

Owen carefully hung the furs on the stair rail. His intention was to dodge out of the back door in search of Tom, when the three females reappeared, all frills, flounces and ribbons. One pretty face with a rosy pouting mouth dashed forward and cried, 'Happy Christmas, Owen!' and a brightly wrapped parcel was thrust into his hand. Owen frowned. Surely he had seen that face only the other day ... Then a little blonde face came forward, surrounded by tight sausage curls. Its owner stood on tiptoe and pressed her warm lips to his cheek. 'Happy Christmas, Owen!' she lisped, handing him another parcel.

Owen was astounded. He stood there wondering what on earth was going on and then a parcel was handed to him by the young woman with dark brown plaits and a thin face. She smiled as she said in a husky voice: 'Compliments of the season, Owen.'

Owen staggered into the kitchen loaded down with presents. His face was deathly pale, so shocked was he by this unexpected female onslaught.

Soon Ma came in, with a white apron covering her Sunday dress. 'Now come and meet my three nieces,' she said. 'Bring the tea tray, and be careful – it's my best china.'

Minutes later they were all sitting demurely upon the sofa. Owen decided now that the visitors looked much less frightening.

'This is Mr Dobbs' sister, Mrs Eva Browne,' Ma said, introducing Owen to a thin scrawny woman with a terrific beak of a nose. Her hair was tightly frizzed and twined into a top knot giving her the fierce look of an aggressive hen.

Mrs Browne held out a droopy hand and gave Owen a quick little smile.

Mrs Browne's daughters all cried in unison. 'We have met Owen decided now that the visitors looked much less frightening.

Hemmed in by buxom Katy and pretty blonde Mary, Owen tried very nervously to sip tea from the dainty china cup. The third girl, Georgina, sat bolt upright in a straight-backed chair, her long legs crossed in spite of the disapproving gaze of her mother. Georgina grinned cheerfully at Owen, her merry brown eyes flashing with defiant humour.

Three sisters, Owen pondered, with three distinct personalities. He would love to have held a conversation with each of them individually but, as always, he was tongue-tied. All he could do was nibble a biscuit and listen to the womanly gossip. He was intrigued to think that here was the dreadful dragon with whom Tom so assiduously avoided contact when they visited her brother's house. It had not previously sunken in that old Dobbs was so closely connected with Tom, but he finally worked out that Mr Browne, Dobbs' partner and the father of these three girls, was Tom's father's brother. Indeed, Georgina had a look about her which reminded Owen of Tom.

When everything had been discussed and the annual greetings exchanged, the afternoon ended. Owen helped the ladies climb back into their pile of wraps. Then, all bound up in fur once more like solemn pussies with a long-tailed mother cat,

Dobbs and shouted in his ear, 'Wakey! Wakey!'

There was no response, so Tom shouted again: 'Anchor's away!'

This yell usually brought some response from Dobbs, if it was only an irritable one, but now there was not a peep.

Owen brought the lamp forward to shine it on the old man's face.

Tom lifted the veined hand and dropped it. It fell back limply.

'Crikey!' cried Tom. 'He ain't with us.'

Owen had seen death before and knew that Tom was right as the lamp shone on the upturned eyes and the tongue that lolled out of the open mouth. 'My God, he's dead,' he whispered, and the two men stared at each other in shocked silence.

'I'll get help,' cried Tom, running out.

Owen rubbed the stiff hands but there was no life, only a kind of peaceful stillness.

The small office was soon filled with people – the doctor, neighbours and the landlord of the Sun Tavern. Gently they laid old Dobbs on a stretcher and carried him for the last time up that steep hill.

Wandering up behind the procession, Owen felt very sad. Dobbs had been a nice old boy, despite everything, and he had been unfailingly good to Owen. He would miss him a lot.

That night going home on the cabbage cart, Owen and Tom sat quietly, unable to talk freely as the spirit of death still hovered about them. Most of all, they worried about how to break the news to Ma.

CHAPTER FOUR

Windfall

On the morning of Dobbs' funeral, events began to take a surprising turn. Dobbs was to be buried out at Halstow, in the family grave in the beautiful churchyard of a Norman church which was overshadowed by a ruined castle.

The Dobbs family had been the old yeomen of England. Dobb's ancestors had first defended that old castle with bows and arrows. Then, under Elizabeth I, an ancestor had returned from a privateer voyage, the part owner of a ship. That was the beginning of the old cargo line.

On this February morning, the last member of the Dobbs family was being laid to rest – his wife lost in childbirth, his only son drowned at sea.

The sun shone over the wide marshland as gulls swooped low over the church tower and the little group of mourners who stood around the open grave. The women were muffled in black crêpe, while the men wore black hats and black bands around their arms.

Owen, Tom and Tom's mother drove out in a hired carriage. This was the first time Owen had seen Ma outside her own hamlet. Dressed, in a little black peaked bonnet with flowing ribbons and a rather fusty black dress that was wide and heavy, Ma reminded Owen of a small mouse. Her bright, alert eyes, shining from her small thin face, darted sharply this way and that.

Tom was looking rather dour in a black hat he had borrowed for the occasion. It was a little too small for his large head, and he kept pulling it down. Tom was bored and fidgety; he hated being hemmed in by all these weeping ladies.

With a melancholic expression on his young face, Owen watched the ceremony and its participants. There was Eva, tall and awkward with a dreadful arrangement of black plumes on her hat, her beaky nose red from constant blowing with a black bordered handkerchief. There was demure little Mary in a black-and-white checked dress and a genuinely sorrowful Katy weeping copiously. And there was Georgina, rather remote, staring sullenly ahead, her hands deep in her coat pockets.

As Owen watched them all, he thought about what an unusual family it was, but in some small way he felt quite involved with it.

Over to the left he could see the smartly dressed Captain Browne, in a uniform with brass buttons and gold braid. Owen had not yet met him. He looked as husky as Tom but more upright. There was a certain likeness in that strong jutting jawline but there the likeness ended, for the Captain's eyes were a keen bright blue with a steady gaze. So this was the father of those vivacious girls, Owen thought, and Tom's father's younger brother.

Soon the carriages, pulled by coal-black horses, were rattling into town and up the steep hill for the funeral tea. Tom had tried to leave the carriage when they got into town but was restrained from doing so by a whack from his mother's furled umbrella. Now looking very sulky, Tom sat glowering across at them.

'We stay to hear the will read,' Ma commanded. 'Is that clear, Tom?'

'Don't see why,' groused her son. 'Old Dobbs had nothing. He boozed it all away.'

'This is family business and I'll see it conducted in a proper manner,' declared his mother.

So they all lapsed into silence until they reached the house on the hill where Owen and Tom used to deposit old Dobbs at the end of each day.

Owen was feeling decidedly uncomfortable. Now he felt like an intruder amidst this close family but Ma held firmly on to his arm.

'You must stay, Owen,' she pleaded. 'I am relying on you to see that I get back home safely.'

Owen and Tom sat in the flower-filled conservatory, while the funeral tea took place. Simpering and giggling now, Katy brought tea and fancy cakes. The large drawing-room was filled with a crowd of gossiping people who, after paying their respects, slowly drifted off, until only the immediate family and very close friends remained.

'Look at 'em,' scowled Tom. 'They're worriting who poor old Dobbs left his share of the business to.'

But Owen was barely listening. He had pulled out his sketch-book and began to draw the ladies in their funeral garb, and then he did a quick sketch of Katy among the flowers.

The portly doctor and the lawyer from town had arrived, as had the landlord of the Sun Tavern, a man who had been a good friend of old Dobbs. The lawyer coughed and rustled his papers as the ladies arranged themselves about the room. Owen and Tom had chosen to remain in the conservatory. The room was completely quiet. At last, the lawyer put on his monacle and proceeded to read out the last will and testament of Josiah Dobbs:

'Two hundred pounds bequeathed to my sister Eva, in the hope that she will find it in her power to pay burying expenses and provide a decent headstone.

'Three separate personal gifts – one telescope, one ivory chess set, and one gold watch, to be shared by the three nieces, Katy, Mary and Georgina.

'Finally, my half interest in the business of Browne & Dobbs, Shipping Agents, to my most efficient clerk and assistant, Owen Oliver.'

There was a gasp and then a shocked silence in the room as the lawyer's words sunk in. People frowned and then began to mutter and shake their heads with indignation.

'Well!' someone said.

'Who would have thought it?' said another.

'Crafty old devil. Just who is this Owen Oliver?'

Tom gave a loud guffaw and thumped Owen on the back. 'Hear that?' he shouted. 'The old boy has left the business to you.'

Owen's knees had gone weak, and his cheeks were flushed red with embarrassment.

'Step forward, young man,' said the lawyer briskly.

Tom propelled Owen forward.

The lawyer took Owen's limp hand and pumped it up and down. 'Congratulations,' he said. 'I'll see you in the office in the morning to complete details. Good day to you all.' Snapping shut his case, the lawyer marched out of the door.

First to recover was Eva. 'Katy!' she shrilled. 'Bring in the sherry! We all need a stimulant. I've never heard such nonsense! My own family business left to a stranger!'

She swept past Owen, her beaky nose in the air. The other ladies gathered their skirts and followed her, muttering loudly as they went.

'Oh, my dear, how dreadful. Of course, you *will* contest the will, Eva, won't you?'

'You'd have thought at least he could have left his portion to the girls.'

One stout man who was not dissimilar to old Dobbs in appearance, stared aggressively at Owen. 'Been some funny business going on here,' he said. 'Who is this fella?'

'Leave him be, Cousin Bertie,' Tom's mother said firmly. 'He lives with me, and if Dobbs left him the business it's because he earned it and deserves it.'

Cousin Bertie narrowed his eyes. 'We'll see about that,' he muttered threateningly as he walked out.

Until now, Captain Browne had hardly said a word. Now he leaned an elbow against the mantelshelf and surveyed with amusement Owen's ashen face and nervous conjectures. 'Well, now, lad,' he said quietly. 'Don't let them worry you. Old Dobbs was no fool. He knew they would all be here like a flock of vultures once he was dead.' He held out a clean broad hand. 'Shake, boy. Now, seeing as we are partners, let's go and have a quiet drink.' He turned to Tom. 'Where is it?' he whispered.

The three men went back into the conservatory and there, from under a large flower pot, Tom produced a bottle of brandy.

'Old Dobbs won't need it now,' grinned the captain. 'Get some glasses, Georgina,' he called to his daughter who was hovering by the door.

Fortified by the liquor, the three men discussed the situation.

'We did not see eye to eye, old Dobbs, and I,' explained the captain. 'He was too set in his ways, so I let him get on with it. I only inherited the half of the business when I married Eva. It doesn't interest me at all – the deep sea is my life. Besides, I couldn't live in this hive of females for all the tea in China.' He laughed loudly.

Owen began to relax. He rather liked this captain.

'Dobbs was not a fool,' broke in Tom. 'And Owen is a very smart lad.'

But Owen shook his head. 'I am a comparative stranger, and this is a family affair. I feel strongly that I should not accept the bequest,' he said.

'Nonsense!' cried Captain Browne. 'Why, who else could run that office as you do? Do you think I don't know that Dobbs did very little towards it?'

'I was only an employee,' Owen replied simply. 'I did my duty.'

'Don't be so smug,' said the captain. 'Who else was there? After all, Tom is a rogue.'

'Thank you, sir,' grinned Tom touching his forelock.

'Cousin Bertie is a gambling scoundrel,' continued Captain Browne, 'and the rest are women. I am convinced that you came along at the right time. It won't take too much to convince Eva that this is so, and I don't think our Katy will need much persuasion.' He winked knowingly, making Owen blush. 'Come on, drink up, lad, now we will join the family,' said the affable captain.

Before spring had painted the orchards with pink blossoms and the blackbird trilled a mating song in the tall chestnut tree, Owen had left Honeysuckle cottage. With great reluctance, he said good-bye, to the warm comforting home that Tom and his mother had provided for him. The reason for the move was that just before the captain returned to sea, he had acquired some chambers in town for Owen.

'Look here, sir,' he had declared. 'I can't have you travelling up to town in the old cabbage cart. It's bad for business. You must act the part, you know.'

Owen had shrugged. 'I am very content to live in Honeysuckle Cottage. I have found much happiness there,' he protested.

'Yes, yes, sister Peg is a grand old lady but it is very important to live in town if you wish to succeed,' insisted the captain.

Owen was not sure if he wanted to succeed on the captain's terms but he meekly relinquished his attic with its view of the marshland for a suite of rooms in town. They were in a narrow, medieval street, facing the Sun Pier, high up over a bookshop with a good view of the river.

The Browne girls helped him with his moving in. Sweet little Mary sewed covers for the chairs, Katy cleaned out the larder and stocked it with jams and jellies while Georgina supervised the spring cleaning.

Soon Tom remarked on the way his cousins had taken over Owen. 'You won't never get me up there,' he grunted. 'If you want me, just leave a message at the Blue Boar.'

The rooms were pleasant with high narrow windows, high ceilings, and gables that jutted out, obscuring the light. But Owen really missed waking up to the birdsong and the cattle lowing on the marsh.

He now drew an excellent allowance each month which enabled him to buy more than his basic requirements. He often wandered about the Saturday markets buying etchings and old silver. Soon his rooms began to take on the air of a gentleman's abode.

Owen's days were full and busy at the office, for now that the captain had a free hand he brought in more skippers, carried more cargo and ran a kind of advisory insurance brokers. He also took on a young lad called Gus, a pleasant, willing boy with bright red hair, who had been to the same charity school that had given the captain his own start in life.

Owen's prospects were so much brighter than they had been that he felt he should have been content with all this, but deep inside, he was aware of a persistent sense of being trapped.

Every Sunday afternoon he was invited to the Brownes' house for tea. Tea was served in the garden or in the conservatory, depending on the weather. As always, Katy blushed and giggled as she cut huge slices of cake to fill Owen's plate. Her round rosy face with its heavy features had come to seem very attractive to Owen and he admired her long black curls which were often tied with a scarlet ribbon. Tall gangly Georgina still lounged about in an ungainly fashion, her legs over the arms of a chair, allowing the flounces of her drawers to show. And after tea, she was often argumentative and aggressive.

But Owen's favourite at this stage was Mary. She was

always so sweet and cheerful, almost skipping about in a pretty, flimsy dress, as light as a feather on her toes. She was always smiling and affectionate.

Their beak-nosed mother would sit in the adjoining parlour on these occasions, often with a Bible on her lap. She would pretend to read but really she was keeping an eye on her bevy of lovely daughters, making sure that they all, especially Georgina, conducted themselves in a sufficiently ladylike manner.

But soon these Sunday teas became very tedious to Owen, and he began to long for five o'clock when the fiercesome Eva would rise ponderously and with mock civility say: 'Now, young ladies, it is time to prepare for dinner.'

Never once was the invitation extended to Owen; Eva had never forgiven him for being her brother's heir, for inheriting the half of the business that had been built up by her beloved father. She made Owen welcome in her house because her husband had demanded it and she was an obedient wife. Also, she had calculated that if Katy really did have her eye on Owen, and she certainly seemed to have, and they joined in marriage, then at least the business would remain in the family. But she would not entertain him herself, nor introduce him to her friends. No, she detested him. He was an interloper.

Owen knew that Eva disliked him but he continued to go regularly to tea at her house because her daughters amused him and there was very little to do in town on Sundays, what with the office and the inns being closed.

On Saturday at lunch time he often met Tom at the Blue Boar, where they would down a few drinks together before Tom went off, with Old Dawg running beside him to his old haunts, out to Rat's Castle and the other merry sporting gentlemen.

One Sunday evening, Owen left the lively company of the Browne girls feeling rather depressed and lonely. With his sketchbook under his arms, he wandered through the deserted streets of town and then walking beside the river. He walked on down to the poorer parts of town, to the wharves and back alleys of the Medway, downhill along the tow-path, past the huge overhead arch which carried the new railway line down to the coast.

Wooden shacks lined the path and rubbish was piled

higgledy-piggledy along the river banks. The waters of the river were green and polluted as they washed the shore.

Owen seated himself on a large block of stone left over by the developers of the railway, and began to draw. Within minutes he had captured the desolate poverty, the stricken surroundings, and a thin mangy cat turning over the rubbish to find a meal of sorts. Far off, he could see a tall chimney belching out evil black smoke from its factory furnace. Then suddenly, behind him, he heard a familiar sound: a dry irritating cough. He knew he had heard it before. He looked behind at several dreary cottages and a long wooden shack which could have been a stable. It was from here that the sound came.

His curiosity getting the better of him, Owen walked alongside the shack and tried to peer in through the shuttered windows. There was something moving inside, but it was hard to see what it was. He heard that dry cough once more. Then there was some rustling, and a little moan as if bodies turned restlessly.

A heavy padlock secured the wooden door, so Owen bent down and put his eye to a chink in the woodwork. An astonishing sight now met his gaze – a line of sleeping children lying on straw. Under old sacks they lay in a communal bed, top and bottom – boys and girls of all ages. And there, on the end, was the head of the silvery-blonde little girl who had fled from Dobbs' office.

Fury and sorrow convulsed Owen. These children were sleeping like animals, locked up in order to be fresh for work on Monday. What kind of human being could do this to another human? The blood in his veins seemed to boil with anger as his fingers grappled with the padlock.

But then suddenly he received a hefty push from behind, almost knocking him off his feet. Turning around, he saw a slovenly girl glaring at him.

'Ere, wot you doing spying on our kids?' she demanded. Before Owen could answer, the girl opened a large mouth and yelled: 'Polly! Come out here! Someone's poking 'is nose in, interfering wiv our kids.'

From one of the cottages a massive woman appeared, rushing forward like a bull. She made a terrifying sight, waving an empty gin bottle in front of her red and mottled face. Her hair was tied in two tangled plaits, and her clothes were a bundle of bulging shirts and bodices.

'What's up, Sophie?' she slurred. Then, seeing Owen, she headed straight for him, yelling: 'Jack! Come out here! We got trouble.'

From behind her dashed a sprightly little man in stockinged feet and shirt sleeves. On his head was a beaver cap with ear flaps that stuck out like animals ears. Owen was stunned by the sight of this couple and just stood opening and shutting his mouth in a stupid manner.

Suddenly the little man stopped in his tracks. He had recognised Owen from the crowd at Rat's Castle. In fact he was an acquaintance of big Tom's. 'Wait a bit, Polly,' he cried. 'This fellow is a gentleman. I knows him.'

Polly snorted. 'Well what's he doing here, then?' she demanded. 'Don't let no one poke around down 'ere.'

''E was peekin' through a crack in the door,' chimed in the young girl.

'All right, calm down, I'll see to it,' said the man waving his hands authoritatively. 'Now, go inside, I'll settle this.'

With a withering look and muttered snarls, the women retired to the cottage doorway from where they could keep watch.

'I am sorry about that, sir,' the man said, touching those grotesque ear flaps respectfully. 'You know what women are like, always jumping to their own conclusions.'

Owen stared at him in horror unable to utter a word.

'Scared yer, did they?' asked the oily little man, rubbing his hands together. 'Yer, shouldn't wander down here, by rights, at least not on your own.'

Still Owen stood speechless.

'I've seen you before,' the man continued. 'Up at Rat's Castle, with big Tom. You're the bloke what does the drawing, ain't yer?' He continued to rub his palms on his pants as though they were too tight.

At last Owen found his voice. 'I am making enquiries about that little blonde girl in there,' he stammered.

A lewd smile appeared on the unpleasant face. 'What girl,' the man asked.

'The tiny one with the silvery-blonde hair,' replied Owen.

'Oh, Tinsel,' the man exclaimed with a grin. 'Now, don't

come that one on me, sir. She is too young and not very healthy. Have Sophie, she will do a bit of housework for you, too. Nice obliging girl, is Sophie.'

He pointed to the blowsy wench at the cottage door standing watching them with her arms akimbo.

The man's evil smile sickened Owen. He wanted to swear, hit someone or even run, but all he did was to say quietly: 'How do I get out of here?'

'Ah! I thought yer had lost yer way,' announced Jack. 'Walk up river and there's the town.'

This time a restless hand was spread out wide, waiting for the coin which Owen then placed there. 'Good day, sir.' He touched his absurd hat ingratiatingly and again that suggestive grin spread over his face.

As he walked away, Owen could hear them cackling loudly at their encounter with him. He set off back for the town and his lonely chambers. The sound of that dry cough and the thought of those children stabled like donkeys remained like a raging fire in his mind.

'I am a coward,' he told himself. 'Why didn't I knock that evil man down?' He cursed himself for his feebleness but he knew that they would have attacked him in force, there was no doubt about that, and then he would have been just another dead body washed up by the river. But what about those children? He had to do something, but what? All night long that blonde head and dry cough haunted his dreams.

On Monday he sent a message to Tom telling him to meet him that evening. Tom was there at the appointed time but he rebuffed Owen's suggestion that they go to the Bull and have a good roast dinner. 'No, thanks, mate,' he said bluntly. 'You may be society now, but I knows me place. It's the Blue Boar, and a beer and sandwich for me.'

So Owen gave in and they were soon installed in the public bar. It was like old times as Tom cracked jokes and gave lurid accounts of Old Dawg's prowess as a killer, munching his sandwich and washing it down all at the same time. For Owen it was good to be with his lively friend once again. He felt so completely relaxed in his raucous company.

'Ma says to come up and have a good Sunday dinner sometime. Never mind those airy fairy cakes and arse parties at the old dragon's.'

Owen laughed heartedly at such daring rudeness.

'That's better, Olly,' said Tom. 'I thought you had forgotten how to laugh since you came into money.'

'I had a rather depressing adventure yesterday,' confided Owen. 'I found that little waif, the one I took in briefly, stabled like an animal down by the river.'

Tom's keen eyes looked at his sharply, 'I know, mate,' he said. 'That girl belongs to Polly, the woman who farms the kids out. It's a bloody disgrace but it's not against the law and no one can touch her.'

'So you've known where that little girl is for all this time,' Owen said reproachfully.

Tom nodded. 'Not a lot goes on in this town what I don't get to know about,' he boasted.

'But surely there's some way to release her,' insisted Owen.

'It's no good, boy. Polly owns those kinds. She bought her from the convent.'

'A religious house that sells children?' Owen was incredulous.

'It's not exactly like that,' explained Tom. 'These are hard times and any orphaned children are left in the nuns' care. The nuns take them in hoping to find a home for them later as a small favour to the families and to help feed the other poor little devils.'

'By God, what a home!' declared Owen.

Tom sighed, a little irritated at Owen's naïvety. 'Look here, mate,' he insisted, 'why don't you try to forget it. We can't afford to dwell on these things. Life is a survival of the fittest, and most of those kids will survive. Proper little thieves, they are. They come nicking down the dockside, they do.'

Owen was silent as his mind dwelt on the fact that Tom filched rum from the bonded warehouse and swapped it with the locals for favours done. Clearly honesty was not the issue in question.

Tom had gone to the bar and returned with two foaming jugs of ale. He set them on the table and looked down at his pal. 'Cheer up, Olly,' he said. 'I told you I'd help if I could. I know that slimy git Jack well. He only lives with Polly. She's the one who owns the kids.'

'What if I offered to buy the girl from them?' ventured Owen.

'It would depend on how much you offered,' replied Tom. 'It would also depend on various things, such as how much work is left in the kid. It sounds to me as if she won't last another winter, so you might well be able to make a deal with them.'

Owen shivered. It was grotesque to even consider bargaining over flesh and blood. His sensitive nature could hardly bear it. He sat head down, his face a pale mask.

Tom slapped him on the back. 'Now come, Olly, don't take on so,' he urged. 'I'll go with you to see Slimy Jack. But what will you do with the kid if you get her?'

Owen shook a bewildered head. He did not know.

'You realise what they will think you want her for?' queried Tom.

Owen looked up at Tom, and knew what he meant by his expression. He was horrified. 'Oh, no, my God, but she's only a baby!' he cried.

'Well, that's how their minds work. If they sell her to you they will wait awhile and then inform the police that she is living on your premises. Then you'll have the police nosing about. I don't think you can afford the notoriety, Olly.'

Loyally, Tom tried to deter him, but it seemed Owen's mind was made up.

'I'll ask Katy to care for her. I'm sure she will,' he said suddenly.

'Hmm, that's possible,' muttered Tom. 'And the old dragon may be strict but at least she is civilised, which is more than you can say about those bastards down by the river.'

So their plans were laid there and then. Tom would negotiate with Slimy Jack and then Tom and Owen would meet later on in the week.

A week later, Tom paid a lunchtime visit to the office. His huge shape in the doorway blocked out the light and Owen looked up from his pile of papers.

'Can't stay,' Tom hollered, 'but we're meeting Jack tonight at the Dockside Tavern. You'd better be there with me, Olly.' With that, he breezed off.

For the rest of the day, Owen felt acutely anxious. It had become vitally important to him that he procure this child.

The bar was a smoke-filled cellar and full of sailors, for the liberty boats docked at this time each night and the bar was the nearest drinking place. Amid the swearing and shouting crowd they found Slimy Jack, picking him out in the crowd by his fur cap.

He looked a little cleaner this time and was wearing a leather coat, but he still had the air of a rascal, and an evil one at that.

Tom caught him roughly by the collar. 'Into the parlour, Jack,' he growled, 'we have business to discuss.'

So Jack had no option but to go into that small room where there was just a piano and a couple of chairs. There the three men sat down close together like three conspirators to discuss the fate of one small girl.

'Polly is none too keen,' began Slimy Jack, 'but since it's for a pal I managed to persuade her – for a price of course,' he added quickly.

'How much?' demanded Tom abruptly.

Jack ignored this question and went on explaining. 'Nice little kid – pretty, ain't she?' he addressed Owen. 'It's that lovely hair that takes the eye. Polly is always threatening to cut it off but I always stop her. The kid's been working regular, she has. In the sack factory. Can't get her out on the fields, bloody wilful, she is.'

'What is it you want,' asked Owen wearily. He hated this coarse fellow and wanted to get away from him as quickly as possible.

'Well, I thought you might make an offer,' said Jack warily.

Tom trod on Owen's foot, warning him to be silent. 'Now how much do you want?' he demanded aggressively of Jack.

'Well, we are very fond of her, and we don't want no harm to come to her,' hedged Jack. 'Of course,' he added with a sly look, 'we all knows that you arty-crafty blokes have got your funny ways.' He almost sniggered.

Owen went deathly white.

'Well,' said Jack, feeling the tension, 'what about twenty quid?'

Owen wanted to puke. This disgusting creature was convinced that he, Owen wanted that child for some sexual perversity. 'Hand over the child to me and I'll produce the money,' he said quietly.

'Right, then,' said Jack, rubbing his hands together. 'That's settled, then. Of course, there will be a little extra for me trouble. If Polly says twenty quid she means it. I won't get a bean out of that, I won't, so if you could find it in your way, sir, just another pound or two . . .' His tone had become crafty and cadging.

But suddenly a big hand came out and pushed Jack flat in the face. Jack's chair went back against the wall, and he hung there, looking very surprised.

'Not another penny!' shouted Tom, rising with a fist waving.

'All right, then,' cried Jack, gesticulating wildly as he came upright. 'I'll settle for a drop of the hard stuff.'

Tom reached into his back pocket and passed Jack a bottle of rum.

'Right, the bargain's made, and no welching,' threatened Tom. 'Come on, Olly, let's get out into the fresh air. This bloke stinks.'

Feeling rather dejected, they walked back through the town to the Blue Boar, but once they were back in those familiar surroundings they relaxed at last. 'Well, the deed is done,' said Tom.

Owen nodded gratefully. 'My sincere thanks to you, Tom, I am sure you will never regret it,' he said. 'I have had that child on my mind for so long.'

Tom shrugged modestly. 'Well, I like to see you happy. Come on, let's drown our cares in good Kentish ale.'

The following afternoon, Tom came into the office carrying in his arms the little blond girl whom he plonked unceremoniously on to the desk. 'Look what Uncle Tom's got!' he cried.

The child had tucked her head tight down under Tom's thick arm and would not look up. Her feet were bare, her knees covered with scabs and she wore an old rag of a frock.

'Got an odd name, it seems. She's called Tinsel,' said Tom. 'She was born on Christmas Eve outside the convent. Her mother was a travelling player on hard times and did not survive.'

Tears wet Owen's eyes as he looked at the child. She had lifted her head at last. Her nose was red and sticky as if she had a permanent cold, but her eyes were as blue as the summer sky, and her hair hung down in a golden mane right to her small waist.

'How old is she?' he asked. 'She's still tiny and seems to have grown very little since I saw her last year.'

'Well, she wouldn't grow, would she?' said Tom stroking her

lovely hair. 'They don't bother to feed the poor little sods, do they?'

Owen surveyed the child, afraid to touch her.

'Polly said she is turned ten,' said Tom, 'and according to her she's a bad-tempered child, and not very healthy. Now there's a bloody good bargain,' he joked. He pulled out a short stick of barley sugar from his pocket and waggled it in front of her. 'Say thank you, Uncle Tom.'

The girl smiled as she grabbed the sweet and popped the whole piece in her mouth. 'Tank oo, Tom,' she muttered, her cheeks bulging. Tom roared with laughter.

'See!' he said. 'I got her trained already.'

'Will you stay with me, Tinsel?' asked Owen when she had finished the sweet.

Tinsel looked straight at him. 'I must,' she said. 'I work for you now.'

'Oh dear,' cried Owen, 'she thinks I'm her new owner.;'

'Well, let her,' muttered Tom. 'If that's what she thinks, then she will stay put. It's what she's used to.'

'I'll send Gus with a message to Katy,' said Owen.

'Do that,' said Tom, 'but first hand me the money. Slimy Jack is waiting in the alley for it, and he's likely to razor me if he thinks we're dodging the pay-off.'

Owen counted out the twenty coins and Tom quickly left.

Tinsel sat demurely in a chair sucking the other piece of barley sugar Tom had left her.

When Gus returned to the office, Owen dispatched him immediately to the Brownes' house with a message for Katy, asking her to come to his chambers that evening for an important reason.

Tinsel gave him no trouble at all, merely clutching at his hand as they walked home. And she was rather afraid of the long gloomy flight of stairs up to Owen's rooms.

Once in the large parlour, Owen lit a fire. He wrapped Tinsel in a rug and she finally stopped coughing and shivering, which, Owen noticed, she seemed to do more when she was nervous. Then he boiled some milk for her, knelt beside her and pressed her to drink from the jug.

Soon the door bell clanged, announcing the arrival of Katy and Georgina, veils obscuring their faces. They glanced to the right and left as though afraid of being seen.

'Oh, Owen,' gasped Georgina, 'I couldn't let Katy come unchaperoned, but I'll wait in the other room if you like.'

Owen looked puzzled as Katy stood before him wide-eyed and flushed, with an adoring look on her face. Suddenly he realised what Georgina meant. It had never occurred to him that she might think that he was about to propose.

'Oh, but I'm delighted you came along too, Georgina,' he said in a rush to explain. 'I have a major problem to settle.'

The women divested themselves of their many wraps and paused when they noticed Tinsel sitting so demurely in the big plush chair.

'Goodness! What's that?' cried Georgina.

'Who is the child?' asked Katy.

'She is mine,' replied Owen artlessly, regretting immediately when he saw how shocked they were.

'Oh, I mean, I bought her for twenty pounds,' he added quickly.

'Why on earth should you buy her?' queried Georgina.

Katy went over to Tinsel and wiped the dewdrop from the little red nose. 'Poor little thing,' she commented. 'She's sadly neglected. Is this the child you saw at the hiring fair, Owen?'

Owen smiled gratefully; he had known that Katy would understand. 'Yes, I paid twenty pounds to get her away from those dreadful people.'

'Well, I'm impressed, Owen,' Georgina said, marching up and down. 'What a magnificent gesture!'

'Get me some nice warm soap and water,' said Katy. 'I'm going to give her a wash and bathe those sore knees.'

Without a murmur, Tinsel resigned herself to being washed and fussed over by these scented ladies. They wiped her limbs and brushed her silken hair, praising its softness.

Owen watched this performance with mixed feelings. It was very touching but was it genuine? At last he asked the question he needed to ask: 'Will your mother take Tinsel in to live with you?'

The girls looked surprised and also very doubtful. 'No one gets into our house unless they have been vetted by at least half a dozen vicars,' Katy murmured wryly. 'Mother is very fussy.'

There was a heavy silence, broken by a bitter sigh from Owen. 'Well, never mind, she can stay here,' he said through clenched teeth. 'What do I care for propriety?'

Katy and Georgina sat together on the sofa and conversed in whispers, their heads close together, curls shaking.

Owen waited patiently for them to speak.

'This is what we have decided, Owen,' said Georgina at last. 'We will smuggle Tinsel into our house and let Mary in on the secret. Mary will ward Mother off. Meanwhile we will clean Tinsel up and dress her respectably. Then Katy will pretend that a friend has asked her to find a home for her. She will say that she has been brought up in a good family who are off to India.' She paused and looked worried. 'It will be awfully wicked to tell so many lies,' she added.

'Never mind,' returned Georgina. 'We know that it will be in a good cause.'

'Once Mother has agreed to look after her she will be good to her, I'm sure of that,' said Katy. The words poured gently from her red rosy mouth, her dark eyes looked somberly at him.

'Oh, thank you, girls!' Owen put an arm about both their shoulders and gave them a brotherly squeeze. Tears of disappointment sprang into Katy's eyes as she finally realised that Tinsel was the sole reason for her summons. She had been so sure that Owen was going to declare his undying love for her.

So Tinsel went off placidly in the pony trap, seated between those two lovely ladies. Her future was being changed by the actions of these benefactors, and she was aware of it.

CHAPTER FIVE

A Home for Tinsel

All that week Owen waited anxiously for news of the child
Tinsel. But there was nothing but silence from the house on
the hill. In the evenings, he would sit in the bay of the narrow
window, puffing thoughtfully on a long pipe, his gaze focused
on the main street. He was always hoping to catch a glimpse of
the girls out shopping or visiting acquaintances. Suppose the
worst happened and they brought the child back? What would
he do with her? In such an event he could try Tom's mother,
but she was getting on a bit and already had the vicar and Tom
to care for.

As Owen thought about his concern to find a place in his
world for that small waif, he wondered why he felt so keenly
about her. He had badly wanted to cuddle her but had been too
shy to show his feelings. He recalled how Katy had fussed
because Tinsel's knees and elbows had been so dirty, they
would not come entirely clean, and the nails on those tiny
hands had been cracked and broken.

The child had shown them wordlessly how she came by
these defects. She had knelt on the floor moving her hands as if
sewing, just as she did in the sack factory where she had been
constantly on her knees and elbows sewing the huge hop bags
together.

As they watched, the adults had at first been amused but
then were terribly shocked. Owen was amazed to see how this
child was too inarticulate to explain verbally, but intelligent
enough to act out the part. She was like an animal in her

57

behaviour, no doubt as a result of the treatment she had received from those fiendish people down by the riverside.

Owen puffed hard at his pipe. The little muscle at the side of his face moving spasmodically as it often did in times of stress. Poor unwanted child! There was no doubt that she reminded Owen of himself. How neurotic he had been in his youth, unable to express himself in words as he wanted to ...

He was started out of his reverie by the loud clatter of a pony trap rattling down the high street. He peered out of the window to see the Brownes' trap, driven by Georgina dressed in a big thick coat and a tweed cap jammed down tightly over her forehead. With brisk movements, she jumped down, tethered the pony and ran swiftly up the steps.

At last! Owen was so relieved to see her. Now he would learn of the verdict.

'Good day, Owen,' Georgina cried boisterously. 'I thought you would like to hear the good news.'

Owen gasped. 'Come in, and welcome, Georgina,' he said.

'Well, it worked. We got mama hooked,' she declared jubilantly, catching her breath. 'Katy wouldn't come because she is suffering from a heavy twinge of conscience,' she explained. 'The weight of the lies was almost too much for her,' she laughed.

'Well, we dressed Tinsel up in a discarded dress of Mary's, then kept her hidden for a day or so while we trained her. She is very bright, you know. She learned everything very fast. Mama was rather suspicious at first, and seemed to recognise the gown but we managed to convince her that Tinsel was a genuine orphan brought up by a schoolfriend of Katy's. And it worked.'

Georgina banged her knee excitedly and lolled back in the armchair. She was very pleased with herself.

'I am extremely grateful to you, Georgina,' murmured Owen. 'Any expense you have incurred I would like to recompense.'

'Don't be silly,' scoffed Georgina. 'Tinsel's going to get a shilling a week. She'll be better off than I am,' she declared ruefully.

Owen sighed. So he had handed Tinsel over from one bondage to another. Well, at least she would be cared for and well fed.

'It was so funny,' continued Georgina. 'Mama kept stuffing medicine down Mary's throat because she was convinced that it was Mary coughing in the night. Mary was far from pleased, I can assure you.'

As Georgina chatted on exuberantly, Owen realised how fond of her he was. She was so unusual and refreshing in what was generally a stuffy world.

'Well, I'd better leave you,' Georgina said. 'I'm supposed to be over at Wright's Farm collecting the butter and eggs. Good day, Owen.'

Owen watched Georgina drive down the main street, scarf flying out and cap awry, and he wondered what lay ahead for his adventurous young friend.

On Sunday Owen took up his standing invitation to Honeysuckle Cottage. He hired an old nag from the stage coach inn and arrived just in time to see that diminutive lady and her huge son coming out of church from the morning service. Framed by the lych-gate and the ivy-covered walls they made a pleasant picture. They waved a cheery greeting to him.

Soon the three of them were all gathered around a well-laden table. There was a cold leg of lamb, baked the previous day, roast potatoes, boiled carrots, turnips and parsnips, and a hot suet pudding, followed by raspberry tart and farm cream. What a feast for Owen whose meagre bachelor meals seldom satisfied his healthy youthful appetite!

'My,' declared Tom's mother as she ladled hot gravy onto his plate, 'I do believe this lad is filling out at last.'

Owen blushed. But she was right. There was no doubt about the fact that he had improved vastly in appearance. His skin was no longer spotty, just clear and sun-tanned, his brown curls thick and glossy, his sideburns long and bushy.

'You are growing into a very handsome man, Owen,' remarked Ma.

Tom was shovelling food into his mouth and as he began to snigger, he almost choked.

'Mind your manners, Tom, or leave the table,' Ma reproved him, and then they all laughed.

That afternoon, Tom and Owen wandered in the orchards as they used to. By six o'clock they were ready for evensong. The church was lit by the late evening sun shining through the stained-glass windows. Once more the villagers' voices joined

in unison in praise of the Lord. And once more it was home to
a supper of cold mutton pie and pickles washed down with
parsnip wine. The vicar and the sexton had joined them and it
was a wonderfully relaxed evening. Ma's face was flushed with
the effects of the wine, as she joked with the guests and teased
Owen. They were happy with such simple pleasures – choice
bits of parish gossip, the recent wedding of a young girl to an
old rich farmer, the bantering, and the joking which was so
happy and spontaneous. Owen felt warm and content, truly at
home, unlike how he felt with the stiff-necked dragon Mrs
Browne and her giggling females.

The vicar told Owen that his university friend had shown
Owen's sketches to a literary acquaintance who had been most
impressed and was anxious to meet Owen himself.

Ma was delighted and proud to hear the news. 'He is a
bright, clever boy,' she boasted, as though he were her son.

At nine o'clock, Owen started back to town feeling greatly
uplifted, and from then on, he began to spend the long summer
weekends out at Honeysuckle Cottage, roaming the marsh-
lands with Tom, fishing and shooting and even going out to
Rat's Castle with Old Dawg for the ratting season.

Owen filled another sketchbook with rustic drawings,
fantastic humorous little figures sprawled everywhere, each
page telling a funny or tragic tale. He had visited the hulks out
in the river and had been appalled at the conditions of the
convicts awaiting transport to Australia. These sentiments
resulted in more sketches, and more captions of life in the raw,
the decrepit, the picturesque, rags, filth and starvation. He
needed to expose all the poverty he saw. His conscience would
not allow otherwise.

One morning he received a letter from London. He gazed at
it in apprehension. Surely no one remembered him from there.
He had been away from it for so long. But he was amazed on
opening the envelope to find that it was from a certain Mr
Greenbanks, who described himself as an artist's and author's
agent, a friend of the vicar's friend who had taken Owen's first
book of sketches to London. Mr. Greenbanks wrote to say that
a certain magazine was interested in his work. Breathless with
excitement, Owen re-read the letter twice. At last someone had
acknowledged the fact that he had something to tell the world!

Owen wrote back to Mr Greenbanks immediately, stating

that he would come to London and meet the gentleman at his earliest convenience.

After he had posted the letter, he felt so elated that all he could do at lunchtime was walk restlessly about – thinking of how he could tell Katy his good news.

Quite suddenly, he realised he had begun to miss her, her motherly attitude, and her understanding ways. How he wished he had the courage to call on her. But he decided to wait at the bottom of the hill so that if they were out visiting he could catch a glimpse of them coming home.

At two o'clock the little pony cart came rattling along, driven by Georgina. Katy was sitting sedately beside her and behind them sat a demure little girl, beautifully dressed and with blonde corkscrew curls tapering from a pretty bonnet. It was Tinsel! Owen hardly recognised her.

'Whoa, there!' Georgina halted the pony. 'Hello, Owen,' she called. 'What a surprise.'

Katy did not look at him. She just hung her head; her normally rosy cheeks were rather pale. When Tinsel saw him, she gave him a mischievous grin. Her widely spaced teeth which had previously been yellow were now a gleaming white. She held a full shopping basket in her lap and boxes and bags from fancy shops were spread around her in the back of the carriage. She looked like a different person to what she had been before. Owen wanted to put that tiny mitten hand to his lips but he suppressed that rash impulse. With those deep-set blue eyes surveying him in a disarmingly adult manner, he pulled himself up quickly.

'How are you, Katy?' he asked.

Katy bowed her head stiffly. 'I am quite well, thank you,' she replied.

Georgina gave an exaggerated shrug. 'We must go, Owen,' she called. 'Mama is waiting with tea for us.'

As the women went rattling away, Owen felt strangely defeated. He realised that he must have offended Katy. But he was not sure exactly how. He decided then that perhaps he ought to call the following Sunday and make his apologies for his absence to Eva Browne. But he was not at all sure about how much he wanted to get involved again. He guessed that Katy had set her cap at him, but he was still only twenty and the last thing he needed was marriage, at least not until he had established himself properly as an artist, as he longed to do.

Thinking of the sight of Tinsel, he smiled. The Brownes had certainly made a fine job of rehabilitating the child. He was extremely grateful to them for that. But, he thought cynically, she probably had to earn her keep, so he should not feel too obliged to them.

Tinsel was certainly a little beauty. Good food and plenty of rest had improved her enormously She seemed to have matured a lot since he last saw her.

Pondering on all these things, Owen returned to the office to make arrangements for his trip to London. And elaborate arrangements they were.

He had left London two years before. Then, he had been without a penny in his pocket, in danger of being arrested for debt, and almost on the point of starvation. His return had to be made in a different style – more befitting his station in life, for this had improved considerably. After all, he was now a person of some importance in this Medway town. Although he had not yet reached his maturity, he was half-owner of a profitable shipping agents and about to discuss the possible publication of his sketches.

First, he decided on a new suit and some fancy waistcoats. A flowing cravat was needed, as was a tall hat in silver grey to match the jacket which fitted tightly at the waist and had long tails which reached over his buttocks. Tight, smooth pants of a deep grey would run down his legs to dapper suede boots. He was going to look like a fine dandy in all this.

The next day, dressed up in all his finery, he placed his new book of sketches on top of the shirts in his travelling bag. He was all set.

As he made his way to the coaching station, he walked with swinging jaunty steps, occasionally catching sight of himself in the shop windows. He felt very pleased with the images he saw in the glass but inwardly he was still anxious. Had it been a good idea to recruit Cousin Bertie, old Dobbs' nephew, to take charge of the office, while he was away for a few days? Bertie had come with pretended reluctance, humming and hawing, and muttering about being used. But a fair sum advanced from the petty cash had settled the question.

At the coaching inn, Owen was asked by the slightly intoxicated coach driver if he would like to travel 'hinside or hout'.

Owen decided upon inside despite the fact that they would all be packed in like sardines trying not to retch at the odour of snuff and lavender water intermixed. Owen squeezed in beside a fat man who belched constantly and his small miserable-looking son. Facing them was the over-dressed wife with a small daughter. The children horsed about. First they made rude faces at each other, and then the girl got a kick in the ankle which made her bawl. They stopped misbehaving when the mother nagged and the man cuffed the boy into submission.

As the coach rattled on down the broad highway to London, Owen began to wish he had opted to travel outside, and the only way he could tolerate the conditions inside was to sit quietly, thinking up the reasons for all these folk travelling. He allowed his strong imagination to weave amazing and fantastic stories about them, elaborating, colouring and expanding. He had expected the big city to be noisy after the peace of the country, but he was quite unprepared for the onslaught of noise that battered his ear drums. Despite his smart new clothes he found his knees trembling as he stood outside the Victorian coaching inn. Then he saw, on the opposite side of the road, the newly opened railway station. Crowds of people stood in the entrance idly watching an engine get up steam. As a huge snake of white smoke sailed over their heads and a strong vibration shook the earth, the crowd shouted and gesticulated wildly. Mothers nervously gathered up their children and others began to run as the big engine moved off.

The air was loaded with a tense excitement which still scared the nervous young Owen. But soon a stout shape came towards him and held out a friendly hand.

'Mr Oliver, I presume,' a pleasant voice said. 'They all gather here to watch the express leave,' he explained. 'I wondered if you might not travel up to London by train.'

'No, sir,' said Owen, 'so far I never have.'

'Well, you should try it,' said the cheery man. 'The steam engine has come to stay, and fortunes are being made every day on railway shares.'

Owen felt as tongue-tied as usual and did not prolong the conversation. For a moment this bluff jovial man looked at him curiously. Owen Oliver may have a lot of talent but he seemed to be completely devoid of charm.

'Come, sir, we will lunch at the Magpie. There, I shall introduce you to some bright young men-about-town – some with genius and some just layabouts.'

The dining room of the Magpie Inn had a low beamed ceiling. Smoke from the cooking encircled the blackened beams, and behind a long, well-scrubbed counter were huge casks of wine. White-aproned waiters dashed here and there carrying huge trays of food to the customers sitting at cloth-covered tables in high-backed seats. The atmosphere was full of good humour and savoury smells. Owen began to feel slightly ill at ease, very conscious of his mode of dress, for most of the men were not at all smartly dressed. Many seemed to wear black coats with shiny elbows and ink-stained, crumpled shirts. Even Mr Greenbanks was dressed in grubby pantaloons and shiny gaiters. And he had gravy stains on his waistcoat.

Owen was quite surprised. These were not exactly his idea of the élite gentlemen of Fleet Street. Some eyes watched Owen with interest as his tall thin figure edged its way nervously through the crowd. They found a remote corner and the tankard of ale and plate of cold beef and salad went down very well.

After lunch, Mr Greenbanks introduced Owen to a husky young man in a battered silk hat lolling drunkenly over the table.

Owen was struck by how dark and blue his eyes were, and how red-rimmed, as if from lack of sleep.

'How are you, you old devil?' the young man shouted at Mr Greenbanks. 'Who are you fleecing today?'

'This is Mr Oliver, the gentleman who drew the cartoons,' replied Mr Greenbanks, ignoring the insult.

Immediately, there was a tremendous response. The young man sat down, poured himself a glass of wine and peered straight at Owen. 'Damned good they were,' he said. 'I can use them. Have you got any more?' Owen nodded but said nothing.

'If you are looking for a regular pitch as an illustrator, why don't you try Deakins? His illustrator just blew his brains out.'

'Now, that is interesting,' declared Mr Greenbanks.

'There is a meeting tonight. Deakins will be doing a reading of his new novel. If you care to come, you will be most welcome.'

Those hard blue eyes took a good look at Owen. Then he

said, 'Got any work with you?'

As Owen put his new book of sketches on the tables, Mr Greenbanks produced an eye glass and carefully inspected them, exclaiming all the time. 'Great work!' He chuckled loudly at the sight of Old Dawg and the inhabitants of Rat's Castle, and he roared at the sight of old Fanny, with her breasts exposed, separating a drunken youth from his wallet.

'You mean to say there really is such a place?' the young man asked gleefully.

Owen's thin face relaxed into a slow charming smile. At last here was someone who truly appreciated his work. The communication between them was instantaneous.

This husky untidy man who looked so tired was called Forest. He was an editor on a popular magazine, and a well-known figure in London's literary circles.

'Our magazine has bought your first book of sketches,' he said. 'We shall be paying you, of course. Come with me tonight, do. I'd like to show old Deakins these new ones. I know he'll be tickled pink.'

Another bottle of wine was produced. Owen's sketches were passed around and much time was given to discussion of them. The debate went on all around him but the strong wine had given Owen a dazed sense that none of this was really happening.

Mr Greenbanks left, making his apologies. His wife, he said, was waiting with dinner for him. Owen sat on, sipping the wine and listening to the voices around him.

'Who is he?'

'Some fellow up from the country ... unknown?'

'Yes, first attempt ... good stuff. My magazine bought his first book.'

'The old man might be interested ... could be ... but I was thinking of our famous novelist. He's looking for an illustrator.'

'He might, but he's a hard taskmaster.'

'Well we can but try ... He's a nice sort of fellow ... Doesn't have much to say, does he?'

So this dialogue went on and on until they all began to argue among themselves on subjects unintelligible to the already inebriated Owen.

Several hours later, somewhat belligerent and argu-

mentative, the group of men gathered up Owen and set off in a
carriage, destined for Lincoln's Inn. There they congregated in
a large, sparsely furnished room with a dozen or so other men
of all ages. They sat quietly in a semi-circle while a tall man
with a striking appearance settled down to read to them from a
work-in-progress. His loud clear voice was very commanding,
causing the atmosphere in the room to become loaded and
tense. It reminded Owen of creeping into church in the middle
of communion service.

Owen was impressed by the man's presence and he thought
that the penetrating gaze and aqualine features were rather
familiar.

The novelist read from his new book entitled *A Parish Boy's
Progress*. Throughout the reading, his audience sat captivated
as they listened, arms folded, and eyes closed as though
some magnetic power held them.

Owen had always imagined this author to be much older but
he was actually not much older than himself – twenty-five,
possibly. Yet he had such power and imagination!

Once the reading was over, there was a friendly discussion
after which pipes were lit and food and drink were brought in.
Then the room split up into little groups for conversation.

Owen still felt horribly shy, and his heart beat fast as Forest
nudged him. 'The great man is coming over to you, now, lad,' he
said. 'Use your head. I'll disappear once I have introduced you.'

'Good evening, Mr Oliver, you're our new guest tonight.'
The novelist grasped Owen's hand firmly and fixed his penetrating eyes on his face. 'I've been looking at your sketches,' he
said. 'You certainly have talent, young man,' he added with a
patronising air. 'I come from your part of the country,' he went
on. 'It's a favourite spot of mine. I might even go back some
day.' His eyes roamed the room as if already seeking someone
else of interest. 'I would like to keep the book of sketches, if
you don't mind,' he said. 'I'll let you know if I can use them.
Make sure that Forest knows where to find you.'

Then Deakins drifted off to the other side of the room and
was soon engaged in a heated discussion with some of his
literary colleagues.

Any confidence Owen may have had, drained from him. He
felt utterly deflated and he wished he were back home in
Chatham.

CHAPTER SIX

The Sleeping Tiger

By the time he had returned home, Owen was feeling even more dejected then ever, having convinced himself that he had been a proper ass in front of all those talented men. He felt that he would never see the great novelist again, and that his sketches would be held up for ridicule. A deep gloom descended upon him as he put away his smart clothes and reverted again to wearing his shabby suit and tall, ink-stained hat.

Then he wandered listlessly back to the office which he found to be in a terrible upheaval.

Cousin Bertie was there, loud and vibrant, sweating profusely as he poured out a long list of complaints about the rudeness of Gus, the office boy, and the shortage of ready cash.

Irritated, Owen paid him off and then ordered Gus to open the windows and clean up the office.

'I'm darned glad to see the back of that Bertie,' muttered the red-headed Gus. 'I couldn't have taken much more of him. Acts as though he owns the place, he does.'

Meanwhile, Cousin Bertie left, muttering to himself that he was going to enlighten the good Captain Browne about the shoddy business methods of this upstart Oliver.

But when he did, Captain Browne simply puffed at his long cigar and looked extremely bored. He was not interested. Recently back from his latest voyage, his main concern was for his little Katy, his favourite daughter. She seemed very pale and unhappy. Captain Browne was irritated because it seemed that the idiot down in the office had not proposed yet. He decided to give Owen a prod. After all, the business had to stay in the family.

So to add to Owen's troubles, the captain breezed in to the office that afternoon.

'Ah! Owen, me lad!' He gave Owen a good hard slap between the shoulders, shaking him from head to foot. 'All ship-shape and Bristol fashion, eh?'

Browne's eyes roved around the files, as he sat in a chair, his long legs spread out. 'I hear you were commissioned to do some sketches, eh?'

'The sale is still pending. I only went up to see the editor,' explained Owen.

'No, mind, but from little acorns big oaks grow,' said the captain cheerfully.

'I should know quite soon,' explained Owen.

Browne shook his head. 'They won't hurry themselves. None more lazy than those tykes, editors and publishers. I shouldn't bank too much on it, lad.'

Owen nodded miserably.

'Now, we must not neglect the real business – ships and cargoes. That's what makes the world go around.'

Owen did not reply. He just continued with his work, checking a list which Bertie had muddled up.

'How's the love life, son?' asked the captain. 'There's not much progress I gather.'

Owen looked up with a puzzled expression.

'Our Katy. You've not asked her yet?' Browne looked him straight in the eye.

Owen's cheeks reddened but he remained silent.

The captain got to his feet and gave Owen another good thump. 'Now, lad, don't be shy with me. Get a move on, pick the cherry while it's still sweet and ripe.'

The blush extended to Owen's ears which grew quite scarlet. Helplessly, he grappled for the right answer.

'All right, lad,' said the captain kindly. 'I'll not pry. Just come up to dinner tonight. Georgina will pick you up.'

Once the captain had left, Owen breathed a deep sigh of relief. What an idiot he was! Of course, it was plain. They expected him to marry Katy. The idea had never really fully sunk in before! Suddenly he felt as though the captain had dropped a huge fishing net over him. He felt quite trapped. He was not in love with Katy. Certainly her womanly charms appealed to him, but he felt for her none of that hot inner passion that he had given to his first love, the one who had mocked and scorned him. Where a warm heart had been there was only a cold stone, an icy void. He felt as though he could never face up to a love affair again.

Owen suddenly realised that he had either to marry Katy or pull up stakes and go. The latter appealed to him even less than the former. After all, he had had such good luck since he had come to the Medway. Perhaps it was only fair to marry Katy, he thought. After all, what he had of the business really belonged to her.

Over and over again, Owen tried to find an easy way out of his dilemma. He was not ready for marriage yet, he knew. In fact, he knew very little about the physical side of life. His first love had been so pure and sacred and he had never had any physical contact with a woman. The nearest he had ever been was when old Fanny at the Rat's Castle had tried to seduce him. Well, he thought, if he proposed to Katy it would probably be quite a while before they actually wed and Katy would be well protected by her mother.

His fate was sealed. That evening he dressed with care, putting on his best suit and choosing a rose from the front garden for his button-hole. All the while he rehearsed his opening speech to Katy in his head.

At last Georgina arrived, signalling her presence with a whistle. She wore a thick flowing cloak as she sprawled in the bouncy little pony trap. As always, Tinsel sat in the back seat with a basket of provisions on her lap. She greeted Owen with a pretty grin and a lingering look. Owen wanted to reach out and stroke that lovely flaxen hair. It was so strange that this child excited him so much.

'Get in!' yelled Georgina. 'Otherwise we'll be late for dinner.'

It was a well-served meal – delicious meats with the best of wines – presided over by that grim dragon who wore plumes in her hair. Katy and Mary looked sweet and pretty with flowers in their thick glossy hair. Georgina, of course, had no time for such frivolities. It was a smart, plain grey dress for her and her hair was pulled back in a tight bun above the merry brown eyes which sparkled from her well-scrubbed rosy face.

The captain drank a good deal, as did his other guest, a retired sea captain. And after dinner, the two old salts went to the library to finish the bottle.

Owen's hostess, the formidable Eva, sat in a straight-backed chair with a watchful expression on her face while Katy played the piano and Mary sang in a high contralto voice. After the entertainment had finished, it was Georgina who suggested they played charades. Owen was paired off with Katy to hide behind the drawing-room curtains while Mary and Georgina prepared their act.

Behind the curtain, Katy leaned close to Owen. She smelled of wood violets, he thought, and the moon cast soft shadows on her young face. Owen suddenly and impulsively held her hand to his lips.

Without hesitation, Katy threw her arms tightly around his neck. 'Owen!' she gasped. 'I thought you were never going to ask me.' Then she burst into a flood of tears.

Owen was appalled. His heart was beating madly with fear. He had inadvertently sprung the trap. What was he to do now?

'Come out, you two!' yelled Georgina. 'We're ready!' Her voice tailed off as she caught the sight of her sister in tears.

Katy fled into her mother's arms. 'Oh, Mama!' she cried. 'Owen proposed!'

After that, it was congratulations and celebrations all round. But Owen felt completely detached from it all, overwhelmed by a feeling of numbness. The captain came from the library, flushed with drink and very jovial, insisting that they all drink to the couple's health.

Amid all the excitement, there was only one person in the room who seemed to react differently. The sky blue eyes stared at Owen, unblinking and condemning.

A slight figure in a cap and apron, with her flaxen hair bound up in a chignon, Tinsel stood in the doorway, watching. The withering look she gave Owen cut straight through to his soul. He knew immediately that she thought him a weak fool.

When Owen at last declared it was time for him to leave, Katy put up her pouting red lips to be kissed. Courteously, Owen responded and then walked home through the cold night air. He felt empty and unrewarded.

News of the betrothal of Owen Oliver and Katy Browne soon spread about the small country town. Soon afterwards

Owen purchased a small knot of diamonds and turquoise to be Katy's engagement ring.

Georgina had gone with him to the jewellers to choose the ring, informing him that Katy had already chosen that particular one from out of the window.

'But it's quite inexpensive,' exclaimed Owen. 'I can afford more than that.'

'That's the one Katy wants, Owen,' said Georgina decisively. 'She likes it because it's so pretty. Why chuck good money away?' laughed the ever practical Georgina.

A party was given for Katy's friends and, looking thin and awkward, Owen stood among those giggling damsels, certainly not at his best.

When the guests had gone, he sat in the twilight garden with Katy while she put her soft arms about his neck.

'Kiss Katy,' she said babyishly.

Owen felt quite nauseated and pushed her unceremoniously away. 'I've got to go, Katy,' he said. 'I don't feel very well.'

From then on, time was rarely his own. He was expected to walk with Katy in town every Saturday, parading in the cathedral gardens, and stopping occasionally to gossip with other couples.

And on Sunday he was expected to attend the church service, sitting in the family pew. Even during the week Katy buzzed in and out of the office, bringing little homemade cakes, and brewing endless cups of tea.

Gradually that long summer waned and the autumn twilight came down. Through the long dreary winter he sat with the girls each evening in the stuffy drawing room under the watchful eye of their mother, listening to Georgina reading in a strong voice from the latest novel by Jane Austen. While her sister read, Katy sat coyly sewing little cloths for her bottom drawer.

Owen did no sketching. He could not. He just sat dumbly listening to Georgina who had a good dramatic sense and almost acted the parts, with her hands waving and her eyes flashing. She was already beginning to find her vocation in life.

Mary skipped about, petting him, while even the dragon seemed more amicable towards him.

Before he had returned to sea, Captain Browne had proclaimed: 'I'll be home for the wedding in the spring. Behave yourself, sir.' As he said it, he almost broke the bones of Owen's hand with a farewell handclasp.

Only his friend Tom was critical on the rare occasions when they managed to get to the Blue Boar together for a drink. 'They've got yer, mate, they have,' Tom declared after taking a long swill of his beer. 'Hog tied and off to the knackers yard, you are, mate.'

'It's not so bad,' protested Owen. 'Katy is a very sweet girl. I wasn't really ready for marriage but I'm getting used to the idea.'

'Don't look that way to me,' replied Tom gloomily. 'Yer don't never do no drawing now. Done for yer, those females have.'

Owen knocked back several large glasses of strong wine to avoid Tom's remarks depressing him even more. And then it became a merry evening until Owen staggered back to his rooms.

The winter became very hard and bitterly cold. The Browne girls stayed at home, all busy with Katy's trousseau and wedding arrangements.

One evening, Owen sat looking out of his window at the swirling snowflakes and the white street when he saw a small fair girl gazing hungrily into a baker's shop window on the other side of the road. He opened the casement window and threw the child some money. She gathered it up quickly, dashed into the shop and bought a huge meat pie. Then she sat down on the kerbside to consume it with great greed. Owen was suddenly filled with an urge to capture this scene. Grabbing his long-abandoned drawing pad, he began to draw, and draw. At last, after six months, Owen Oliver had begun another book of sketches.

He drew hungry ragged children who contrasted with corpulent overfed shopkeepers, windows full of Christmas fare being stared at by thin, starving beggars.

All through that bad winter and into spring, he filled that book with humanity at its worst, while Katy remained indoors sewing and dreaming of bonnie babies, her life as smooth and unruffled as it was for any well-fed middle-class Victorian.

In January, Mary was taken ill. Then Katy, who had nursed her solicitously through her illness, went down with the same severe chill. During this time Owen was often visited by

Georgina who came several times a week to his rooms, always accompanied by Tinsel. With her legs spread out in an unmaidenly manner and her coat unbuttoned, Georgina would indulge in a good gossip with Owen, while Tinsel was kept busy tidying the rooms or refurbishing his linen and food store.

Every week, Tinsel collected Owen's dirty linen and replaced it with the freshly laundered clothes, and the dirty clothes were taken home to be washed by the servants at the Browne residence. Softly and silently Tinsel worked. Owen would close his eyes and imagine Tinsel dressed in a fairy costume, while Georgina chattered on about her passion for the theatre. 'You've only got to mention that someone is an actress and right away she's classed as a whore,' declared Georgina indignantly.

Owen opened his eyes and looked alarmed. Georgina's frequent free expression often shocked him.

'It's all a question of art,' continued Georgina. 'Either you can do it, or you can't. Oh, I'd give anything to get up on that stage and say my piece.'

Owen looked at her. 'Yes, Georgi, I think you have a flair for it,' he laughed.

'I'm not jesting, Owen,' she replied grumpily, 'I really mean it.'

Owen looked contemplatively at her. 'Why don't you try writing?' he suggested gently.

'Why, no!' Georgina cried. 'I could no more sit down all day scribbling than I could marry a rich old man for his money!'

Owen smiled his slow charming smile which always lit up the rather austere face, 'No, Georgi, I don't think you could.'

'What I would like to do, is direct,' continued Georgina. 'To instruct and gather talent. I want to create with people and not words.'

'It is an ambition that is not popular in your social circles, Georgi,' Owen advised.

'What do I care?' announced Georgina. 'You know,' she said, lowering her tone, 'I'm already taking drama and elocution lessons during the times when I'm supposed to be learning music.' She chuckled. 'And I'm training young Tinsel. Come here, little one,' she called dramatically.

Tinsel had been wandering around the room flicking a feather duster.

'Put the duster down,' ordered Georgina, 'and do it.'

With an amused glint in her bright blue eyes, Tinsel waved her arms slowly in a willowy fashion. Daintily her arms flew up and down like wings, she pointed her toe and started to recite in a clear, ringing voice:

> I know a bank where wild thyme grows,
> Foxgloves and the nodding violet blows,
> Quite over canopied with vine,
> With sweet mush rose and eglantine.

'Right, that's enough,' commanded Georgina proudly, and Tinsel skipped away as if off-stage.

'Isn't she good?' exclaimed Georgina.

Owen was truly astounded. He had never heard Tinsel utter more than two words before.

'I taught her,' declared Georgina.

In Owen's mind's eye he could see the picture of Tinsel poised like a fairy. His heart had begun to beat very fast, as he thought about those intense eyes, her already well-formed young bust and the long line of her slim white legs as she held up her skirt and skipped out. 'Marvellous, Georgi,' he said. 'How did you manage it?' he asked politely, once his composure had recovered.

'Ah! That's a secret, Owen,' Georgina cried jubilantly. 'Tinsel is a natural. Her mother was a performer and God knows who her father was. She can't read or write but she can memorise every word you teach her. And she is a lot older than we think.'

'How old is she?' Owen asked. He had always wondered.

'She's fourteen. But being so small she looks much younger.'

'Well, you amaze me,' exclaimed Owen. 'She's almost a woman,' he said. 'I can't believe it.'

'But believe me, she is no fool. And I have grown very fond of her,' announced Georgina.

After the women had left, Owen felt very restless. He realised that he was actually sexually frustrated, something that he had never felt before. He wondered if he really missed Katy, although their innocent petting did little to satisfy him. Within him was a sleeping tiger which had begun to stir.

In February Katy and Mary were sent off on a recuperative holiday with their mother to Bath to take benefit from the healing waters. Every week Katy sent Owen a perfumed love letter, telling him her heart's desires and how she was looking forward to their wedding day, fixed for April.

During this time Owen began to enjoy his freedom once more, going nightly to the Bull to dine expensively or to drink at the Blue Boar with Tom.

One Saturday afternoon, hazy with drink, he rolled up the front steps of his rooms to be confronted by the demure shape of Tinsel, dressed in straw bonnet trimmed with blue ribbons and blue dress with a small lacy apron in front. On her arm was the basket of linen.

'Well, this is a surprise,' said Owen, looking around for Georgina.

'Georgnia isn't coming,' replied Tinsel. 'She's gone to her lessons. I am to look after your linen.'

Owen took the basket from her and inserted the key in the door. He suddenly felt shy and awkward, and he was not sure why.

Tinsel grinned up at him, and her arm brushed his hand. Owen took hold of the girl's elbow and escorted her upstairs. His heart was beating madly. On the top stairs he felt a strong urge to stroke her soft flaxen hair.

Tinsel stopped and stood very still. She looked straight into his face. Owen staggered slightly as they entered the room.

'Have you been drinking?' she asked. 'Lie down and I'll make you some coffee.'

Owen lay on the couch, half dozing, and watched Tinsel preparing the coffee. Presently she brought him a cup of the hot drink and knelt down beside him. 'Drink this, sir,' she said. 'It will do you good.'

Her voice sounded angelic to his ears. Owen opened his heavy lids. He was astonished by what he saw. Tinsel had removed her bonnet and her pretty dress and was now covered by a large white apron. Her hair hung down her back in a golden cascade. Her arms were bare and she held her small white face close to him.

Owen did not take the coffee. Instead, he placed his hand on those thin arms and edged it towards the small firm breasts. Tinsel did not retreat, but she placed the coffee on the floor and leaned forward. Her scented hair covered his face.

The sleeping tiger had fully awoken and was crouched, ready to spring. Now he crushed her passionately to him as she allowed him to, moving even closer.

Not a word was spoken between them as he removed that large white apron and kissed and caressed her tiny breasts. Tinsel trembled violently, not with fear but with love. Her hand and her lips were seeking, finding. In spite of her appearance, she was a mature woman, hungry for love and not unversed in the sexual act.

Owen rose into an unknown heaven with this tiny child-woman. It was a sexual awakening he was never to forget.

It was dark when he roused himself. Tinsel was still asleep beside him. The tiger was quiet. Owen got up and paced the room. Sobs of misery rasped his dry throat. 'Oh, my God, what have I done?' he murmured as he gazed down at the sleeping angel, that little waif he had now destroyed.

Tinsel raised her heavy golden lashes and smiled up at him. Owen fell on his knees and begged forgiveness, as the tiny hand stroked his brow.

'It's all right, Owen,' she said in her soft voice. 'I wanted it this way. I belong to you. You have always owned me.'

Owen pressed her to his heart again as the tiger stirred. He was so overcome with emotion that the urge to make love was almost unbearable. But Tinsel gently restrained him.

'I'll come back tomorrow,' she whispered. She went into the other room to put on her dress.

'It's a black night out there,' Owen told her. 'I cannot let you walk home alone.'

For a moment Tinsel looked afraid. 'Georgina will be looking for me,' she said.

Owen bent down and he kissed her on the lips.

'I don't know what devil possessed me, Tinsel, but you must not tell a soul,' he said. A wise look appeared and those strange eyes glinted.

'What kind of a fool do you think I am?' she said sharply.

They walked hand in hand back to the house on the hill, holding no conversation as each was lost in private thoughts.

At the gate Owen turned and left her. As he was walking away, he suddenly heard the strident tones of Georgina. 'Why, you little slut! Where have you been?' She had dashed from the house in a violent temper and grabbed hold of Tinsel, twisting her arm spitefully behind her back. In a terrible passion she shouted at her, 'Where have you been?'

From the shadows where he stood, Owen heard Tinsel whimper in pain. He had to help her, and he stepped out towards them.

'Oh! It's you, Owen,' cried Georgina in astonishment. 'I've been frantic with worry. Tinsel has been gone for hours.'

'Go in, Tinsel,' he said. 'I'll talk to Georgina.'

'Oh, it's all right if she's been with you, Owen,' protested Georgina, 'but why keep her out so late?'

'I happened to be out myself,' he lied, 'and found her asleep on my doorstep when I came home.'

'Silly girl! Why didn't she come back?' complained Georgina. 'But I won't beat her, Owen, I promise. Honest to God, I really thought she was out with some low-class boy from the town. I was quite beside myself,' she told him.

Owen dropped his gaze, embarrassed by Georgina's attitude. It was almost as if she was jealous.

'Goodnight, Georgina,' he said coolly. 'Perhaps Tinsel could pick up my shirts on Monday.'

The beast within him had already begun to lick its lips at the prospect of another meal.

As Owen walked home he was filled with remorse that he could lie so easily; yet he looked forward to another visit from Tinsel.

Once home he lay awake lashing himself with guilty feelings. How could he marry the sweet virginal Katy now? Was he in love with this immature child, Tinsel? She had certainly always excited him. She had been more than willing and seemed to know what it was all about. But what a way for him to behave! What should he do? Cut his throat? Hang himself? Such morbid thoughts filled his mind.

The next day being Sunday, Tinsel did not come, so he had the whole day to reach his final decision. When Katy returned to town, he would tell her that he could not honourably marry her.

On Monday when he returned from the office he was surprised to find Tinsel already installed in his room. Little blushes coloured her pale cheeks as she stored the linen. The coffee was brewing on the stove.

'How did you get in?' he asked.

'I've got Katy's key,' she answered pertly.

Owen took off his coat, wondering how to put her off. This situation could not continue. He had decided that.

But the golden head came snuggling softly under his arm. 'Don't you love me any more, Owen?' Tinsel asked wistfully.

Owen pulled her close, feeling terribly distressed.

'Don't cry,' she whispered. 'We must be very happy, you and I.'

'How can I, Tinsel?' he wept. 'By rights I should marry you but I cannot betray Katy.'

Somehow Tinsel had contrived to get him sitting down on the bed. 'Why get so upset? There is no harm in what we did.' She stared at him like a wide-eyed child. 'I will not tell Katy. Many people do that act and do not marry.'

Owen looked at her in shocked silence. 'Are you trying to tell me that it happened to you before?' he blustered.

'Well, not in the way we did it,' she replied dreamily. She looked up at him in that soulful way.

Unconsciously, his hands fondled her legs and gradually they grew closer together. Once more their lips clung, and waves of fire filled his brain. Within seconds, his feelings had overcome his conscience and they made love more passionately than ever.

Later, Tinsel lay peaceful and exhausted by his side. She was completely naked. Owen stroked the small pale face. 'Tell me the truth, Tinsel,' he said. 'You are so young and not a virgin. With whom did you do this?' There was a hint of jealousy in his tone.

'I was raped by a sailor when I first went to Polly's,' she said. 'It was terrible and I was very much afraid. But that was a long time ago. When I was older I did it with a nice boy who was Sophie's brother. He slept in our bed. He was nice but with *you*, it is real love. It will never die.'

Incredulously Owen listened to this description of cruelty and corruption. 'Oh, my God!' he cried. 'You poor little darling. You have been exploited all your life, and now, I, who considered myself your saviour, have added to your misery.'

Tinsel's hand roamed over his body. 'Don't be silly, Owen,' she murmured. 'We have found happiness because you really need me.'

'But I cannot protect you,' he whispered urgently.

'I don't care, so why should you?' Tinsel asked, winding her arms tightly about his neck. 'Love me, Owen, I belong to you, you bought me,' she urged.

Hopelessly infatuated, Owen gave in to the beast within. They made love once more and he was still sleeping when she crept out of his bed and returned to the house on the hill on time.

CHAPTER SEVEN

On the Road to Fame

Several weeks had passed and Katy had still not returned from Bath. At last Owen received a long letter of explanation. Mary had become ill again, Katy wrote, and her mother had decided that she should not risk travelling while the weather was so cold.

Owen was filled with a sense of relief mixed with dismay, for now he was so involved with Tinsel that the thought of informing the good-living Katy that he had betrayed her for a serving girl filled him with apprehension.

Tinsel now came to Owen's lodgings twice a week, having got an extra half day off from Georgina. Owen had recently discovered that Tinsel loved the candy from the confectioners near East Gate. These she gobbled up as avidly as she made love – enjoying every minute of it.

In his leisure time, Owen sketched Tinsel with her clothes on and off and in all sorts of poses. She made an excellent model. Today she sat wrapped only in an old plaid shawl which he had provided for her. With her long mane of silvery golden hair hanging down to her waist, she sat crossed-legged, as he worked, ramming the huge candies into her mouth and savouring every one.

It was because she had been so deprived that she was so greedy, he told himself. She fascinated him now more than ever.

It was not, however, long before he discovered that her small tongue was spliced with malice. She had a tendency to repeat tales about everyone in a most spiteful manner. She complained of 'that silly, fat Katy,' who chided her about her laziness; or, 'that spiteful Mary' who pinched her arm; or her mistress, who was a religious old skinflint, and Georgina, who bullied her. She disliked all the Brownes. She seemed incapable of coming out with even one word of gratitude for the good home and good food she received. Owen listened to Tinsel's chatter in amazement.

One day he asked: 'This boy who made love with you, where is he now?'

'Jack killed him,' Tinsel replied flatly.

'Now, Tinsel, don't be foolish, you know that's untrue.'

'It's as true as I am sitting here,' she told him.

Owen stopped drawing and sat beside her, stroking her slim legs. 'Listen to me, dear, you must not tell so many lies.'

Tinsel stared back at him in the strange adult way she had. 'Jack did it. I saw him. I know where the boy's buried,' she announced.

Owen put his hands over his ears. 'Hush, I'll not listen to another word,' he said.

But the thin penetrating voice went on regardless. 'Jack wanted to make him different, you know, go to sea and oblige the skipper. 'That's for you, little nipper,' he used to say to him.

'Stop!' Owen looked very shocked. 'This is nonsense, Tinsel. What are you talking about?'

'All right,' she cried pertly. 'Don't believe me.'

'Get off home!' he said angrily. 'Georgina will be on your tail.'

'No she won't,' Tinsel declared defiantly.

'What do you mean? Where is Georgina?' he asked, puzzled. 'If she's minding the home, she must be there.'

'No, she's not,' retorted Tinsel and, grinning mischievously, she stepped into her dress.

'Well, where is she?' he queried.

'I know a secret,' said Tinsel jubilantly.

'Now, darling, don't confuse me with any more lurid stories,' Owen said with better humour.

'Please yourself,' she answered, 'but there is going to be hell to pay when her mother finds out.'

'Well, come on, tell me, then,' he said.

'She goes to the circus every day,' declared Tinsel dramatically. 'I'm not supposed to tell, that's why she gave me an extra half day off.'

'The circus? Whatever for?' Owen was very bewildered.

'It's down on the waste ground. She's got a man who's teaching her acting.'

'You mean a travelling show? Are you sure?' Owen was incredulous.

'Quite struck on this man, she is,' grinned Tinsel.

A bell went off in Owen's head. Oh dear, he thought. Surely not sensible, level-headed Georgina. 'I don't believe you,' he said suddenly. 'You're a little liar. She would not go unchaperoned to a place like that, she's too well brought up.'

'That's the secret,' cried Tinsel, going off into a cascade of giggles, 'she goes dressed as a boy.'

Owen walked to the end of the lane with Tinsel and then returned home feeling very unsure. He definitely loved Tinsel but her youth spent with those dreadful riverside folk had apparently left its mark. And now he was worrying about Georgina for whom he felt slightly responsible since her parents were away. But surely she would not compromise herself . . . But then who was he to interfere? Much of what he had been up to in the past month would not bear scrutiny.

In bed he tossed and turned all night. In the morning he decided he would find Georgina and tackle her on the subject of her indiscretions. He also found himself worrying how much Georgina knew of his affair with Tinsel. Was she really trustworthy?

In the morning a messenger came to the office with a banker's draught for thirty pounds as payment for Owen's second book of sketches. After all this time, here was a request from the famous author asking if he would care to join him as an official illustrator and travel with him to Yorkshire.

Owen leaped from his stool. 'Hurrah!' he yelled like a schoolboy. Gus the office boy looked astonished. 'Fame at last!' cried his boss. 'Now take a message to Cousin Bertie, will you, Gus. I'm off to Yorkshire in the morning.'

With Tinsel and Georgina both temporarily forgotten, Owen made his plans to leave.

Cousin Bertie came with sham reluctance. There was no time for good-byes. Owen threw a few things in a bag and dashed off.

★

Twenty-four hours later, he was on his way up north, travelling in a comfortable carriage with the dynamic young writer whose eyes gleamed excitedly as he outlined his plan to his new illustrator. His recently published novel had been read in instalments in a favourite paper of the middle classes and his popularity had risen with each issue. People loved his novels, fascinated by the plight of society's poor persecuted children, and the ugly social injustice that the smug Victorian moralists tried so hard to cover up. Now his active mind was seeking new material. He intended breaking down the secret lives of so-called school masters, people who advertised for schoolchildren by promising them a good home and a good education.

'You would never believe the plight of some of these children,' he informed Owen. 'I have visited these so-called schools where unwanted children are sent to rot. They are a disgrace and I will be eternally grateful to you if you can illustrate them as well as you did those maltreated youngsters in the brick fields.'

'I will endeavour to do my best,' said Owen quietly and politely.

'I've heard of a particularly vicious type,' the author continued, 'who resides in Yorkshire. As a child I was sent to one of these so-called educational premises so this research will be of a personal interest to me.'

Owen listened in respectful silence.

'Relax, sir,' said Deakins suddenly. 'Let's have a good time together. We're both very ambitious and the world is our oyster.'

Owen smiled his slow smile and the ice was broken. Soon the two men were like old friends.

At each overnight stop the pair prowled the town, eating and drinking, and chatting to the locals. Owen always had his book open, ready to do his lightning sketches.

Deakins was usually a bright, intelligent companion to Owen, but he could also be surly and moody when things were not to his satisfaction. He was not much older than Owen and unhappily married. Also, a recent bereavement had upset him considerably.

'I simply had to escape for a while,' he confided in Owen.

'She was so good and so beautiful, and only seventeen. She died in my arms.'

They visited a school high up on a lonely moor. Owen wandered around the grounds, sketching the thin, ragged boys and the evil-looking school masters. While he did that, Deakins entered the school and under the pretence of placing a younger brother there, interviewed the rascal of a headmaster. He then returned looking very pleased with this encounter; the visit had been very fruitful.

In the company of this pleasant vibrant character Owen's mind did not once dwell on anyone in Chatham – not Tinsel, Georgina, or Katy. He was completely absorbed in the fascinating work.

In the third week, the pair returned to London where Owen stayed for several nights with Forest, that virile bully of a newspaperman. Forest was an excellent host and Owen met all the literary lions once more. To his amazement, he found that he actually felt quite self-assured among them. It was as if some of the novelist's talent had rubbed off onto him, now that he was the present illustrator to the great master.

He returned home bursting with self confidence. His first stop was the office, where he arrived dressed in his best grey suit and twirling a silver-knobbed cane which he had acquired on his travels.

'Ho! Ho!' exclaimed Cousin Bertie. 'Hif it isn't his lordship come back at last.'

'How is everything?' Owen asked brightly, choosing to ignore Bertie's sarcasm.

'Wery, wery poor, things have been,' complained Bertie.

Owen immediately felt a sense of dismay, scanning the untidy office in search of the faithful Gus with his tousled head.

'Gus has been and gone,' declared the pompous Bertie. 'It's no use looking for him. Skedaddled, took off back to sea, he did. I'd have the law on him if I was you, seeing as he signed apprentice papers.'

Owen sighed and hung up his best coat. Then he put his hat and stick on the stand with the air of a prince.

'Dearie me,' blurted Bertie, puffing out his cheeks. 'High and mighty, aren't we? But I warn you, I don't take on this lousy job any more. A gentleman of means, I ham, no need for me to 'umble myself and get no return.'

Owen pondered on how Bertie managed to drop aitches and then add them where they did not belong. Bertie had definitely become very aggressive. But inwardly Owen fumed, for everyone knew that Bertie was a pauper and overfond of his drink, as his late uncle had been. But he did not reply, for Owen tended to become tongue-tied when involved in an argument. Eventually he asked: 'How much do I owe you, Bertie?'

'Ho! Ho! No you don't,' exclaimed Bertie, pushing out his blue chin and fat belly aggressively. Owen stepped back in alarm. 'I hain't being paid orf by the likes of you,' blustered Bertie. 'Captain Browne is home again, *and* Miss Katy. They are waiting for you hup at the house. It's curtains for you this time, Mr High and Mighty,' he threatened. Having said his piece, he toddled off to the adjoining room where he had probably hidden a bottle of Dutch courage.

Owen sat down and thoughtfully twiddled with his quill pen. He knew he had to face up to Katy as well as little Tinsel. He wondered if she had told the Browne family her tale of woe.

Eventually he got to his feet, replaced his hat and coat and, swinging his silver-knobbed cane – but not quite so jauntily this time, he began to walk up the long hill to the house.

The weather as bright and sunny. In the distance he could see the windmill perched high on a neighbouring hill. The fields were strewn with workers and the air was sweet with the scent of flowers. If he married Katy perhaps it would be possible to build a house of their own high up on that other hill outside the town.

He strolled leisurely down the laurel-lined drive where he had first bumped into Katy. Now he knew that he dreaded meeting her again.

There she was, bursting with joy as he entered the hall. In spite of the remonstrances of her parents, she could not contain herself. 'Oh! Owen!' she cried, 'I missed you so much!' She flung her arms about his neck and covered his face with kisses.

Owen was momentarily stunned, but he recovered slightly to return her embrace and say politely: 'How are you, Katy?'

In the hall just behind Katy stood a small figure, her mouth curled in a knowing grin as she held out her hand to receive his hat. The sight of that pale face and golden hair washed over him like a bucket of cold water.

The evening passed quickly enough. Katy was constantly at his side, simpering and giggling, while the dragon eyed him with infinite suspicion. Captain Browne quizzed him about his trip up north, and was as smiling and brusque as ever. 'Yes, sir, great man, that Deakins,' he muttered, 'but too maudlin for my taste.'

'I am now his official illustrator,' Owen boasted quietly.

'Oh!' squealed Katy. 'You won't go away again, will you, Owen? We've fixed our wedding date only yesterday. In three weeks I'll be your bride.' She looked as if she might explode with happiness.

Owen passed his hand over his hot brow. The gallant Captain Browne had done more than drop anchor; he had condemned Owen for life. 'Where's Georgi?' he asked. He could think of nothing else to say.

'Oh, she's got this urge for extra music lessons. You know what Georgi is . . .' said Katy. 'Mary is still in Bath, but they'll both be here for our wedding. Isn't everything absolutely scrumptious?' she burbled on.

After dinner, over the port and cigars in the library, the captain discussed the business, a subject he usually managed to avoid. 'You are a bright clever lad and my Katy's settled, so that suits me,' he told Owen in his direct manner, 'but we must talk about this business of Cousin Bertie.'

The corners of Owen's mouth twitched.

'Yes, yes,' exclaimed the captain. 'We all know that he's a dreadful old bore, snuff and booze all over the place. Indeed, I would never have him aboard my ship.'

'He chased out my clerk Gus, who was a good boy,' protested Owen glumly.

'Don't I know, sir,' continued Browne, 'did I not recommend that lad myself? But he was a young and enthusiastic boy so I admit I made it comparatively easy for him to go back to sea. He's going to train as ship's writer.'

'But I need an assistant down there, sir,' complained Owen. 'Besides running the business, I have in my spare time to illustrate a whole novel.'

'Yes, yes,' replied the captain. 'I had thought you might turn to that, but will it provide sufficient income for both you and Katy?'

'Well, I hope so,' pondered Owen, 'especially since the business is declining.'

'Yes, the business isn't what it used to be. This kind of trade is declining. The old skippers are going out of business and the new ones are so keen on these modern steam ships, they'll take over in the end.'

'Well, if you suggest that we sell out, sir, that's all right by me,' said Owen.

'No, lad, I believe there is need for a little patience. Myself, I do not rely on the business for my living but at the same time we are an old fashioned line and it has been in the family many years. No, lad, I think we will hold the rudder steady until the right time comes.'

'As you wish, sir,' agreed Owen.

'If I were you,' continued Captain Browne, 'I'd let old Bertie muddle along a bit. He seems to think that he's entitled to something better. You do the accounts and check the manifests. That'll give you more time to concentrate on your drawing, and I wish you every success.'

'As you wish, sir,' said Owen, feeling quite relieved.

They parted on good terms. Owen felt a warm sense of gratitude and respect for his future father-in-law. Owen gave Katy a mild good-night kiss and listened to all her chatter about the grand wedding she was planning. Then he progressed back down hill to his rooms, still feeling ill at ease.

As he turned the key in the lock, a small figure glided from the shadows and a tiny white face looked pathetically up at him. There was Tinsel wrapped in that old plaid shawl. She came up close to him without saying a word. Her fragrance was enough to set his pulse racing, that strange sweet smell which always lingered on her flaxen hair and was fire to his body and brain. He reached out to her, the door swung open and they climbed the stairs. Owen unwound her from the tight shawl and she put her cool hands on his face.

'I knew you still belonged to me,' she said passionately, trembling and hungry to be loved. Nothing or nobody could have stopped them then, so great was their need for each other.

Later, she sat like a little elf, knees huddled up to her chin. Owen lay beside her with his head pressed to the pillow. His eyes were closed and tears trembled on his dark lashes.

With a tiny finger Tinsel wiped one away. 'You cry very easily,' she said quietly.

'Oh, my love, what am I going to do about you?' he snivelled.

Her small face looked very serious, her lips were pressed tight. After a moment's silence, she said: 'You know, I can't cry.'

Owen looked up into the brighter eyes that were like a sunny winter sky. She was so loving, passionate and loyal. What more could he ask for?

'It's strange,' continued Tinsel, 'when I am upset I cough, and I don't think I can laugh very well either.'

Owen stared at her in amazement. She seemed to have forgotten those past wonderful moments, her mind was on another track. 'I must face up to the fact that I cannot marry Katy,' he muttered pitifully.

'But you're so fond of Katy,' she said, 'and you already own me. So where's the problem?'

'Tinsel, my love, how can you be willing to share me? I wonder if you realise that should it become known of what I did to you I should be ruined. I would probably be driven out of town.'

Tinsel yawned, and stretched as if bored with the conversation. 'Shall I come tomorrow?' she asked.

'I don't care what goes on in that den of iniquity. I have a different standard of morality – at least I did have,' he added gloomily.

Tinsel yawned, and stretched as if bored with the conversation. 'Shall I come tomorrow?' she asked.

Infuriated, Owen grabbed hold of her and shook her like a rag doll until she was limp and clinging. She smiled up at him through semi-closed lids. Then, trembling, he ran his hands over her body. Suddenly he groaned and let her go, dashing his face to the wall, and banging on the wooden panels until his fists bled.

'Go, Tinsel!' he moaned. 'And stay away. This is more than I can bear!'

Slowly she buttoned up her nightdress and wound the old plaid shawl around her. Then silently she disappeared out of the door.

There was no more sleep for Owen that night as he lay

thinking and worrying. Then, as the grey dawn crept in through the windows, he started to work on the manuscript that the publisher had sent him. He drew caricatures that turned sadness into humour – Tinsel, Cousin Bertie, the old dragon – they all lived under his pen and fitted perfectly with the novel that the great Deakins had written.

When he had finished he sprawled his signature, Owen, across the bottom of the last page.

CHAPTER EIGHT

The Honey Pot

For two weeks Owen kept his nose to the grindstone,
completing the first two instalments of the book and then
starting on the third. Inbetween he handled the financial side
of the business, balancing the books and paying the bills. He
never went near Bertie, who reigned supreme in the dusty
office and got more muddled every day.

Occasionally Katy put her head in through Bertie's door and
sniffed before she asked: 'How are you, Cousin Bertie?' But
she would pull her head back out again quickly when the
stench of snuff, alcohol and body odour became too much for
her.

On Sundays Owen was practically forced to attend the
service at the cathedral, accompanied by Katy and her mother.
He sat in the family pew and after the service was fawned upon
by the toothy avaricious vicar.

One Monday, when Katy and Georgina came as usual to
collect Owen's linen, there was no sign of Tinsel with them.
Katy was inspecting the rooms thoroughly and Georgina
seemed very quiet. She looked unusually spruce and had
adopted a new hair style. Her long hair was tightly wound into
a bun which rested on the back of her long slim neck. Little
curls escaped and dangled on each side of her cheeks. They
suited her to perfection. She wore a tight, tailored skirt and a
high-necked plain blouse.

Owen was very conscious of his own unshaven face and the
grubby shirt which he worked and slept in. He avoided

Georgina's eyes but he knew that there was certainly something different about her.

'Tinsel not with you?' he asked casually as he rammed his dirty linen into the basket they brought with them.

'Oh, she has been a very naughty girl,' said Katy. 'Such tantrums!'

Owen's heart sank. 'What has she been up to?' he asked.

'Up to? My goodness!' declared Katy. 'She was found out in the garden early one morning wearing her nightdress and wrapped in a big plaid shawl.'

'She said that she was walking in her sleep,' said Georgina.

'Yes, but Mama didn't believe her. She locked her up at night and she has been demoted to working in the scullery. It serves her right. Give these girls an inch and they take a mile,' declared Katy very bossily.

Owen and Georgina made no comment but looked at each other in sympathy.

'You know, Owen,' said Katy, flushed with the exertion of inspecting the whole premises. 'I have been having a good look round here because we may have to live here together for a while. I haven't seen the house I care to live in just yet.'

Owen looked depressed.

'Well, come on, Owen,' Katy prodded him playfully. 'Do we start off here or not?'

'Please yourself, Katy,' he replied aimlessly.

'Oh, what a hopeless man you are!' Katy cried, rumpling his hair. 'Do I have to do everything for you?'

Georgina's hazel eyes sought his, still full of sympathy.

'I'll tell Mama. She will send in the decorators,' said Katy. 'You'll have to push about a bit for a few weeks, Owen.'

Without fail, the following day, painters, paperhangers and carpenters arrived, along with labourers, pots of paint, buckets and ladders. Owen nervously gathered up all his papers and went up into the dusty old attic which at least had a couch in it. And, amid all the rubbish which collects in attics, he tried desperately to complete his work.

He did not emerge all day, except to creep out to join Tom in the Blue Boar every evening. One Saturday he had a prearranged meeting with Tom and found him leaning on the parapet of the bridge. Old Dawg, red-eyed and slavering at the mouth, sat beside him. After a friendly hand clasp, they walked along together to the high wood that looked down on the town.

Owen looked rather seedy with his shoulders bowed and a remorseful expression on is face, while in contrast, Tom was big and upright, whistling cheerfully as he walked along.

'Don't look so glum, lad,' he told Owen.

'Had a heavy night. I don't feel so good,' complained Owen.

'A man ought to be able to take his beer,' said Tom. 'You worries too much, boy.'

They had reached the crest of the hill. Behind them was thick dark woodland while in front of them were the green rolling hills of the heath dotted with clumps of yellow gorse and golden primroses. Beyond, there was a crystal clear view over the estuary and the red-sailed barges breezing up the river.

Tom breathed deeply. 'Isn't this fine? Where on this earth would you get a view as good as this?'

Old Dawg suddenly went rampaging off into the woods as the men lay down on the moist grass. They said very little as they just relaxed. A long time had elapsed when Owen finally said: 'You know, I'm getting married next Saturday, Tom.'

'I wish you joy,' replied Tom in an noncommital tone as he chewed thoughtfully on a piece of grass, and stared steadily out to sea.

'I'm not overkeen, you know, Tom,' said Owen lamely.

'Well, don't do it then, lad,' was the laconic reply.

'It's not that easy to back out.'

Tom took the strip of grass from his lips and eyed Owen keenly. 'Katy is a bonny enough girl. What's changed your mind?'

Owen sighed. 'I'm not in love with her, and never was. And now I am involved with another.'

Tom stared at Owen in disbelief. 'Well, well, lad, I just don't know what to say. I never loved anyone but me mother and Old Dawg.'

'That's what I mean,' said Owen. 'I have no wish to marry anyone. I would rather remain free. How the devil I managed to get mixed up with two women, I'll never know.'

'Well, boy,' Tom was very amused, 'you've had the sweet, now you must taste the sour. But you can't marry two, it's against the law.' There was a decided twinkle in those merry brown eyes.

'It's no laughing matter, my friend,' said Owen, full of self-pity. 'Also, I'm being pushed into a corner of my chambers while they're being decorated.'

'Well, now, boy, if I was you I'd pull up anchor and sail away. One woman is too many, but two is a disaster,' warned Tom.

'You could be right,' said Owen moodily. Nothing had been solved but he felt a lot easier having talked to his friend.

'It's my opinion ...' said Tom, weighing his words carefully. 'I'm only an ignorant fellow, mind you, so it don't really matter what I think, but this being in love is nought to do with what goes on in bed.'

Owen looked at him earnestly. There was an earthy wisdom in those words. Tom put his fingers to his lips and blasted out a shrill whistle. Within seconds Old Dawg emerged, mud-covered, from the woods. They both got slowly to their feet and Tom screwed up his eyes to look at the opposite shore. 'There's rain on the river. I feel it in the air. Come on, boy, let's go down before we get drowned.'

Huge spots suddenly started to pelt down. Owen would have liked to stay up there on the hill. He did not want to go down again into the valley.

They were soaked by the time they reached the Blue Boar. They shook the rain from their coats and filled themselves with Kentish cider.

'I won't come to your wedding, boy,' declared Tom, 'but I'll willingly give you a last night out with Billy Bentley and the boys.'

Sadly the promised stag night never materialised. For the whole of next week, Owen was taken over by his future family. The builders clumped about his premises shouting and singing and making a dreadful racket. At one point they were on the roof banging and knocking down soot all over his papers. Georgina and Katy popped in and out, excitedly talking about the grand preparations for the wedding. And there was never a trace of Tinsel.

'Where is she?' he demanded of Georgina.

'She's still in disgrace,' Georgina told him sheepishly. 'She has to work in the kitchen.'

'She's got a bit too cheeky lately,' said Katy. 'She won't get out at night anymore. She has to sleep in the attic with the old washer woman.'

Georgina looked sad and embarrassed and Owen's brow wore a puzzled frown. But Katy, busily measuring the armchairs for new covers, was quite unconcerned.

On Friday evening, Captain Browne called, bringing with him a distant cousin called Norman who had been chosen as Owen's best man. The very idea was not to be entertained. This man was tall, thin and austere in appearance. He had a nose just like the dragon, long and tilted at the end, and he spoke as if his mouth were full of peas. Owen hated him on sight. But in spite of his protests, he was whisked off to the Army and Navy Club to drink with the captain and his old comrades until early morning.

The captain's drinking friends declared Owen to be a dry old stick. He fell into bed in the early hours to be rudely awakened only a few hours later by the long thin man, who was laying out his wedding clothes and preparing his bath. Owen felt dazed as he was hustled and bustled to get to the church on time.

Fiery brandy had been forced on him. 'Hair of the dog, old boy,' gabbled Norman. In a confused state he stood at the altar awaiting the arrival of sweet, virginal Katy.

Katy was a vision of white loveliness as she came down the aisle on her distinguished father's arm. Owen felt a strong urge to run away but his feet felt as though they were anchored to the carpet where he stood. The hum of the organ and the clang of the bells whirled about his head, as he meekly and graciously took the hand of his bride. They were married as planned.

After the ceremony, the family adjourned to a fancy restaurant by the Gate House. Their guests at the reception were some of the most prominent people of the town. For Owen there was only one pair of sympathetic eyes, those of Georgina. He felt very strongly that she understood his silent reluctance.

The long coach ride to Broadstairs, seemed like a dream, in an ancient hired vehicle whose springs rattled and swayed until he thought his head would burst. Katy sat facing him, all fur and feathers as she smiled and cooed at him constantly. He had an overwhelming feeling of embarrassment in the red-carpeted, stuffy hotel. People in the lounge sat and stared at them curiously as they crept furtively up the wide stairs.

As the servant closed the door to their room, Owen sank

down on the bed, as pale as death, holding his hands to his head.

'Oh, Owen, what's the matter, dear?' cried Katy. 'You don't look well.'

'It's all right,' he said. 'I've just got a headache,' he added irritably.

'Oh, silly boy,' Katy said, divesting herself of her cloak. 'You've been drinking too much. I'll mix you a nice powder.' Muttering sweet nothings all the time, she mixed something up in a glass. 'Now drink this, it will do you good,' she insisted.

As the evil-smelling potion was forced on him, Owen wanted to shout, scream and swear. But he patiently closed his eyes and did as he was bid.

'Now, be a good boy and get a good night's sleep,' Katy told him as she helped him into a robe. 'Then you'll be as fit as a fiddle in the morning.'

Owen slipped between the cool sheets and pressed his aching head to the pillow. He had a faint memory of Katy in a long white nightie, all lace-trimmed with ribbons and bows, getting heavily into bed beside him and cuddling him to her ample bosom. 'Silly boy,' she simpered, 'Katy's with you now.'

He slept like a baby.

During their quiet honeymoon, Owen saw his new wife in a different light. She was like a tonic, calm, and cool, and rather bossy, but in a sweet way. She watched what they ate, making sure that the food was fresh and that they did not eat the same thing two days running.

'Liver was on yesterday, was it not, Owen?'

Owen would not answer; he was above such trifles.

'Well, it won't be fresh today,' Katy would continue. 'I'll order beef.'

After luncheon, she would buzz down to the shops and buy little mementoes of Broadstairs. But she appreciated Owen's need to work and she found a private spot in the hotel garden where he could take himself to draw and sketch.

She was neat and tidy and always ready to attend his many needs. In many ways the honeymoon was a success. The only drawback was that they did not consummate the marriage until the very end, when Owen drank a whole bottle of wine at dinner and made love to Katy in a polite, restrained manner. He knew that this was expected of him.

With her shy manner, Katy did not attract or excite him. And all the time they were making love, Owen kept thinking about Tinsel and her passionate embraces. The image was like a red hot wound imprinted in the back of his mind.

They came back from their honeymoon happy and healthy. Katy was positively blooming. Now that she was a real wife, she had no complaints.

Owen's chambers were unrecognisable. The walls were covered with rich, exotic wallpaper, the windows covered by velvet drapes. All around there were huge pots of ferns and aspidistras, stuffed birds in cages, vases with dingle dangles hanging from them, brass whatnots, bamboo tables and framed photographs of Katy's family everywhere. All Katy's treasures had been assembled with loving care by her sisters. A wizened old woman greeted them and presented herself as the housekeeper.

Owen was astonished by the transformation of his rooms. He allowed Katy to take off his shoes and help him on with his fancy slippers and smoking jacket.

'Now, dear, make yourself nice and comfortable. I'll organise some supper for us,' she said, clucking like a mother hen.

Slowly the knot that had been so reluctantly tied settled into position; their marriage became sealed. Katy took good care of her young husband and Owen happily accepted all she offered, wallowing in these home comforts and settling down to finish illustrating the novel for Deakins. When thoughts of Tinsel crept into his mind, he resolutely pushed them away.

Every day Katy ventured into the town wearing her wide crinoline. There she would shop and greet everyone she knew, as befitted her position as a married lady. Every day she visited her old home on the hill, and brought back news of all the family to relate to an indifferent Owen.

Owen was not unhappy about these arrangements. He felt quite content and pleased to have the opportunity to work. But deep within he still felt a great sense of guilt when he thought, as he could not help doing, of Tinsel. He had decided to avoid all contact with her now; this was the only way he could cope with his past misdeeds. So far, avoidance had worked.

It did not take long for Katy to involve herself in the business affairs. She marched down to the office and unmuddled Cousin Bertie.

'Oh, what a mess!' she said later to Owen. 'Bottles, cigar butts everywhere, and letters piled high; unopened. I'm getting Bertie a boy to help with the mail whether he likes it or not.'

Owen grinned slyly as he imagined a perspiring Bertie being bullied to a standstill by Katy.

In the end, the office was tidied up and a bright boy installed. He was just a back-street urchin who could neither read nor write, but he was intelligent and willing, and Katy, from her own purse, paid the schoolmaster to instruct the boy in his spare time.

Bertie was furious. He complained to Owen immediately. 'What is the world coming to?' he gasped. 'Taking them off the streets and educating them. There will be a revolution, a bloody massacre soon, mark my words.'

Owen ignored his protests. 'You needed an assistant down there,' he said. 'Now you've got one. So just get on with it.'

So the red-faced Bertie was left to go puffing away, muttering about radicals and revolutions.

Spring had burst forth into summer and Owen had turned the big attic into a studio. The long window gave him a good view of the river. Recently he had begun to experiment with canvas and oils and was currently working on a picture of Katy.

'Oh, it's beautiful, Owen,' cried his delighted wife. 'You'll have to paint my sisters next, and then all our friends. You could get some good commissions in this town.' Her shrewd mind was working overtime. 'If you charged a fair price, we might make a good bit of money.'

At this remark, Owen looked at her coldly. His gaze was scornful, for he could think of no worse occupation than to paint for money, especially the society women.

Later that day, Katy sailed off on her errands to visit her family. She came home a few hours later with a pale tear-stained face. 'Oh, Owen,' she cried, 'something terrible has happened at home . . .'

Owen surveyed her anxiously.

'Oh, poor Mama, what will Papa say?' she moaned.

'Whatever is it, Katy?' Owen demanded.

'It's Georgina. She's run away, gone to be an actress. Isn't it dreadful? Oh,' she sobbed, 'we will never live it down.'

Something warm stirred within Owen when he heard this.

At last someone had the courage to do as they wished. How he admired Georgi!

'She has taken that little madam Tinsel with her,' continued Katy. 'Tinsel is probably at the bottom of it all, the sly little minx. Well, I never trusted her.'

Owen listened with interest. So Tinsel had fled too. He suddenly felt very sad.

'Well, say something, Owen,' wailed Katy in desperation. 'What can we do?'

'Perhaps I had better hear the whole story before I make any decisions,' he said calmly.

Katy trembled with temper, 'How can you remain so unconcerned? This is a terrible catastrophe.'

'Oh, for God's sake, stop snivelling,' Owen snapped. 'Now explain actually what happened.'

'Well,' Katy began, 'there has been a lot of trouble at home. An acquaintance of Papa's spotted Georgi at a travelling show in town,' she said. 'Oh, it's awful,' she blubbed. 'Apparently Georgi was dressed like a man and was actually helping backstage. She was supposed to be taking extra music tuition for all this time but in fact has been doing this. So, of course, Mama was very angry indeed. She and Georgi had a heated argument about the rights of women, whatever that is,' babbled the distressed Katy. 'Mama forbade Georgi to go out and locked her in her room. But that little minx Tinsel let her out, and they both ran away. Oh, dearie, me.' Katy paused for breath and sighed heavily.

Owen grinned, 'Hurrah for Georgi!' he cried.

Katy stared at him in disbelief, and collapsed in a terrific hail of weeping as Owen gave a resigned shrug and went back to work. 'It is time for coffee, isn't it?' he asked as he went.

After this exchange, the atmosphere in the home became very tense. Katy flounced about red-eyed and bad-tempered while an unbothered Owen worked quietly on a new assignment he had just been sent.

The assignment was from Forest who wanted some amusing cartoons on an electioneering campaign for his magazine.

'Make it humorous and make it soon,' he had written.

All over the page, Owen drew sprawling fat men, thin, flag-waving youths, cats and dogs, people fighting and pushing, and waving banners.

As he worked, he ignored Katy's jibes. At last she put on her cloak. 'Well, if you won't help Mama, I will. An urgent message must be sent to Papa. I don't know when he'll be back.' With an angry sniff, Katy turned and flounced out of the door.

'It's not my affair,' Owen called after her mildly.

When twilight came and he could no longer work in comfort, Owen put down his pen and went down to the Blue Boar.

CHAPTER NINE

The Pilgrims' Way

The narrow twisting road that winds over the Weald of Kent was first trodden by the pilgrims on their way to Canterbury. Along it now on this bright morning rolled a heavy wagon drawn by two wide-backed grey mares, their dappled coats wet with the morning dew. The horses strained at the harness, which twinkled with brasses in the bright sunlight. As the wagon rumbled along, the hedgerows brushed the sides of the wagon, scratching the painted letters which read: 'Silver & Dillon, Theatrical Show'.

On the high driving seat, a slim youth held the reins. His short brown curls peeped out from beneath a floppy black hat. He wore a spotless white shirt and linen trousers held up by a wide leather belt. The youth whistled a merry tune as, with strong gentle hands, he urged the mares along.

Beside him sat a good-looking middle-aged man whose hoarse voice occasionally wheezed out encouraging remarks. 'That's it, boy, give 'em their head,' he muttered. 'They practically know the way.'

There was an unusual intonation in the deep voice. The man had a noble face. His skin was dark, his hair black and an open-necked shirt exposed a very hairy chest. His right arm was fitted into a bright red choker, acting as a sling about his neck. 'There's a nasty bend ahead, George, take it slow, boy,' he advised.

The youth eased on the reins. 'Whoa there, Lady, whoa there, Bess,' he called in a strong voice. His eyes were shining, his cheeks glowing. It was clear that he was enjoying himself.

Sitting in the back and on the tailboard of the wagon were half a dozen small children with dark, tousled heads. Among them Tinsel's silvery crown stood out.

Tinsel sat wrapped in her old plaid shawl, surrounded by the children. A few yards behind the wagon was a wobbly old gypsy caravan pulled by a strong mule called Alphonso. The caravan contained two women. One had a large frame, auburn hair and was in her mid thirties. Her smile was wide and charming. Beneath the freckles, her skin was as white as snow. And her thick hair was bound up in a green scarf. Her name was Moira Dillon.

In the driving seat next to Moira, and idly holding the reins, was Rosita Silver. Rosita was older, but smaller and darker than the other woman. Her skirts hid a twisted, deformed leg. At her breast, a child was strapped with a sash to her thin body. This was Rosita's ninth child in as many years. Not all the children had survived this hard life but still, at forty, Rosita herself was healthy and fit. Next to the caravan walked her husband. He was thin and wiry, his dark hair glinting with grey. He had long Latin features and black button eyes. This was Sam Silver, bred and born in a travelling show.

Now Rosita had begun to sing snatches from an Italian opera in a beautiful contralto voice. Sam took his concertina down from his shoulders and began to play. Then the tune switched to Irish music. Moira's strong brogue was then transmitted to the children who picked up the lively sound. Soon the lanes of Kent rang with song as George and Fred Dillon in the front of the first wagon joined in too.

Georgina whistled contentedly. She had no regrets at all. She was now a member of this little travelling show, most of whom regarded her as a boy. This suited her to perfection. As she sang along with all the others, she thought back to those days just before she had decided to make the break from home. Just for a bit of fun she had dressed up as a boy, paraded the town, and made the acquaintance of young Jan Silver, who was only sixteen. They had chatted about the stage and Jan had introduced her to his parents, owners of a travelling show.

From that day on Georgina had become fascinated and could not stay away from the Silvers. Twice a week she had gone down to the wasteground, where they were pitched, to watch the show. Rosita had been expecting this last baby so the group had stayed longer than usual, putting on a different show each night, ranging from light opera to morbid melodrama. All members of the group took part, even the tiniest toddler. Everyone had a place in keeping the show on the road. It always got very hot in the crowded marquee, and paraffin flares lit up the stage. The audience were rough but not unappreciative.

Georgina was in her element in this atmosphere. She hung about in the wings, helping whenever she could, buttoning a dress or straightening a prop.

One heavy night, the crowd was particularly drunk and rowdy. It was the custom to throw pennies on to the stage inbetween the acts, and the tiny children of the company would dash on stage and pick the pennies up. But on this night, the audience threw the money wildly, spinning the coins violently in order to hit the children. One little girl received a long cut on her face.

Seeing the child injured, Georgina dashed on stage from her place in the wings. 'Hold it!' she hollered. 'Don't hurt the children!'

From that night on, Georgina became popular with both families, and was accepted as a sort of impromptu stage manager. She was invited to share their merry suppers after the show.

The supper was cooked in a field kitchen and eaten around a big camp fire. To Georgina, raised in a middle-class Victorian home, this was the life – full of adventure. She would not have missed it for anything. With her long hair concealed under a big cap and in a smart trouser suit she allowed everyone to address her as George. They all seemed ready to treat her as male.

But Moira, in her rich brogue and jesting manner, had thought George a little odd at first. 'By Jesus,' she said, 'he's a queer kind of fella.'

Rosita defended her protegée. 'In my opinion, he's a nice, clean living lad.'

Sam also thought something was amiss. 'To tell you the truth,' he said. 'I ain't sure what sex he is. But I like him, or her, whatever it is.'

Everyone laughed.

'He's a willing, hard-working chap, so we won't pry,' boomed Fred Dillon.

So Georgina was accepted into the close community and shared their work and their leisure.

It was the big, thick-set Cockney, Fred Dillon, whom Georgina admired most. Fred was strong, steady and reliable and it was he who kept the show going, even in times of hardship. Fred was capable of keeping the show going under any amount of stress. She had seen him play a merry Falstaff, a sly Shylock, a buccaneering pirate. He did them all with equal skill. He could carry any part and memorise the script word for word. To the stage-struck Georgina, Fred was a wonder. Her admiration for him knew no bounds.

Georgina's decision to join the travelling show had been entirely unforeseen. Rosita was now out of child bed and the group had made plans to move on. On that last night, Georgina had watched over the restless audience, thinking how bored she was going to be when the show pulled up stakes and moved on.

It was Friday night and the audience was made up mostly of sailors. A big warship had docked recently, spilling its crew out for the night. Drunkenly, the sailors had roared for the show to begin. Georgina had watched from the wings as the audience fooled around, aiming orange peel at the closed curtains. Then one wag jumped up to the front and danced a hornpipe but as he leaped down, he overturned a paraffin flare. A blue flame raced along the floor catching the fringe of the curtains.

Without hesitating, Georgina raced forward with a sack to put out the fire. As she leaned over the blazing canister, her floppy cap fell off her head. Her long hair fell forward and caught alight. A muscular man in the front row rushed forward and clenched her burning tresses in his bare hands. In no time, the flames in her hair were out. Georgina swung round to gaze at a familiar face. He was an old acquaintance of her father's, having been mate on a previous ship . . .

At this moment, Fred Dillon had rushed up to put out the other flames that were still burning. Order was restored but Fred had burned his hands.

The show went on and 'Maria Marten' was murdered in the 'Red Barn' without a hitch, in spite of Fred's injury.

After the show, Moira cut the scorched ends of Georgina's

hair off very short. 'To be sure it's a fella you will be now, whether it's true or false,' Moira jested.

Rosita was attending to Fred's hands. 'We will not be able to move out tomorrow, Fred,' she said, 'You'll never drive the nags with those burned hands. And I don't think Jan is capable. The wagon is too heavy for him to handle.'

Everyone was worried, including Georgina, who had her own problems. She had to think of some excuse to give her mother for the loss of her lovely long hair.

The next morning Georgina stayed in her room to avoid questioning. But at eleven o'clock, her mother had a caller, in the form of the wife of Papa's old sailor friend. The wife lost no time in communicating her husband's experience at the travelling show the night before.

Thinking back to the fiery exchange with her mother, Georgina now had a few qualms. She wondered, for instance, if she should have been so hasty in taking Tinsel from a secure place. Tinsel had always declared that once Georgina had gone she would run off anyway, so Georgina had allowed her to leave with her in the dead of the night. In fact, Tinsel had fitted in marvellously with the show, and had taken to acting like a duck to water.

'Gee up,' cried Georgina, giving a good flick on the reins. No, she had no regrets. And her strong wrists had come in handy. She could drive the wagon while Fred's hands were getting a rest. At last she was free, unhampered by long skirts, or long hair. Yes, this was the life for her!

So along the green lanes the merry company travelled. They camped that evening in a chalk pit just outside Canterbury. The next day, the show went into action. With Georgina leading Alphonso, they paraded the town. Tinsel perched on the mule's back as the original fairy queen, Titania, while the children, dressed as pixies and fairies, romped along beside her. Fred wore a huge ass's head and walked among the curious crowds and larked with the town's folk while Sam played his concertina.

Roaring through a paper trumpet, Georgina announced the forthcoming performance of *A Midsummer Night's Dream*. The actual performance had little to do with the original play but it went down very well with the audience.

It was not long before Georgina discovered how limited the

group's repertoire was. It was only the talented little cripple Rosita who was well read. All the rest had learned their parts by ear, from tattered old scripts that belonged to her old Italian father who had been both musician and composer. But it did not matter. Their audiences did not read either, and were happy with the shilling's worth of entertainment they got.

It seemed that in spite of her lame leg and her brood of children, Rosita was the body and brains of the show, while Moira, with her flamboyant hair and her expressive green eyes, was the star. Her vibrant style won her the hearts of the audience in spite of the fact that she often muffed it when she was too full of gin.

Between them, Rosita and Moira groomed Tinsel, who soon learned to swoon like a lady, scream and swear like a harridan, and sing and dance like a beautiful butterfly. Georgina was amazed at Tinsel's rapid progress.

From Canterbury they travelled to the coast, staying at Folkestone and then travelled along to every coastal resort all the way up to the north.

All through the summer, Georgina worked like a Trojan, helping to keep this tattered show on the road. Driving the wagon, erecting the marquees, supervising the rehearsals, she loved every minute of it. She was also popular with everyone but young Jan Silver.

Jan had taken a shine to Tinsel and the girl brazenly encouraged him.

Georgina had come down on him very heavily. 'There's no time for such nonsense,' she said. 'Tinsel is under my protection and she is very young.'

With a surly grunt Jan muttered back: 'Mind your own business.' He was a dark, good-looking lad, and Sam Silver's eldest son. He was also lazy and insolent.

Georgina worried a lot about the two youngsters and what they got up to.

Tinsel's ethereal beauty which had so impressed her audience had begun to fade of late. She seemed to be getting podgy and extremely lazy, and was often to be discovered sitting in a quiet corner and scoffing sweetmeats, which Georgina had forbidden.

In the autumn, when nature had begun to paint its golden landscape, the group had just left Yarmouth and the weather was still good. Rosita had a serious look on her dark face when she called in Georgina one day.

'Come into the van, George, I want to talk to you,' she said, indicating the gypsy van where Moira and Rosita spent most of their time when not acting.

Georgina climbed the three steps. It was pokey inside. Coloured souvenirs of various performances in different towns covered the walls. There was one large double bunk and several small ones. On one of these beds sat the big red-faced Moira, a bottle of gin beside her. Moira started to get up.

'Don't go, Moira,' said Rosita quietly. 'I'd like you to stay.'

Moira gave a nonchalant shrug and remained seated.

'Something is wrong. What is it?' Georgina demanded.

'It's about Tinsel,' said Rosita gently.

'Well, what has she been up to?' Georgina asked.

Moira started to cackle and almost choked on her gin.

Rosita's voice was soft and gentle. 'We would not want to worry you, George, but we think you ought to know.'

'Know what?' Georgina looked startled.

'That Tinsel is pregnant,' answered Rosita.

'Goodness!' yelled Georgina. 'Who says so?'

'I do,' said Moira defiantly.

'Why, that young Jan, I'll break his neck,' threatened Georgina.

Rosita placed a restraining hand on her shoulder. 'You mustn't blame my son. He's only a young lad and the girl was already with child when she came here.'

'That's a lie!' cried Georgina, overcome with temper.

'You have only been with us three months, George,' said Rosita, 'and according to my reckoning Tinsel is already four months gone.'

'It's not possible,' gasped Georgina. 'She's only a child. She was well protected in my own home.'

'Not unless you had a sex change,' giggled Moira.

Georgina blushed scarlet and looked at Moira in disgust.

'Leave us now, there's a good girl, Moira,' urged Rosita.

Moira obediently picked up her bottle and with her wide hips swinging, climbed out of the van.

Georgina stood silently, stunned and disgusted.

'Sit down,' said Rosita, patting the bed.

Almost in a trance, Georgina obliged.

'Look here, dear, I am a woman of the world and it is because I realise that you are not, that you must accept my help and advice,' said Rosita. 'Take no notice of Moira, she's very common. But I assure you it is true about Tinsel. She herself informed me that the gentleman who is now married to your sister raped her.'

'God in heaven! Not Owen! That's unbelievable!' wailed Georgina. 'The girl's a liar, but she won't get away with it,' Georgina's temper rose.

'Calm yourself,' urged Rosita. 'What is done, is done. It is not the end of the world. I had my first child at the roadside when I was not much older than she is.'

'She looks so young. No one could possibly have forseen it,' murmured Georgina.

Rosita shrugged. 'Jan loves her, so there is no problem. Once she has had the child they can marry and she will be protected. She is an asset to our show and by then she will be older and wiser. There's nothing to worry about, George,' Rosita tried hard to console her.

Georgina found Tinsel in the marquee sitting on a packing case and eating sweets. She strode up, grabbed Tinsel by the wrist and dragged her out of the marquee into the sunlight. She pushed her against a tree and scrutinised her. 'What's all this I hear?' she demanded.

Tinsel's thin lips tightened and her cold blue eyes stared at Georgina defiantly. 'It's not your business,' she cried.

'Not my business, when you go around saying that my brother-in-law raped you and that now you bear his child?'

'Well, it's true,' declared Tinsel.

Georgina flew at her, slapping her face hard, and leaving a long angry weal. 'You whore!' she cried, her temper getting the better of her. 'Some oaf from the town did it, admit it!'

'No, no Georgi,' sobbed Tinsel rubbing her cheek. 'It was Owen. He loves me, and I want to go back to him.'

'Be quiet!' roared Georgina. 'Owen is Katy's husband.'

'But I belong to him, he owns me,' persisted Tinsel.

Georgina clenched her fists. 'You damned little liar! Tell the truth or I'll kill you,' she threatened.

But as she spoke, two firm arms came around her. 'Now George, let the kid be,' a thick hoarse voice said. Fred led Georgina into the wagon and for the first time for many years, she burst into uncontrollable sobs.

'That's it, let it go. You will feel much better,' said Fred comfortably.

The show had to go on, so that night they took to the road again. Rosita moved Tinsel from the wagon to new quarters in the warm van with the babies and away from Georgina's wrath.

While Jan Silver tossed and turned all night in the sleeping tent with the older boys, Georgina lay awake in the wagon. But she was up at dawn brushing and feeding the mares. By now her decision was made. She *would* stay with the show and never contact her family again. She had made a life with Tinsel and the show folk. She would never turn back. But God help the next man who tried to corrupt Tinsel! A burning hatred consumed Georgina and she vowed to protect Tinsel and her child with her own life.

So little Maisie Dillon, Fred's eldest girl, was trained for the part of Titania and Tinsel moved to less active jobs such as dressing and caring for the little kids. As the year waned, the group moved up to the Scottish borders. On the wild wind-swept moors, they were installed in a warm barn for the winter.

More than a hundred miles away back in Chatham, Owen's marriage had sadly deteriorated. During the first weeks after the disappearance of Georgina and Tinsel, things rapidly became gloomy. Katy still sulked and left the house after breakfast each day, stating that someone had to comfort her poor mother. At about midday Owen's chambers became extremely hot and stuffy, particularly since he was too idle to open the windows or make himself a cool drink, as Katy had lovingly done for him in happier days. Now he just went down to the Blue Boar haggard and unshaven, ate sandwiches for lunch and drank many pints of ale. He spent the whole after-noon there, playing games with the locals – darts and shove ha'penny – and was joined by Tom at eventide.

Of late Tom had not been his usual cheery self. His mother, who had never had a day's illness before, had recently devel-oped an arthritic knee, which had not improved her temper. Now, he complained, he was constantly in the dog house.

'That makes two of us,' replied Owen bitterly. 'Anyone would think that I did away with those two girls personally, the way Katy regards me,' he informed Tom.

'Should never have got mixed up with them females. I did warn you,' said Tom.

So the two men commiserated with each other, drowning their sorrows in ale until it was time to help Tom get on the cabbage cart back to his village.

Then Owen would wander aimlessly about the town until he saw Katy come home. Supper nowadays usually consisted of something from home which could be heated up.

'It doesn't look as though you did much work today,' Katy would comment sharply, her eyes surveying the room.

Drunkenly Owen would accept the stodgy food and the obvious contempt of Katy.

'Papa will be home next week,' she announced one evening, plonking a leathery omelette in front of him.

Slowly and methodically, like a cow chewing the cud, Owen disposed of the food, and looked at his wife. He had never noticed how Katy's tummy protruded before.

'I don't know what Papa is going to say,' continued Katy. 'I feel positively ill each time I think about it.'

Owen did not comment.

'Oh, poor Georgi,' Katy began to wail again. 'She might have been murdered by those ruffians, for all you care,' she accused him.

'Don't keep on, Katy,' Owen pleaded. But night after night it was a repeat performance. Her tear-filled eyes and her head of curls waggling reproachfully at him. Owen was beginning to feel the effects and felt that he was suffering a dreadful mental strain. And deep down, he was aware of a gnawing hungry feeling. He longed for the sight and sound of Tinsel, to hear that thin, high-pitched voice, to stroke that wealth of flaxen hair. But every time he thought about her, he wrestled madly with his conscience. Where was she? What was she doing? As far as he knew she had gone out into the world penniless and without any protection. No doubt Georgina would endeavour to take care of her, but what chance did someone like Georgina have? A woman with such advanced ideas stood little chance of success in this man's world. Nought but ridicule would be her reward.

Perhaps Katy was right, he thought gloomily. Perhaps he should not have been such a moral coward. A different man would have immediately assumed the family's responsibility and gone in search of the girls. He wondered whether it was too late to begin now. He never could make up his mind and inevitably hung on lamely until Captain Browne's return.

In due course the captain came home and immediately requested the presence of Owen at his house. This was Owen's first visit since Georgina had left. As he entered the door, the stuffy atmosphere overwhelmed him. The silence, the smell of floor polish and those dreadful pictures in the hall of Grecian maidens holding urns on their shoulders, all repelled him.

Katy was sitting with her mother in the parlour, stiff and upright amid the potted palms. Owen was suddenly struck by how alike they looked, hands crossed on their laps, mouths turned down primly.

The captain marched up and down in front of the fireplace. He was wearing his uniform, all brass and gold braid. His hands were locked behind his back. His brow was creased as he contemplated the mutiny which had broken out in his own home here. He had to get to the bottom of it.

Owen had yet to meet the brave captain in a bad temper. He had always been so jovial before. But as soon as Owen appeared, Browne roared out: 'What's all this I hear, Oliver?'

Owen opened his mouth but no words came out.

The captain had a good supply. 'My daughter has gone off and you have done nothing to prevent it. Now I learn also that that wretched child placed by you in this house came from a down-town slum. What have you to say for yourself, sir?'

Owen was shocked. Katy had betrayed him. 'I did not consider it my business, sir,' he said. 'Georgina left home and took her servant with her. I regarded it as of her own free will, so why should I interfere?'

'Well, well, I must say,' said the captain, 'I have been very wrong about you.' He surveyed Owen sternly. 'There are no guts in you, sir. You are weak and indecisive.'

This was a blow that struck home. Owen flushed but remained silent.

'When you asked for Katy's hand I was sure you would be an asset to my family while I was away at sea. It seems I was sadly mistaken,' continued the captain. 'You left that dear child to shoulder the burden all alone and did nothing to console my wife. I must say, sir, that you are a very shiftless young man.'

So on and on went the reprimand. Owen shot an angry glance at Katy who sat furtively wiping her eyes. 'I am very sorry that I did not come up to your expectations of me, sir,' he muttered.

'Sorry! It's too late to be sorry,' grumbled the captain. 'Where Georgina got these ideas defeats me,' he said. 'I understand that she used to go to town dressed as a boy. It's preposterous! I have sent the police to find them. I also intend to complain to them about the amount of vice and drunkenness to be found in this town. I am damned if I won't get this place cleaned up. Now, Katy,' he said firmly, 'go home with your husband and let's have no more nonsense.'

Katy looked so pathetically at Owen that his conscience pricked him. He took her hand and courteously helped her on with her cloak and escorted her out.

In the cab home, she wept copiously.

'Don't cry so, Katy,' Owen begged.

'But you don't love me,' she sobbed. 'Perhaps you never did.'

'Oh, don't be foolish. Of course I do,' Owen felt his voice was not his own.

Katy threw her arms about him, knocking his breath away. 'Oh, Owen,' she wailed, 'I'm sorry that I told Papa about Tinsel.'

'It's all right, it's done with now,' he said briskly. He did not want to dwell on it.

Back home, Katy was her old self once more. Owen's slippers were warmed, his coffee hot. Sweet and coy, dressed in a snow-white flowing nightgown with pink bows, she waited patiently in bed for him each night. And with a guilty feeling Owen crept in beside her. The domestic crisis over.

Owen settled down to work once more and life quietened down. Neither the police nor a private agent could find Georgina. The countryside was scoured without success. Soon the case was closed. The captain's complaints about the vice in the town resulted in some 'cleaning up'. Owen was saddened to witness the arrest of various women, including Polly, Sophie and old Fan from Rat's Castle, who were marched off to prison. People gathered to throw filth at them. After sentencing by a judge, they were then carted off to the hulks to await transport to Australia.

CHAPTER TEN

Silent Night

The air was very still, the night cold and frosty. As she lay tossing restlessly on the prickly straw bed, Tinsel could see that bright shining star through a chink in the door. On the other side of the barn, the two old grey mares had settled down for the night, while a couple of young goats poked out their white noses for a pathetic good night bleat.

It was Christmas Eve and all the others had gone to a local farmhouse to put on a Christmas show. There was also to be a grand party afterwards.

How Tinsel would have liked to have joined them! But the baby was due soon and she did not feel up to it. She had been so languid that day and constantly twinged with pain. In the circumstances Rosita had considered it wiser for Tinsel to stay at home. Her time was very near.

So in a byre in that warm barn she now lay. Outside on the bleak moor, silver frost lay on the ground and long icicles hung from the trees.

Tinsel shivered and snuggled down under the coarse blanket, trying to accept the waves of pain. How she wanted this baby to be born! She was fed up with being fat, ungainly and unable to act. She wondered what Owen was doing, and whether he ever thought about her. She felt desperately lonely and sad. Perhaps she would die from complications of childbirth, just as her mother had done, soon after she had left the baby Tinsel on the convent doorstep with a note pinned on her.

Waves of sorrow swept over her as Tinsel found herself

reliving her youth: Polly driving her out in the cold air with a huge stick; a great bewhiskered sailor getting on top of her and ripping her small body apart.

The images were unbearable. Sweating and shivering, she called out for Jan. He had promised to return once the show was over. But there was no answer, only a deep silence suddenly broken by the ringing of a distant church bell to herald the birth of Christ.

Tinsel seemed to lose all control as fear overcame her. She sobbed and screamed, rolling over and over desperately in the straw as pain surged through her. She banged her small fists violently against the wall and worked herself up into an hysterical fit while the child kicked feebly within her.

Suddenly the door burst open and young Jan appeared, 'Tiny, Tiny.' He called his pet name for her. 'Whatever is the matter?'

He knelt down beside her, a great burly robust lad who was as gentle as a lamb and so unlike his minute, fiery parents. 'Hush, don't take on so. Where does it hurt?'

Frantically Tinsel clung to him. 'I'm afraid,' she cried. 'I'm going to die as my mother did.'

'Now, Tiny, calm down,' Jan said reassuringly. 'Mother's on her way. She won't be long.' He held her hands tight as the storm within her died.

Rosita arrived shortly afterwards as she had promised, her face pale and weary after a long struggle through the snow with her crippled leg and a heavy child strapped to her back. She released the straps. 'Put the bairn to bed, Jan. I'll see to Tinsel.' With gentle touch Rosita felt over Tinsel's small body, running her hands over the extended stomach. 'Your baby is nearly here, Tinsel,' she told her. 'Be a brave girl and it will soon be over.'

From a bag laid ready, she pulled some brown paper and large white sheets. 'Bring the hot water, Jan,' she called, 'and then wait outside. It will soon be over.'

With great skill Rosita drew the baby from Tinsel's body. But the child was still; it did not cry. It was a tiny doll-like figure with golden downy hair. Rosita slapped it and held it upside down. But to no avail.

With a deep sigh, Rosita wrapped it in a towel. 'Take it

away, Jan,' she said, 'it does not live.'

Jan held out his arms for that tiny body as large tears fell from his eyes onto the white towel.

'Your child was born dead, Tinsel,' Rosita informed her. Quietly she sponged the fevered brow but the little mother did not cry out or utter a word. She just stared back at Rosita with cold blue eyes.

It was well past midnight when the rest of the family arrived home. Fred and Moira arrived first in a farm cart drawn by Alphonso. Georgina came immediately afterwards. She was walking home and playing snowballs with the children. She rushed in through the gates, her cheeks glowing with health. The charcoal brazier was blazing to warm the barn and all the hurricane lamps had been lit. There was also a good fire going in the gypsy caravan where Rosita boiled up a giblet soup, hoping to get Tinsel to drink a little.

After the night out, Fred was bright and breezy while Moira was very drunk.

'Merry Christmas, everyone,' Georgina yelled. But the cry died in her throat at the sight of young Jan sitting on the top of the caravan steps, a look of deep depression on his youthful face. In his arms he held a small white bundle.

There was no noise from the barn now, since Tinsel had dropped off to sleep.

'God in heaven, what's that?' demanded Moira.

'A stillborn child,' replied Jan faintly.

'Oh, my God!' cried Moira, crossing herself. 'Born on Christmas Eve! It's an omen.'

Georgina dashed into the barn to see Tinsel. Looking down at the girl's angelic white face, she stroked her mane of flaxen hair spread over the straw.

'What happened?' she asked Rosita who had followed her into the barn. 'Is she all right?'

'She's fine,' said Rosita, 'but she will need to sleep a while. The child was born dead. There was absolutely nothing I could do.'

Georgina's lips tightened. 'Good,' she said quickly. 'Now she will recover and get back to normal.'

Rosita looked at Georgina quizzically. How callous, Georgina was.

★

The Christmas festivities could only be subdued after the death of the baby, which was put in a box and buried in a wood as though it were a kitten.

'We don't need a doctor now,' said the practical Rosita. 'That would be an unnecessary expense. Besides, George, we all know that you have run away from your family. Having any contact with the authorities would be the quickest way to put them on your track.' Georgina looked shame-faced.

Everyone agreed that the baby should be buried.

'Without a prayer? But that's too awful,' wailed Moira. She had been brought up in Catholic Ireland and often had bouts of religious fervour when sober.

'Let those that believe do the praying,' growled Fred.

So in the end, the tiny body was buried by young Jan without any ceremony. Jan sobbed, and salty tears poured from his eyes.

On Christmas morning, Moira decided to take all the children into the town to attend mass at the Catholic church. Rosita was not sorry to get this excited tribe of show children from under her feet and readily agreed.

So, with Alphonso hitched to a rickety cart built from parts salvaged from a ditch, the warmly-wrapped youngsters climbed aboard. Moira climbed in beside them, dressed in a moth-eaten fur coat and a large hat with a green feather. Her face looked very serious and sober.

Fred and Sam lit a big camp fire to spit-roast the two large fowls that the farmer had given them for Christmas, and an awning was erected between the wagon and the barn to make a cosy windproof spot.

Georgina sat there the next day, looking completely unrecognisable. She was dressed in a long navy jersey and wearing a white untreated wool cap that a small Dillon girl had knitted for her as a present. Her cheeks were ruddy and weatherbeaten, her hands all split and cracked. But she looked extremely content and positively radiated happiness as she busily scrubbed very large potatoes to roast in the hot ashes of the fire.

Rosita sat in the entrance of the barn next to her much loved charcoal brazier. She was watched by a frail Tinsel, who had developed a cough.

'There was a time,' remarked Georgina, 'when I never believed anyone who told me that they camped out in mid-winter.'

'We have done so for many years,' Fred said. 'We couldn't afford to do otherwise.'

'It's crucial that we put on a show tonight,' joined in Rosita. 'The kitty is very low.'

'Not to worry,' piped up Sam. 'I've managed to hire the village hall.'

'Not sure what to give them yet,' pondered Fred.

'Better mix it,' said Sam. 'A few clown acts, a bit of a panto. It's Boxing Day and folk will be in holiday mood.'

'The children can do a few fairy and elves acts to amuse the other youngsters,' suggested Rosita.

Georgina sat dreamily listening to their voices. It seemed so unreal to sit here in the depth of winter beside an open fire and scraping spuds. Mother, Katy and Mary would be shocked if they saw her now. But she worried. It concerned her to hear the others talk of the show in this way. It sounded as though it was on the rocks. So far both Tinsel and she had been housed and fed in return for their services, and recently Tinsel had contributed little. But no one had uttered one word of complaint.

'Look here,' she said abruptly, 'I'd like to help you through the winter. So far I've not given anything towards my keep.'

'You and your little friend have earned it,' growled Fred.

'Not to worry, George gets results,' said Sam in his warm and generous manner.

'I know you're short of ready cash and I want to put my share in,' insisted Georgina.

Rosita's dark eyes surveyed her shrewdly, 'Well, can you afford anything?' she asked shortly.

'I can well afford it,' replied Georgina. 'My father is a ship's captain and each time he returned from sea he gave us all a sovereign. My sisters had brooches made, or spent it on rubbish, but I saved every one of mine. I've still got them,' she announced.

Everyone looked startled.

'Well, you dark horse, George,' said Rosita. 'How much have you got?'

'Twenty-five sovereigns,' cried Georgina jubilantly. 'And I am perfectly willing to put it all in the show to tide you over the winter.'

Fred raised a large calloused hand in protest. 'No, George, I've survived many winters and I'll keep going through this one. You keep your money, you might need it.'

'Five sovereigns would be a fortune to us at the moment, George,' remarked Rosita.

'I think you have certainly earned a piece of the show, George,' said Sam. 'Why not buy a share? It will be profitable when the good days come.'

'When will the good days come for us?' cried Rosita with a sneer. 'It's been hand-to-mouth for a long time.'

'Don't complain,' growled Fred. 'By now you should be used to it.'

Georgina quietly left the fireside and went to her own quarters in the back of the wagon where her few possessions were kept. She brought back a handkerchief tied up by its four corners. With her strong white teeth, she tackled the knots and then poured the golden sovereigns out on to the ground.

'There they are! They're all yours, and you're welcome!' she cried.

For a moment there was an embarrassed silence. Then Rosita got up and put the money into the little black apron she always wore. 'Thank you, George,' she said. 'I never look a gift horse in the mouth but I'll not forget your generosity.'

'Well that's it, George, you are part of our show now,' cried Fred.

'Take my hand on it,' declared Sam as he jumped about like a wiry little monkey.

'I'll put it in a safe place,' said Rosita, her apron heavy with the coins. 'See to the dinner. The children will be very hungry.'

Georgina went to sit with Tinsel who was now sitting up and looking more like her old self, though that irritating dry cough had returned with a vengeance. Georgina looked at her with concern but obeyed when Tinsel asked her to brush her hair. She produced a brush and sat grooming the golden hair and then tied it back with a white ribbon.

Whatever Tinsel's feelings, she did not show them as she sat up and ate her dinner. And it seemed to Jan that she looked more delectable than ever before.

That afternoon they all gathered in the barn to rehearse the show. It was good fun and ended with an impromptu concert in which all the children sang and danced or played a musical instrument.

In spite of the dead baby, to Georgina it was the happiest Christmas she had ever spent. By the New Year Tinsel was recuperating well and Georgina was working like a Trojan to repair and renovate costumes, paint scenery and recite to the others lines from her own book of modern plays. Advising and teaching involved body and soul in this small decrepit travelling show.

In February, when the nights got lighter and the snows melted on the hills, making the swollen streams rush down the valleys, it was time to move on. So the travelling group said goodbye to their winter quarters and were back on the road again. This time they headed south through the Lake District and towards the west coast. There was money enough in the kitty and Tinsel was on her feet once more.

As Tinsel was giving birth to her stillborn child, Owen wandered about Chatham. Melancholia had taken him for her own and his gaunt face was set in a morbid mask. His thin slovenly figure was well known by the locals as he slouched through the main street, sketchbook under his arm, or stood propped up in a doorway drawing the population as they passed by. He drew the destitute ragged boys who swept the snow from the crossing, and hungry ten-year-old girls, often with baby siblings in their arms and ragged toddlers hanging on to their grubby skirts. He sketched an old man in a ditch who had died from exposure. He captured on paper the long line of people outside the soup kitchen – fieldworkers who got no sustenance during the winter and survived as best they could on charity hand-outs. On and on Owen went, seeking out and immortalising this stark ghost of poverty.

Little grotesque figures filled his book, with hollow eyes and stick-like limbs. In all weathers, wet and cold, he prowled everywhere. He drew shop windows bursting with Christmas fare, a sharp contrast to the poverty of many of the characters on the streets. A blind match-seller, a prostitute, a group of beggars, all became his models and acquaintances.

Katy was getting very worried. 'Must you draw all this misery?' she begged. 'Why do you stay out in the cold all day?' she nagged. He stared at her vacantly, noting vaguely, as he had before, that she had got very plump and was most decidedly over-dressed. But he said nothing.

'All right,' she continued in a complaining voice, 'don't answer me, but I am telling you for your own good, people are beginning to talk.'

'People? What people?' he asked slowly, as his thoughts drifted to the queue outside the soup kitchen.

'Mother's friends,' Katy declared in a high tone. 'They can see you lounging about the town. It's a disgrace.'

Owen shot his wife a disdainful look and grabbed his battered hat. Then he picked up his sketchbook and set off for his daily patrol of the town.

Katy sighed. Picking up her feather duster, she flicked it over her prized china and her aspidistra plants, and then went off up the hill to visit her mother.

So on that Christmas Eve when the Cathedral bell toiled out the good tidings, Owen stood outside the Blue Boar with big Tom, who nursed a bloody nose which he had got in a fight with some locals.

Owen was intoxicated and he swayed back and forth clutching his sketchbook. 'Happy Christmas, Tom,' he slurred.

'The same to you, old pal,' Tom returned his greeting in a maudlin manner.

Then Owen left Tom and began to wander, or stagger, slowly home. As he drew near his chambers, in his befuddled state of mind, he imagined that Tinsel was waiting at home for him. He rubbed his hand over the iron knob on the gate post, and could see as clear as day, her flaxen hair and sky blue eyes. Then he realised that it was not real. He hung on to the post and wept.

Katy came down the steps in her flowing nightdress and gently escorted him inside to put him to bed.

Over a boring Christmas dinner at the house on the hill, Owen sat pale-faced and silent. The captain was in great form, entertaining another skipper and his wife. They were Americans from that progressive new country and were lively and very talkative. But Owen found that he could not communicate with them. He sat at the table with a sullen expression on his face, while his mother-in-law's beady eyes seemed to penetrate his brain.

'Oh, how she detests me,' he thought miserably. 'What a horrible predicament for me to be in.'

Plans were being made for Captain Browne to go to America to discuss an interest in a new steamship line. By the end of the dinner it had been decided that he should take the trip in the New Year and take his wife and young Mary with them. Owen felt relieved but Katy seemed distracted.

'You can go too, if you want to,' Owen informed her.

'Don't be silly, Owen,' Katy replied. 'Someone must see to things here. I'll miss them terribly but Mother certainly needs a holiday after that dreadful affair with Georgina.' Once more tears fell from her eyes like rain.

Owen hid his scorn from her but showed no sympathy.

In late January when the rest of the family had left on their travels, Owen decided to take his finished work to London.

'Don't stay long, Owen,' begged Katy. 'I'd come with you but someone has to mind the house and give eye to the office.'

Owen did not seem to be listening. He simply gave Katy's cheek a peck and slid out of the front door.

This time he travelled on the new railway which he enjoyed enormously. He found it all very stimulating with the smooth flow of the train, the continuous grind on the track of the wheels which said over and over again, 'We're going away, we're going away.'

He leaned back, listening to the swish of the wheels and watching the green countryside rolling past. In his compartment he listened with interest to a conversation between his fellow passengers on the comparative merits of the steam horse and the real animal. Yes, in all it was a very agreeable journey.

As bright and breezy as ever, Forest was now installed in Fleet Street in an untidy newspaper office. He greeted Owen as an old friend, took him to lunch at the Magpie and introduced him to a lively old man with a big bushy moustache and long white hair. He was Smiley, the oldest illustrator in the business. Owen had always admired this distinguished man's work. In Smiley's time he had caricatured kings, queens and princes and once had been imprisoned for his audacity. Smiley admired Owen's new book of sketches and promised to recommend him to a certain lord he knew who campaigned to help the poor and oppressed, especially children. Owen was delighted with this reception.

That evening Owen went with Forest to a private reading of Deakins' new novel. All the old literary gang were there and Owen received another commission from the great novelist to illustrate his latest work. Deakins informed him that he too was leaving for America the following week, determined to probe that radical new country.

For Owen the days passed quickly in this stimulating company. He stayed in Forest's rooms in Gravesend and lazed about the city all day and half the night. He wrote a note to Katy informing her that pressure of work held him, but in fact it was only selfish ambition that held him in town, and a desire to hobnob with the famous. He went to parts of the city he had never been to before, over to the south bank, mixing with the *hoi polloi* of Southwark. For weeks he lingered on until the buds on the plane trees in the London squares were bursting forth.

Finally, it was time for him to return to Chatham.

Owen climbed the steps to Pier Chambers with a heavy step and opened the front door. As he did so, from the shop on the ground floor emerged a little wizened woman with no teeth. 'Ain't no one up there, sir,' she called.

Owen turned to look at her. He did not understand. 'Me and me son lives down here now,' she said. 'We got to look after the new tenant when he comes.'

Owen ignored her and ran lightly up the stairs. He was appalled to see that his rooms were virtually empty. All the best furniture, the drapes, and even his own possessions had disappeared. He dashed downstairs again.

'Where is my wife?' he demanded.

'I told yer, sir,' the old woman whined. 'Madam has gone to live in her old home at the top of the hill.'

Owen snorted angrily. 'How dare she move me out of my own chambers!' he roared.

At the top of the hill a demure but defiant Katy greeted him.

'What on earth have you moved out for?' Owen demanded.

'Now, now. Sit down, Owen,' Katy said. 'Don't lose your temper.' She took off his coat and pushed him firmly into a chair. 'If you had communicated with me more often and not taken such a long time to come home, I would have informed you of my plans,' she said. 'I wrote several times to you but got no reply.'

'I was moving around,' Owen lied, thinking of the pile of unopened letters he left behind in Forest's house.

'I got an excellent rent for those rooms from a solicitor,' she informed him. 'The old man in the shop below died so I bought the lease of the premises and put Billy and his mother in the downstairs to help look after the new tenant. That way it pays for itself and gives me a little bit to spare, which I intend to save up to buy some land. Then we'll build our own house just how we want to,' Katy explained excitedly.

Owen looked depressed. 'Why was I not consulted?' he asked.

'I wrote to you about all this, but you never answered,' Katy informed him. 'Don't worry so, Owen, my parents intend to go on to visit Canada so they'll not be home just yet. We can save money by living here in their home.'

Owen felt relieved that his dragon of a mother-in-law would not be returning just yet, but he also felt manipulated.

'Please yourself,' he said sulkily.

'Don't be so off-hand, Owen,' Katy begged. 'It's for our own benefit that I did it. Now you're getting so successful it will be nice to have a house of our own. Billy is a useful lad in the office and he really appreciated me giving the place to his mother.'

Owen shrugged. It was no good fighting Katy. She knelt to untie his boot laces, brought him his slippers and chattered to him in sweet baby talk. By the end of the evening, Owen felt he had no power left to fight that sweet cloying woman.

She fussed over him, and made his life so comfortable that he stopped roaming the streets. Every day he worked in the captain's warm library while Katy crept about the house trying not to disturb him, and telling the servants to do the same. But most of the time Owen just sat idly doodling and filling up the waste paper basket with his scribbles. He felt like a fly enmeshed in a web waiting to be gobbled up.

CHAPTER ELEVEN

On With The Show

The spring came in with all its glory. The hedgerows were a bright green, dotted with the jewel-like colours of tiny wild flowers. In the woods primroses and wood violets made a luxury carpet of gold and blue. That spring day was simply made for lovers. The blackbird sang a full-throated mating song, while the cuckoo called from across the valley. Tinsel danced hand in hand through the woods with young Jan.

Jan had grown tall, gawky and rather silent, while Tinsel was full of the joys of spring. Her high-pitched voice echoed through the tall trees.

'Oh, it's so grand up here, isn't it,?' she cried. 'I feel so free and happy. I want to shout out to Mother Nature to tell her how clever she is!'

Jan looked slightly bewildered and clung desperately to Tinsel's hand as she skipped over the last year's ferns, her head held high, her long hair shining in the spring sunshine.

'Flowers, they come and go each year. I can't see what's exciting about them,' he muttered.

'Oh, you oaf, you are a dear, darling oaf,' exclaimed Tinsel. 'But I love you.' She put her arms tightly about his neck and they stood still, lovers lost in a long kiss.

'Come, Tinsel,' Jan said, 'let's lie down under a tree and let me really love you,' he pleaded.

'Don't be foolish, Jan.' Tinsel pushed him impatiently away. 'You know you promised never to mention such things.'

'Darling,' he groaned, 'how can I just kiss and fondle you?

I'm only human, and this love play is getting impossible.'

'Well, Jan, you have a choice,' Tinsel said, stamping her feet defiantly. 'I have sworn that I will never do that again except with Owen, to whom I really belong.'

At these words, Jan's face went white with passion. Jealousy glowed in his usually mild eyes. 'I'll kill that damned fellow!' he muttered. 'Why do you say such things, Tinsel? I swear I'll do for him when I find out who he is,' he threatened.

Tinsel pulled away from him. Her thin lips had tightened. 'Well, I'll never ever tell and if you was to hurt him, I'd kill you.'

'But Tiny,' Jan begged, 'he raped and deserted you. He took advantage of your innocence.'

'Mind your own business,' Tinsel replied tartly. 'When Owen comes for me, I'll go to him – just like that.' She snapped her delicate fingers under his nose.

'All right,' Jan muttered, defeated, 'let's go back and stop this silly squabbling. How we can play Romeo and Juliet together beats me, for they really loved each other.'

'Me,' boasted Tinsel, 'I can play *any* part once I'm up on stage.'

'I don't doubt it,' murmured Jan despondently.

A very grim-faced Georgina waited at the edge of the wood. 'Where have you been?' she asked Tinsel fiercely.

'Just for a walk,' replied Tinsel with wide-eyed innocence.

'Well, get going! We're ready to move on,' Georgina ordered.

Quite soon the show was on the move once more – through the rural lakelands towards the west coast, and the seaside resorts where they planned to put on a super big show which they had been rehearsing continuously the last few weeks. Business had picked up recently, helped by the input of Georgina's fantastic new ideas and terrific drive. And with Tinsel as star of the show again.

'We will hire some casual actors,' Georgina suggested, 'and make it a full cast. It will be worthwhile with Jan and Tinsel playing the lead.'

'No, there have never been such star-crossed lovers,' jested Fred.

Such remarks irritated Georgina. 'I'll have to be after them,' she grumbled. 'I'm afraid they're getting bloody lazy, the pair of them.'

Fred puffed at his pipe and scrutinised Georgina shrewdly. Was she jealous of these young lovers who played their part so well on and off the stage? His thoughts ran on. Georgina not only acted but looked like a male, with her husky voice and strong body, but she was unreasonably possessive of Tinsel. Still, she had also trained Tinsel to be a fine actress. That was impressive indeed.

During her time with the group, Georgina had built up a good collection of costumes which she worked very hard to maintain – altering, designing, making up and repairing. It was a whole year now since she had left home. The time had matured her. Her skin was rough and tanned, she wore shirt sleeves and riding breeches, highly-coloured cravats and a *pince-nez* on the end of her nose. Her chestnut hair was still short and had grown very curly. And always there was an alertness about her, a sort of readiness to jump into action, like a caged lioness.

Both Georgina and Tinsel had permanent quarters in the back of the old wagon. It was a pokey spot among the props and the wardrobes, just two bunks one above the other. A mirror and a small cupboard were the only furniture.

Tinsel was now sitting on the bottom bunk in a cross-legged position, scoffing the sweets that Jan had given her as a peace offering.

'Don't let me catch you slipping off to the woods with young Jan again,' threatened Georgina. 'I've warned you. I want no more trouble from you.'

'Wha'foor?' cried Tinsel with her mouth full.

Georgina's eyes flashed fire. 'You know quite well what for, you damned silly girl. You're not safe with any man.'

'I want to go home,' declared Tinsel defiantly. 'I want to be with Owen.'

Quick as a flash, Georgina reached over, caught Tinsel's tiny arm and twisted it behind her back. Tinsel yelled, almost choking on the sweet in her mouth.

'Don't you dare mention that name,' shouted Georgina. 'How many times do I have to tell you that that episode is over and done with. You have a career ahead of you, and by God, I'll see you stick at it.' She gave Tinsel's arm a vicious twist.

'Oh! Oh, Georgi, you're hurting me,' yelled Tinsel. Sweat rolled down Georgina's brow. Her eyes had a strange glazed look. Then suddenly she dropped her hold on that thin arm.

'Oh, my God, why do you provoke me?' she cried.

'Sorry, Georgi,' snivelled Tinsel. 'Let's kiss and make up,' she said, pouting her rosy lips to be kissed.

Georgina placed her lips on Tinsel's but hers was a long kiss of a lover not a peck of friendship.

Tinsel's tiny hands smoothed her chestnut hair as Georgina cuddled her close.

Suddenly Georgina pushed her away with brutal force. 'Give over, Tinsel!' she yelled. 'Get out there and rehearse your act! If you sit about here eating so many sweets like that, you'll get as fat as a pig.'

Tinsel wriggled off the bunk. There was a knowing expression in her deep-set eyes. 'Don't get bad-tempered Georgi,' she said. 'I'm just going.' But there was an undertone of triumph in her voice. She flounced out, leaving Georgina, clutching her pinking shears so tightly that her knuckles were white.

So successful was the show in Blackpool that they stayed on for six weeks, almost to the end of the summer season. *Romeo and Juliet* was extremely popular, with the young star-crossed lovers reducing the audience to tears. And every night, Georgina sat in the wings chewing her nails with jealousy.

In late August they moved to Birmingham where again the theatre was full every performance.

Georgina suggested that after Birmingham the group should push on to London and spend the next winter there. She thought that it would be better to keep working than to rest up all the winter, as they usually did.

There was considerable dissent about this idea. Rosita hated London, having had a rough time there once when an audience ran wild and wrecked the show.

Moira protested against it too, but she was protesting against everything, it seemed, particularly since she was fed up with getting the mature roles now that Tinsel was established as the leading lady.

Sam was not too keen on the classics and wanted to return to ''orrible murders' as he called those Victorian blood-and-thunder stories, while Fred was ambitious for them all and thought they should try the big city.

But at last, with much persuasion from Georgina, they did all agree to move on to London.

Georgina was delighted and promised to read up some modern plays and come up with something different for them to perform.

Then, quite suddenly, there was mutiny in the camp. Young Jan announced that he would not go with them unless he was allowed to marry Tinsel.

'Don't be a fool, boy,' roared Sam. 'You're not even seventeen yet.'

'Why not let him?' said Rosita. 'It might settle several problems.'

Georgina stared vacantly over at young Jan then back at Tinsel who stood poised like a nymph, a mischievous smile on her face.

'Tinsel will not be marrying anyone,' Georgina said coldly. 'She has a career ahead of her.'

Young Jan dashed towards Georgina, his face convulsed with fury. With his fists waving, he yelled: 'What's it to you, you kinky old crow? You don't own her!'

Taken aback by the venom of his tone, Georgina was speechless. She just stared at him. Then, suddenly, all hell was let loose as Jan hurled himself on Georgina and caught her a blow on the jaw that sent her spinning. Fred rushed at Jan, Sam intervened, and in no time at all the women, men and children were fighting, screeching and yelling.

Georgina rose to her feet and looked at this dreadful scene with horror. She had never seen such expressions of emotion. Tinsel stood on the side, laughing and clapping her hands with glee and with excitement as she saw this pile of writhing fighting men and weeping women. She was really enjoying the situation.

Georgina was disgusted. Reaching out, she fetched Tinsel a stinging blow across the cheek. Tinsel fled, crying loudly.

'Hi! Hi!' yelled Georgina, wading into the fray. 'Give over! Stop this scrapping!' She dragged out little Sam and hauled Jan to his feet. Jan was bloody-nosed and still struggling but the battle was over. Tempers were already subsiding.

'For Christ's sake!' roared Georgina. 'Let's discuss the matter like human beings, not animals. Get the camp fire going, Teddy,' she told Jan's small brother. 'We'll hold a general meeting.'

Jan sulkily wiped the blood from his nose while Fred got out the bottle which was kept for emergencies.

Within ten minutes they were all settled around the camp fire – women and men with the little children on their laps. Georgina surveyed them all soberly, and whispered a quiet prayer to God to give her the courage to settle this dispute. She was sure that Tinsel was responsible for it.

Rosita, the most level-headed spoke first. 'We all like and respect you, George, but we must face the fact that we have a real problem on our hands.'

'I agree,' said Georgina. 'What do you suggest? Perhaps Tinsel and I should leave the show.'

'Oh, no, not that!'

There were cries of dissent even from the young children.

'It's better that *I* go,' announced the sulky Jan. 'But if I do, Tinsel goes with me,' he added.

'Peace, peace,' cried Fred, afraid that the quarrel would break out again. 'I'm still the guv'nor, and I shall decide who stays and who goes.'

'To be sure, what harm is there in the kids getting married?' muttered Moira, already slightly woozy from the booze.

Georgina's obstinate square chin stuck out aggressively.

'Tinsel is under my protection and I forbid it,' she said firmly.

'Who are you to forbid anything?' sneered young Jan. 'Half man, half woman, and no good to either one.'

Georgina flushed a deep red.

'Now, Jan, that's enough,' warned his father.

'I suggest we let Tinsel speak for herself,' said Rosita.

'Good idea,' growled Fred. 'Now, Tiny, what have you to say?'

Tinsel stood up. She was dressed in the short white shift that she had rehearsed in, and the fire-light outlined her well-formed body and gave her hair a red glow. For a moment there was a hushed silence as if her presence over-powered them.

'Well, get on with it! Say your piece,' ordered Fred.

Tinsel swayed back and forth. She looked at Jan and then at Georgina. Suddenly she burst into a wail of misery. 'I want to go home!' she cried. 'I want to be with my Owen. He owns me.'

Everyone looked shocked. Jan leapt up. 'Oh, Tiny, don't say that! I love you so. I'll kill myself if you won't marry me.' He threw himself dramatically at her feet.

But Georgina got up and ran straight at Tinsel. 'You bloody little devil!' she yelled. Tinsel took one glance at Georgina and fled.

Fred put out a firm arm to prevent Georgina following her, and he stirred the prostrate Jan with his foot.

'Get up!' he ordered. 'Be a man. As far as I can tell, you are all being influenced by a damned good actress.'

In subdued silence, the company broke up. They all went off to bed with no decision having been made. Georgina took a blanket and lay all night beside the camp fire.

At dawn, Fred stoked the fire and began to prepare coffee. When Georgina awoke, he said: 'We have all agreed. Jan is leaving.'

After breakfast, Georgina stood with Fred and watched young Jan go down the road with his parents. At the end of the lane they would say farewell to their errant first born son. The sweet-natured Rosita was a small limping figure with a black shawl held tightly about her frail shoulders, while his father Sam looked a small figure in shabby clothes and swinging step. Between them walked the tall, gawky Jan. The haversack on his back contained all his wordly possessions as he went out into the wide universe alone. He looked dejected, with his shoulders bowed, and he did not look back once.

From the wagon came a dry rasping sound. Tinsel did not easily weep real tears but she had a disturbing cough when she was genuinely upset.

Deep sadness overwhelmed Georgina. 'I did not want him to go, Fred,' she said.

'It's better this way,' Fred replied. 'He was never whole-heartedly with us, and there is a wide world out there waiting for him.'

'I feel so guilty,' declared Georgina.

'There's no need for that,' replied Fred. 'Believe me, Jan is better out of it. That little girl is not consistent and she would've only brought him sorrow.'

'By God I'll make her work now. I'll grind that little monkey into the ground,' Georgina threatened.

Fred shot her a shrewd look. 'Let's hope you can settle your own problems so easily,' he said.

'You heard what he called me?' she asked ruefully. 'I

suppose it's true. Sometimes I am afraid of life. It's as if there's no place for me.'

'This is certainly a man's world, Georgina, women have little opportunity,' agreed Fred.

'But I *am* an oddity, I feel neither one nor the other,' she said sadly.

Fred patted Georgina's shoulder. 'Not to worry, lad, it takes all kinds to make up this world. That's the joy of it all.'

CHAPTER TWELVE

The Road to London

Once young Jan had left the show there was no one to play Romeo to Tinsel's Juliet, so the most successful of the group's ventures had to be scrapped. It was decided to return to one-night shows in various towns, with comedy, strong acts and melodrama.

The show made fair progress even if the friendly atmosphere within the group had disappeared. Indeed, there was now a distinct air of distrust between the families. Moira was spiteful and extremely catty towards Tinsel, while Fred and Sam often exchanged angry words. Only Rosita reigned peaceful and serene. Her expressive dark eyes were extremely sad but with admirable calm she held the rest of them together and thrilled the audience with her rich contralto voice as she entertained them with the ballads she had gathered on her world-wide travels during her nomadic youth.

Georgina murmured apologetically one evening: 'I am truly sorry that your son was forced to leave us, Rosita.'

Rosita sighed and stirred the fire with a stick. It was a habit she had when preoccupied. 'No matter, I have other sons,' she replied quietly.

In November they left St Albans and made their way to London. They approached by way of Romford and then on to Stratford. By then they were cold and travel-weary. The November mists had enveloped the big city. Fred found them a piece of waste ground, and stables were found for the two mares and the mule, Alphonso. The land they camped on was flat and marshy, and close to the river. It was very damp. Tinsel immediately developed a cough and the small children caught a strange fever. There was an air of dejection about their camp fire in the evenings. And hordes of ragged local children hung about the camp, watching them curiously. They laughed and jeered as Fred chased them off.

It was so miserable that for the first time in eighteen months Georgina felt the need for a secure roof over her head and longed for the privacy of a hot bath.

'Look here, Fred,' she challenged him one day. 'I am going to try and rent a house for us for the winter. We did so well over the summer, we can afford it now.'

Fred was doubtful. 'I don't think Sam and Rosita would live in a house. They've spent so many years in that old caravan, they've got well used to it.'

'Well, I will persuade them,' said Georgina firmly. 'It's unhealthy in this marsh, and it stinks to high heaven.'

The next day, clad in her long sailor's jersey and a woolly cap, she scoured the area in search of an empty house. She soon found a tall, three-storeyed tenement. It was in a very depressed area and was dirty but it was vacant and the rent was reasonable. Georgina leaped at it and, with her usual energy and help from the small boys, she cleaned it up thoroughly.

And all the cast did move in. Sam and Rosita were reluctant about it but they were so worried about the youngest babe who had developed a bronchial infection that they accepted Georgina's good advice.

The smaller children had lots of fun running in and out the large empty rooms, their feet clattering on the bare floorboards. Down in the basement a communal kitchen was set up. There a huge wood fire was always burning. In the kitchen there was also an old tin bath in which the kids were all well scrubbed before being put to bed. In the evening, the adults had the big and only meal of the day, sitting around a rickety old table discussing the house and the affairs of the show.

'Well how about it?' asked Georgina. 'This place is better than the old barn for the winter, eh?'

The others nodded in agreement except Rosita, who muttered glumly: 'Well, at least the children will be warm.'

'I've decided to open with a Christmas show,' said Georgina. 'What do you think, Fred?'

'It's fine with me, Georgina,' replied Fred.

'I've collected a lot of old magazines,' she informed them. 'This one runs a serial story every week, mostly stuff by modern writers.' She produced the pile of old magazines bought from a second-hand stall.

'We will study them,' stated Georgina. 'Those who can't read can look at the pictures. Between the lot of us we may get a good idea for a new show.'

During those long dark evenings, they had a lot of fun. Fred read out the jokes to the others in a loud voice, and all the kids peeped and giggled at the pictures of voluptuous half-clad ladies. The serials were systematically put in order.

It was Tinsel who made the discovery. One day she pointed to an illustration of a thin fair girl with long hair gazing hungrily into a baker's shop window. 'That's me,' she informed the children. 'My Owen did that.'

Georgina snatched the magazine from her hand and, sure enough, the signature leaped out at her: Owen. Well, this was one of the stories Owen had illustrated. Georgina began to read the story and as she read on she suddenly realised that here was the essence of the new show.

When Georgina's creative energy reared into action, there was no stopping her, and her cleverness was remarkable. The title was changed and the story cut and rewritten so as not to be too easily recognisable.

In the second week in December, the show opened in a marquee on the waste lands. 'A Very Merry Christmas' contained pathos and humour, and it was a great success. The audiences were poor and ragged but they all came in droves with their meagre pennies into that brightly lit tent. Sam was the miser, Fred the clown, Tinsel the waif and all the children various Christmas spirits. Moira was a large and buxom Christmas fairy, dressed in a short frilly skirt and sporting a large wand which she used with force, tapping the members of the audience as she greeted them with Christmas Spirit.

The audiences were very appreciative and laughed until they cried. Then they brought their friends the next evening wanting to get the full benefit of this hilarious entertainment which brightened up their dull lives. Oh, they were great times, and Georgina felt very fulfilled. Even Tinsel seemed to settle down. She became more serious, more absorbed in her work,

and she had ceased to torment Georgina. She also loved
shopping and enjoyed wandering about the market. Delighted
with Tinsel's change, Georgina was happy to give her money
to buy 'pretties' as she called the ribbon and beads and other
junk she liked.

There was no doubt that Tinsel was a natural actress. Once
on stage, she became quite alive. It was as if a peculiar radiance
issued from her.

It was not long before this small travelling show drew the
attention of the more prominent local citizens, affluent business people who came to the show with their families. Then a
local newspaper gave them a good review.

But this brought them to the attention of the local church.
Within days, the parson was organising a campaign to banish
these frivolities from his parish. He yelled from his pulpit about
the sinful practices that kept his congregation from church and
ranted and raved about it until Georgina sweet-talked him and
put money in his poor box. For a while this established a truce
with him.

Once the parson had calmed down, the only annoying factor
in their lives came from the over-crowded tenements all around
their house. On each street corner was a gin palace outside
which drunks lay in the road and small children staggered
about, wild with drink. All around, ragged, loud-mouthed
women stood on doorsteps and screamed abuse at the 'gypos',
as they called the show folk. 'Whores, tarts and didicoys!' they
yelled. 'Get back where you came from!'

When off-stage, Moira got well boozed and returned these
insults with equal fury. Rosita cursed in several languages and
the children fought with the local youngsters. But it was
Georgina who invited most derision. Nonchalantly she would
stroll down the street on her way to the big marquee which
served as a theatre, dressed in a loud checked shirt and knee
breeches.

'Look aaht,' the neighbours called, ''ere 'e comes, that queer
fella!'

'Oh dear, ain't we grand?'

'Nancy boy! Nancy boy!' cried the cockney kids marching in
a throng behind her.

Coolly and calmly, Georgina ignored them and went on her
way. It amused her that they took her for an effeminate boy.

Rosita and Tinsel were afraid of the mob and longed for the spring so that they could be on the move once more. But Georgina had other ideas. She was determined to stay put, to get a permanent site and run a legitimate show.

As always, Fred was doubtful when she presented her plan to him.

'Will it cost a lot, George? Once we give up the old trailer, we're anchored. And we won't be able to move even if we want to.'

'Look here, Fred,' sniffed Georgina. 'Do you want your kids to go to school? They will get some sort of education even if you stay put only for a year or two.'

'Well,' he pondered, 'there's that aspect, indeed, but I don't believe we'll be able to stay here, not with the local feeling as it is.'

'We'll see about that,' Georgina replied obstinately.

In her spare time Georgina began to look for suitable premises to convert into a theatre. At last, she found an old one-storey wheelwright's shed. It was a large rectangular room where the large wagon wheels had once been assembled. Attached to the shed was a ramshackle collection of outbuildings. The owner was old and wanted to retire. After much haggling, Georgina managed to take a lease on the place for three years. Well pleased with herself, she stood with her hands on hips surveying the derelict buildings. In her mind's eye, a grand theatre rose up, with plush seats and bright lights. It was going to be a lot of work but who cared? Ambition would conquer all.

Slowly the travelling group settled into the house on the corner and was gradually accepted by the local community. On Sundays there was no show so everyone slept late. After a communal meal, if the weather was fine, they all sat out in the back yard. Fred had rigged up a makeshift trapeze for the small children and everyone gathered to watch their acrobatic antics. Rosita lit up her charcoal brazier and crouched over it dreamily, the old black shawl wound tightly about her body. Fred and Georgina talked shop, and Sam and Moira entertained them all with music and songs. Sam perched on the top step with his concertina while Moira moved around, singing the rich songs of her Irish homeland.

This free show was greatly appreciated by their neighbours'

children who climbed on the wall and joined in the singing. Meanwhile, their mothers listened cheerfully as they hung out from upstairs windows, and on the street corners men whistled in tune. In time there was less hostility and derision, and even some admiration. Soon the 'gypos' were preferred to the Salvation Army Band, which had until then, been the extent of the Londoners' musical education.

Tough necks were heard to shout: 'Leave those poor bleeders alone, will yer!' And they were the law in this poverty-stricken slum where the fist and the weapon ruled the roost. But unfortunately this singing on Sunday did jeopardise the fragile truce with the parson.

During holiday time, Georgina put on a special afternoon matinee with much clowning and humour. She went around like the Pied Piper, collecting up all the ragged children and marching them inside the marquee where they were presented with an orange and a bag of sweets bought from her own pocket. On those afternoons she was curiously uplifted. Fred noticed how elated she was leading the children in song like this.

From then on Georgina became very popular in Stratford and her popularity spread throughout the East End.

After the late show on their first Christmas Eve, the family staged a little party. The show children, who usually went to sleep in the prop basket, were roused to meet Fred disguised as Father Christmas and all were handed little gifts wrapped in bright paper by Georgina. After the younger ones had settled down again, the adults sat about the kitchen table for a glass of cider while Georgina presented her new idea. With excitement in her voice, she told the others about her plans to establish a permanent site for the theatre.

'We will call it the Variety and put on mixed performances, the kind that attract both rich and poor. Raise your glasses!' Georgina cried jubilantly, 'and drink to our very own theatre.'

The others drank reluctantly. Rosita looked sad and distant, Tinsel very sulky.

'Well,' muttered Fred, 'I suppose something must be said for progress.'

'Well, George,' Sam finally murmured, 'we can but give it a try.'

Rosita retired to her corner by the fire. She never said

anything about it, but the extreme cold affected her lame leg and she liked to huddle close to the flames.

As the bells tolled out into the night, Georgina cried, 'A Merry Christmas, everyone!'

Moira leapt up and swung her hefty legs in the air in an impromptu dance. She was full of good cider.

Rosita looked even sadder and whispered to herself: 'I wonder where my Jan is now.'

With a high-pitched wail, Tinsel threw herself down on the floor, a heart-rending cry coming from her lips. 'I want to go home! I want to be with my Owen!'

Georgina was used to Tinsel's dramatics by now. She pulled her up and slapped her. 'Get up!' she said firmly. 'You are not on the stage now. I want no histrionics from you.'

But did Tinsel's strange cry reach the ears of Owen Oliver by some telepathic power? For at that very moment back in Chatham, Owen suddenly felt startled. He was sitting in his mother-in-law's stuffy sitting room, surrounded by nick-nacks, stuffed birds and heavy velvet drapes, when something made him leap from his chair and knock over a bamboo table. The massive aspidistra crashed to the floor, scattering earth all over the deep pile red carpet. With a wild look in his eye, Owen crashed through the French windows out into the garden and stood looking up at the frosty starlit sky.

Upstairs Katy heard the commotion and came running down. She was dressed in flowing nightrobes and a big lacy cap full of stiffly starched frills and bows. Astonishment was written all over her plump features. She looked down at the scattered earth on the carpet and at the open French window. The lace curtains were flapping loudly in the night air. 'Owen,' she trilled, 'where are you? What are you doing out there?'

When there was no response, Katy violently pulled at the rope that held the servant's bell. A sleepy-eyed girl came in.

'Where is your master and what is the meaning of all this mess?' demanded Katy.

'Doan' know, Marm,' stammered the girl. 'Maister, he was her jus' naow.'

'Well, what's happened?' demanded Katy.

'Oi wis awightin' for 'im to go oop so as oi could get ta bed,' mumbled the country lass.

'Oh, dear, oh, dearie me,' complained Katy loudly.

'Clean up this mess and get to bed.' She closed the window. 'He's gone off walking, I expect.'

Tutting and fussing, Katy returned to her bed, her wide hips waddling from side to side as she puffed back up the stairs. In two years, Katy had put on a lot of weight.

Outside Owen had leaped over the gate, and set off up the hill. He wore neither hat nor coat, and his long legs readily covered the frosty ground. He headed for the windmill which stood looking over the town, and once he had reached it, he halted. Standing with his shoulders hunched, he looked out over the river, oblivious to the icy wind which blew about his head. There was some strong urge inside him. He felt that if he waved his arms around he could fly just like a bird, over that grey misty river to the other shore.

Time had not changed him. He was still very thin and his hair was long and untidy. His face was drawn and haggard. A silver moon had risen and painted each tiny leaf on the holly trees. The solemn stillness in the air told him that he was completely alone, alone with the earth and his conscience. How easy it would be to end it all, he thought gloomily.

Suddenly his mood changed. With his head bent and his hands thrust deep into his pockets, he slowly began to descend the hill. He was shivering when he quietly crept in through the front door, wet, cold and almost weeping.

'Is that you, Owen?' slurred his sleepy wife.

'It is,' Owen replied coldly, and then he went off to his own room.

Katy's parents had not yet returned. The latest family news from Canada was that Mary had become engaged to an English baronet. Every afternoon in her parents' house, Katy entertained a bevy of ladies who arrived dressed in wide skirts and feather bows. They all struck Owen like a string of quacking ducks. Katy was engaged in many good charitable works, just like her mother, in fact. The only difference between mother and daughter, Owen once remarked to his friend Tom, was that the dragon was thin while Katy was fat.

Much of Owen's leisure time was now spent in the taverns. Money was no problem; he was well paid for his skilled illustrations of popular novels. Unshaven and often unkempt, Owen still wandered about the town, mooching around the sleazier spots, with his notebook and pencil at the ready. Fame had caught up with him but it made very little difference to his peace of mind. He still found life very difficult to cope with. He had a strong aversion to his own middle-class background and only ever felt happy in the company of thieves, drunkards and vagabonds. He knew that he was known locally as a melancholy fellow but he did not care. He had no concerns about others' opinions of him. He spent his time at weekends with Tom out at Rat's Castle, and all the week in the Blue Boar.

Of late Tom was working less regularly. His mother was now crippled with arthritis, and Tom took great care of her. He also tended the garden and cottage, and raised money to live on by poaching or betting at Rat's Castle. Tom was bigger and huskier and more carefree than ever. Only with Tom could Owen really relax. And he now admitted that he found Katy's company intolerable. At least she had given up wanting to have a baby.

When they were first married, Katy was obsessed with the idea of getting pregnant. Owen had endeavoured to oblige, but like most things he did for Katy, it had been a complete fiasco. Every month Katy would decide that she was definitely pregnant. Her feet would be put up on a cushion because she had to have plenty of rest and no worries, and then suddenly it was all clearly her imagination. After two years, Owen had given up. He refused to co-operate any more and had retired to a room of his own, in spite of Katy's protests. So poor Katy had grown fat and discontented. And yet, she and Owen rubbed along, and there seemed little that would snap them out of their odd existence. His dull life was a burden. The only true escape he had came through his creativity.

CHAPTER THIRTEEN

Murder Out at Rat's Castle

On Boxing Day Owen sat in the bar at the Blue Boar reading the *Medway Times*, as he waited for Tom. The paper ran a long, detailed report of the murder of a certain well-bred young man from a large estate outside the town. The victim, a lord of some sort, had been found in a ditch with his throat slit from ear to ear. He had also been robbed of all his personal possessions. There was, the report added, a man in detention helping the police with their inquiries.

Owen read this story with some interest for he had known the murder victim. He was a pest, always coming out to Rat's Castle drunk and throwing his money around. It seemed to Owen that he had courted trouble for some time.

Owen sat steadily drinking, wondering where Tom was.

At two o'clock, the landlord came from behind his counter. A white apron was stretched tight over his fat belly, and there was an expression of quiet concern on his ruddy features. 'I must tell you, sir,' he said, 'seeing as you are a close acquaintance of big Tom ...'

Owen looked up suspiciously. Something had happened. Tom was always so punctual.

'The police took Tom,' said the landlord. 'They went out to his cottage and arrested him.'

'For God's sake, why?' cried Owen in astonishment.

'The murder of Lord Buckley, sir. They say he done it.'

Owen's face paled. 'Who said so?' he cried, springing to his feet.

'Calm down, sir,' begged the landlord. 'It may only be

hearsay. A fella just told me over the bar.'

'Tom cut a man's throat and rob him? What a lot of bloody nonsense!' yelled Owen. He got up and marched straight down to the police station. He was not allowed to see Tom in spite of his loud protests on behalf of Tom's innocence. The police politely moved Owen on.

He returned home and sat slumped in his chair, drinking whisky and racking his brains about how to help his only friend.

Katy was not much help. 'It's only to be expected,' she said primly, 'what with the company he keeps.' It meant nothing to her that Tom was a family relative.

The next day Owen was sober when he read the latest account of the murder in the *Medway Times*. That morning they published big Tom's name as the man accused of the crime. The report said that the victim had gambled very heavily at Rat's Castle. On the night of his death he had gone out there straight from a party. He was drunk and erratically driving a gig with a frisky horse that had returned to the stables trailing broken shafts. His Lordship had been discovered at daybreak, lying in a ditch and badly mutilated.

It was a gruesome crime, and the newspapers were having a field day describing the sordid details.

Owen felt sick with apprehension. Tom was violent but he was no razor man, as many men out at Rat's Castle were, that motley crowd of seamen and smugglers, rogues and rascals, farmers and gentlemen all bent on a hectic night out.

Owen decided that he had to seek advice on how to help Tom. He would go to see Forest, now editor of the *Daily News*. He would know of a good defence for Tom.

In no time, Owen had shaved and washed. He looked like an entirely different person.

'I am going to London,' he informed Katy.

Katy was still in her bed eating breakfast. A bright yellow dribble of egg yolk ran down her chin. 'Owen,' she spluttered, 'I forbid you. You are not to get mixed up in this nasty business.'

The slam of the door was her answer.

Forest was glad to see Owen looking so spruce and sober. He always had time for this clever lad. Over coffee they discussed the murder case.

'This young blue blood has often been in the news,'

remarked Forest. 'I'm not surprised that he came to a sticky end.'

'Yes, I knew him,' replied Owen. 'He was always a bit of a nuisance.'

'This character, Tom Browne, you say you know him well?'

Owen nodded. 'He is my one and only true friend in Chatham,' he said.

'We could investigate. It might be possible to run it with another angle,' pondered Forest. The journalist instinct was always there. 'We might even recruit Deakins for this. He's back from America. He's interested in prisons at the moment.'

In no time at all, strings were being pulled, and a good lawyer was retained to defend Tom. Owen was so determined to free his friend that it never occured to him to have a drink. This came as a complete surprise to his literary friends who were quite used to old Owen always being half boozed and caring for nothing but his sketches. He seemed like a different person. He was a wide awake man with a purpose. No time or expense mattered. His enthusiasm was catching. Articles appeared in several newspapers of police brutality, wrongful arrest, the bad conditions of the prisons and the long wait before the prisoners were brought to trial.

As Tom's case became more controversial, the Medway police transferred him to Newgate prison. Owen went with Deakins and Forest to visit Tom there. It was a soul-destroying experience which made a lasting impression on Owen. He pulled out his book and sketched the prisoners marching round and round a small enclosure behind high walls, many just miserable debtors who had run out of luck. A whole new series of pictures of social injustice issued dramatically from that clever pen.

Seeing big Tom with his shoulders hunched and his face creased in grief affected Owen considerably.

Tom asked how his mother was.

'Katy has been to see her,' Owen said. 'And she's got a nurse to care for her.'

'Thanks mate,' said Tom huskily. 'And how is Old Dawg?'

'Fine,' lied Owen. He dared not tell Tom that Old Dawg had gone missing, that he had gone off to the woods and hadn't come back.

'I never did it,' whispered Tom. 'But I know who did.'

Slowly his fingers spelt out the word in the air, JACK.

Owen nodded. He could well recall that slimy individual who had sold Tinsel to him years ago. Like a flash of light, he suddenly knew what he had to do. 'I'll find him, Tom,' he promised.

'He hopped off to sea,' whispered Tom.

'Don't worry, I'll get him,' repeated Owen.

When Tom came up for an initial hearing, most of the literary world and its associates attended to hear how young Lord Buckley had won money from Tom at Rat's Castle. They had words, it seemed, and then Tom left to walk home. On his way, his lordship drove past him dangerously close. He nearly ran down Tom's dog. The horse had shied and bolted, throwing Lord Buckley into a ditch.

'Serve you right, you bastard,' Tom had said and turned off to walk home across the heath, as he often did.

But no one had seen any of this and no one came forward to verify it, so Tom was the only suspect.

Tom was remanded in custody again and Owen returned to Chatham, feeling very depressed. He prowled all the old haunts, always on the look-out for Slimy Jack or for the tiniest clue as to what had really happened on that Christmas Eve out at Rat's Castle.

He got no sympathy from Katy, who remained convinced of Tom's guilt. It seemed that most people felt the same way. Tom was generally regarded as a layabout, a drunkard and an aggressive man. Only the landlord of the Blue Boar was truly anxious to help Tom.

So while Owen searched for Jack and more clues, Tom languished in prison and his little mother almost faded away. Owen visited her frequently taking her little comforts and sweetmeats. Old Dawg had fortunately returned. He looked permanently battered and lay quietly under the kitchen table and rarely went out.

'I always knew Tom would get into trouble one day,' Mrs Browne said. 'You shouldn't go troubling yourself over Tom, Owen. You're a clever boy with a career ahead of you.'

'He's my best and only friend,' replied Owen. 'And we all know that he didn't do this dastardly thing.'

Mrs Browne wiped away a tear from her cheek with her apron. 'Yes, I know he's a bad boy, but I really miss him.'

'He will be home, Ma,' Owen said reassuringly, that I

promise you. And without a stain on his character,' he vowed.

'Good lad, Owen,' Ma said weakly.

But after several weeks Owen began to lose heart and feel that he was never going to accomplish what he had set out to do. One evening, he wandered despondently down to the river bank, to Six Bells lane and the vicinity of Polly's abode, where he had found Tinsel amongst all those other slave children. It was a bleak day in February and the river swirled yellow and muddy at full ebb. Polly's old shack was derelict and the cottages were empty. The whole place seemed to cry out its misery. Owen sat down by the river and watched a train speed over the bridge. The dark arch below rumbled and vibrated with sound. Owen found that he was thinking of Tinsel. He woundered how she was. She must be around seventeen by now, he thought, recalling her high-pitched voice and flaxen hair. Whatever had happened to her and Georgina? They seemed to have vanished off the face of the earth.

His mind moved on, brooding over various things that Tinsel had told him. He had not really believed her at the time but as he recalled the details, a sick disgust filled his soul. What a monster that Slimy Jack was, a man who collected up children and sold them to brothels! How he wished he could now lay hands on him! He suddenly remembered Tinsel's chatter about Sophie's brother. Jack had killed him, she had told him. Owen could remember her trilling voice saying: 'I know where he's buried.'

Had it just been her childish imagination? Had Jack really killed the boy? If he had, then the law would help find him. Owen walked around this desolate spot, poking the soft ground with his stick. If Jack had killed the boy and buried him, the grave must have been around here, for how would the slave children have seen him otherwise?

In Owen's mind was Tinsel's constant chatter. 'He was nice . . . Jack killed him . . . I saw him. I know where the boy's buried.'

At the time, Owen had silenced her and not allowed himself to listen to her. Yet now he had come to believe that out of that child's mouth had come the truth.

Owen strolled slowly home, back to the boring gloom, and the soul-destroying atmosphere of the house on the hill. By the time he reached the doorstep he had reached a decision. He would begin to write anonymous letters, to the police, to the local paper and to the *Daily News*. He would continue with the letters until attention was drawn to the true facts, that a murdered boy lay buried in an unhallowed grave, that a local youth, an orphan in the care of the authorities, had been brutally seduced and finally murdered. Perhaps something would come of such a campaign.

And something did indeed happen. In response to Owen's anonymous letters, other letters appeared in the *Medway Times* requesting that the writer come forward if his conscience was clear. The *Daily News* asked for information on brutality to children, stating that they intended to run a campaign on England's slave children. But still Owen remained anonymous. Then Owen drew a detailed map of the place where the murder had been committed and sent copies to the police, prominent citizens and the newspapers. Within hours, the shallow grave was discovered. The remains of the boy were exhumed.

'God bless you little Tinsel,' muttered Owen when he heard the news. 'God bless you, wherever you are.'

That night the papers contained an account of the finding of a child's skeleton at Six Bells. Murder was suspected. Police were making further enquiries.

Owen immediately boarded the train back to London to lay his own findings before Forest and Tom's clever lawyer.

'That's good,' said Forest. 'It will be a scoop. We must now endeavour to find the sister, Sophie,' he said. 'And it would be even better if we could get the girl who actually witnessed the killing.'

Owen grimaced. He always felt sad and confused when he remembered Tinsel and Georgina. 'There's never been a sign of them,' he said. 'For two-and-a-half years, all the information I have had is that Georgina was mixed up in some sort of travelling show.'

'Well, chum, get up off your arse and start looking,' yelled Forest with his usual ferocity.

Sending a quick note to Katy stating that he was detained in London, Owen systematically went to every show and every circus within the vicinity of the town. Then he travelled to Liverpool, Leeds, Birmingham and all big cities, visiting inns and advertising agents. Nothing turned up until after two months, in Blackpool, Owen found himself talking to a man in a bar. The man's skin seemed prematurely aged, so cracked and lined was it by cheap grease paint. 'I did some casual work last year,' he informed Owen, 'for a travelling company. The chap who employed me was called Fred Dillon, a real old showman he was. There was a pretty little girl in the show, like the one you describe. She was a great actress, but a bit bent, I think. A fella called George seemed to own her. Queer sod, he was. I could not make head nor tail of him but he was a grand worker. He ran that tinpot show like a professional.'

'Where are they now?' asked Owen, his excitement mounting.

'Don't ask me, mate, they ain't come back this year.'

'But where were they going?' cried Owen.

'Heading for London, of course, but they could be touring on the continent now, or gone broke. Yer can't tell with these travelling companies.'

'Thanks a lot,' said Owen, handing the man some money. 'Have a drink, I've got to be on my way.' At last he had a clue! Feeling very excited, Owen headed back to London and the *Daily News*.

'Dillon?' muttered Forest. 'The name sounds familiar.' Now they went around all the agents and theatre bars until at last they came across an old billhead that read at the very bottom in small print: Dillon & Silver, Strong Arm Act. However, according to the age of the billhead, that was ten years ago. Since then, they had passed into oblivion. No one seemed to know where they were now.

Sick with disappointment, Owen went on a real bender. He got stupidly drunk and stayed that way for days. Katy's letters demanding his return were ignored.

A dreadful melancholy possessed him as he hung about outside Newgate Prison, imagining Tom inside walking round and round like an animal in a cage. Yet according to Forest, who kept in with the police, a search of all ships and ports was in process for Slimy Jack. So Owen's time had not been wasted. Then out of the blue, they found Sophie who now lived in Tonbridge and was respectably married with two children. For a good price she was willing to tell her story but all she said was that when her brother disappeared, she had been told that he had gone to sea.

'There are still no real witnesses to the murder,' Owen told Forest, with real disappointment.

'Yes, it's difficult,' replied Forest. 'The slave children story will make headlines but how it will help Tom Browne, I can't think. But not to worry, lad, we will win in the end,' he said optimistically. 'I got some tickets tonight for a new kind of show down in the East End. Variety, they call it. Join me. I'll pick you up in the bar. It should be interesting. I hear it's a rough audience but *The Star* gave it a good write-up.'

So Owen rather reluctantly went off with Forest that evening to this downtown variety show. He felt very moody and melancholy, convinced that his search for Tinsel had been a failure. Perhaps the show would cheer him up, he thought. These little places of entertainment were springing up all over London. This one was in a very low class state and in a ramshackle building but, judging from the number of people queuing to get in, it was very popular indeed.

They had some time to kill before the show began. Owen and Forest crossed the road to have a drink in a rowdy bar in which there were medical students, prostitutes, stevedores and even businessmen with their fancy women. The custom was to fill up with liquor before crossing the road to the new show spot and play up merry hell.

Most of the audience stood packed into a circular wooden booth, and there were a few side seats for the priviledged ticket holders. It was in these that Forest and Owen found themselves seated before the curtain went up. A youth in a brightly coloured shirt opened the show with a loud clear voice.

'Ladies and all the rest . . .'

Loud boos.

'We hope you will be patient with us as we are about to give you a new kind of entertainment . . .'

Loud yells of 'Get on with it' came from the audience.

Owen stared at the youth. There was something familiar about him. Out came the sketchbook and he started to draw.

The show was bright and breezy, full of fast-moving comedy, magic feats, singing and dancing. It was great fun. A lovely red-head sang popular songs and Irish ballads in a full-throated voice and tiny children tumbled about doing acrobatic feats. Then a tiny blonde recited dreadful poetry made up of broadsheet material of horrible murders, sex and crime. The narrator's demeanour was so naïve that the audience howled with glee.

But Owen was transfixed. He stared at this creature in

astonishment. By the time she was halfway through her act, he knew that it was Tinsel. Only Tinsel could generate that peculiar radiance and hold such a rough audience.

'I'm going backstage,' he whispered to Forest near the end of the act. His long legs became entangled with the scenery as he struggled behind stage into a little cubicle which was obviously a dressing room. It was empty. The rest of the cast were standing in the wings watching Tinsel. Tinsel's act was just finishing. As she curtsied and left the stage, she was showered with orange peel. Tearfully she ran into the dressing room and straight into Owen's arms.

'Tinsel, my love!' he cried, holding her tight.

Tinsel gasped. 'Owen! Owen! Can it really be you?' She flung her arms about Owen's neck and the two of them stood locked in a passionate embrace.

Then suddenly, from the door, someone lunged at them and pulled them apart, slapping Tinsel on the cheek as they did so. 'What have I told you?' the person yelled. 'No men back stage, you little pest!'

Owen stood back open-mouthed. He was astounded to gaze into the blazing hazel eyes of Georgina.

'Oh, Owen!' Georgina murmured. 'My God, it cannot be.'

'Yes, it is, Georgi,' returned Owen. 'I should never have known you.'

Georgina looked down and then sniffed. 'Look here, I've a show to put on. I don't think that you and I have a lot to say to each other, anymore. Now, get off, Tinsel, you have still got another act.'

'I'll wait,' he murmured.

'But outside,' Georgina said sharply. 'We only have one dressing room.'

Feeling quite nonplussed, Owen went back to his seat. He was very shaken by the sight of Tinsel, crouching white-faced and miserable beside the dressing-table mirror. Well, he had got a very cool reception from Georgina. What was behind all that?

Forest was convulsed with laughter at Fred and Sam's strong-arm act. Dressed up as a clown, Fred put small Sam in a bag clad only in a long pair of drawers and tied him up with heavy chains. Then Fred sealed the bag and called on the audience to witness how genuine it all was. He claimed that at a given signal Sam would free himself from his chains and escape from the bag.

The first time they did this act, it had come to grief. Sam had very cleverly divested himself of his bonds but also, unknown to himself, his long drawers. Thus he emerged from the sack to take the applause completely starkers. As the men roared and women screamed, Sam crawled back into the bag muttering: 'Get me nicks! Get me nicks!' With expert showmanship, Fred managed to cover up the mistake and keep the audience amused until Sam was decent again.

The act was so popular with their audience that it was performed this way every night, but Sam made sure that he wore a pair of flesh-coloured tights to appease any prudes in the audience.

Forest was doubled up with mirth as Sam rolled about the stage in that huge sack screaming for his drawers and pretending that he couldn't find them. Owen sat glum and unsmiling beside him.

'Great act,' said Forest at the end of it. 'I haven't laughed so much in years.'

'I've found her,' Owen said quietly.

'Who?' asked his companion without interest.

'The girl who witnessed that boy being murdered. That's her on the stage.' Owen pointed at Tinsel, who was now doing a fairy dance in a filmy costume.

'That's splendid,' said Forest, rubbing his hands together with glee. 'Perhaps now we can get down to some real work.'

Owen did not reply. He sat quietly, wallowing in his own misery.

'Cheer up, you gloomy tyke,' exclaimed Forest. 'A pretty little girl like that – she's just like a china doll. I'm certainly going to enjoy interviewing her.'

'I'll need to talk with her alone after the show,' said Owen.

'Please yourself,' replied his companion, 'but don't lose her again. I know what a sentimental ass you are,' he warned.

The show was over. The curtains had come down, and the boys in the orchestra pit were packing up.

'I'll wait over the road in the bar for you,' said Forest as Owen made his way backstage once more.

There was no sign of Tinsel anywhere. In fact most of the cast had disappeared.

Owen found Georgina in the box office calmly checking the takings. 'Tinsel has gone home,' she said abruptly. 'And that's where I'm going too in a moment.'

Owen looked lost and hurt.

Georgina stared at him for a moment and then sniffed. 'Oh, for Christ's sake, sit down,' she said irritably.

Owen obeyed but he looked at her with hurt expression in his eyes.

'Well, don't sit there like a bloody stray dog,' snapped Georgina. 'State the reason you came.'

'I was so thrilled to see you both again, Georgi,' said Owen, 'But I didn't expect such a cool reception.'

Georgina's eyes narrowed as she stared at him almost in hatred. 'Don't give me that, Owen. After what you did to Tinsel I've lost all the respect I ever had for you.'

Owen went white. 'She told you?' he asked. His voice was a whisper.

'Told me? God, how naïve can you get? She gave birth to your stillborn child at Christmas that year.'

Owen groaned and put his hands over his face. 'Oh, no, I can't believe it.'

'Well, you can take my word for it, because I was there and any feeling I had for you died that night.'

Owen put his hands over his eyes and wept.

'It's too late for that, Owen. It's no good crying now,' Georgina said harshly. 'All the tears she shed did not recompense her.'

'Georgi, what can I do?' he cried.

'Nothing,' Georgina replied brutally. 'We are on our feet now and I'm going to make sure we stay that way.'

'But I must speak with her, Georgi,' Owen pleaded. 'Don't be so hard, I have also suffered, and I love her.'

Georgina rattled the bag of coins in her hand with a sudden violence. 'Well, good night, Owen. I hope that in future you will forget you ever found us.'

'Georgi, it's not for myself alone,' he pleaded. 'A life is at stake here.'

For a moment, Georgina stared at him suspiciously. 'What nonsense! You don't get round me like that, Owen.'

'I beg of you, Georgi, I swear before God I'll never harm Tinsel. I am still married to Katy, and even I will not break a marriage vow.'

Georgina looked sad when he mentioned her sister. There was some flash of feeling in those hard hazel eyes. 'All right,' she said, 'come back home with me. But I swear to you, Owen, by all that's holy, it will never happen to her again, not while I live.'

Owen regarded Georgina carefully. There was so much heated passion in those words and manner that she reminded him of a jealous lover.

As they left the theatre, he noticed the poor structure of the building and the shabby stage sets once the lights were out. 'Do you own this place, Georgi?' he asked.

Georgina nodded. 'I'm a partner with two others but it was my original idea.'

'But why this kind of show?' he asked. 'I should have thought that straight plays would have been more in your line.'

'I can't get a licence to run a legitimate place,' she told him bitterly. 'And this kind of variety programme doesn't need one.'

They had now reached their destination, a tall corner house, with a flight of stone steps going up to the front door. The house had rather a derelict air about it but once the heavy street door was opened a warm lively atmosphere was released. There was a delicious spicy smell of cooking, the chatter of the children and the sound of music. The clatter of crocks and a babble of voices drifted up from the basement where the families had settled down to supper.

Owen followed Georgina down a long passage lit by a tiny oil lamp, and down a narrow flight of stairs to the warmth of the big kitchen below.

Around a large table the two families were seated. Tiny children played on the floor while the older ones and their parents sat waiting for Rosita to ladle out the bowls of hot nourishing soup. They were all chattering and laughing, all but Tinsel who crouched like a gnome in front of the fire.

'We didn't wait, George,' said Fred apologetically. Seeing her guest, he sprang up to welcome him.

'This is an old friend of mine,' said Georgina casually as she introduced Owen to the assembled people. They all moved along the bench to make room for him.

'Fetch a clean plate,' ordered Rosita.

A small girl pulled a clean plate from the dresser and placed it in front of Owen. Then they all went on with the meal as if he was not there.

Tinsel did not move. 'Not eating?' Georgina asked her, but Tinsel did not reply.

'She's got a fit of the doldrums,' said Rosita. 'Leave her alone.'

Owen's hand was trembling so much that the spoon rattled against the plate. Georgina sat at the head of the table staring malevolently at him. After the soup came plates of beef and dishes of vegetables. The group continued to eat mostly in silence.

At the end, Fred got up. 'We will go, George. We can wash-up tomorrow.'

The room gradually emptied, leaving just Owen, Georgina and Tinsel, who had not moved an inch. Then suddenly, like a rabbit, Tinsel hopped over to Owen and clutched him tightly. 'Owen, Owen,' she whimpered, 'don't let her hurt me. You know I belong to you.'

Owen put out an arm and held her shivering body close, just as he had done that first day on the cabbage cart.

On the other side of the room, Georgina's lips tightened. 'Stop it, Tinsel!' she commanded. 'Behave yourself!' But Tinsel crept closer to him.

'You see how difficult she is,' exclaimed Georgina, extremely annoyed. 'She has the mind of a child, in spite of that womanly body.'

'Come, Tinsel,' Owen whispered gently. 'You're shivering. Let's go and sit by the fire.' He guided her over to that long fireside bench and sat her on his lap. With a deep sigh, she placed her head on his shoulder.

Georgina poured herself a cup of coffee from a big iron pot, lit up a long black cigarette and sat facing them. 'This,' she said, spreading her hands wide, 'is now my life, Owen. I've no desire for any other.'

'I don't blame you for dropping out, Georgi,' said Owen. 'I never did, and that's why I didn't come seeking you earlier. But something has cropped up out of Tinsel's past and only she can help me.'

With Tinsel clinging tight to him, Owen recounted the story of Tom's arrest.

It turned out that Georgina knew about the case, having

read about it in the paper. 'I always thought that Tom courted trouble,' she said.

'But I can assure you that he's innocent,' declared Owen.

Georgina just shrugged nonchalantly.

'Do you remember Jack who brought you to my office?' Owen whispered to Tinsel. He tried to raise her head from his shoulder but she would not move. 'That Jack is a rascal, Georgi, a thief and procurer of children, and responsible for many crimes. Tinsel told me once how he killed a boy. That is true, they found the body, and they are now scouring the countryside for this Slimy Jack.'

'Yes,' said Tinsel with sudden interest, 'poor Sophie's brother, I saw him.'

Georgina had begun to take an interest. 'But what do you want of us?'

'I want Tinsel to be a witness for the Crown when they get Jack. I am sure that they will, and I intend to put so much pressure on him that he will confess to other crimes he has committed, including the murder of Lord Buckley.'

'Well, I wish you luck,' Georgina said sarcastically, 'but I'm afraid that Tinsel will not leave my side and that no one is dragging her through a court scene.'

Owen looked crestfallen. Tinsel sat up and kissed him on the cheek. 'I knew you would find me. I'll do just what you want, Owen.'

'You will *not*,' cried Georgina.

The silence was loaded with tension as Owen and Georgina stared at each other with mutual hostility. But it was Georgina's will that was the strongest.

Tinsel continued to cling to Owen. 'Don't leave me anymore,' she wept.

Owen shook his head. 'Look, Georgi, we cannot come to any clear decisions tonight.' he said. He had just remembered Forest was waiting for him in that seedy bar. 'Let's sleep on it,' he pleaded. 'I'll see you tomorrow.'

He picked up Tinsel and placed her on the edge of the table where she sat dangling her slim legs like a child.

'Goodnight, Georgi, I'll not disturb your life. I am too fond of you to do that.'

Georgina grimaced and shot out a hand to grasp his. 'Oh, Owen, for old time's sake, don't let us hurt each other.'

'I'll endeavour not to, Georgi,' he said. 'Let's talk it over tomorrow.'

He made his way to the front door and went out just in time to see Forest getting into a cab. Which was just as well, Owen thought. He was in no mood to cope with the newspaper man that night.

CHAPTER FOURTEEN

The Variety

Owen walked along the damp London streets thinking about the extraordinary evening. He frowned as he thought about the dramatic meeting with Tinsel and the coldness of Georgina, whose masculine traits were more evident than ever.

At seventeen Tinsel had become a rare beauty but she was strange and wayward like a spoiled child, yet almost completely dominated by Georgina. His mind travelled back to those warm spring evenings when Tinsel had shared his bed. His heart beat wildly as he remembered the happiness he had never known before or since. She had only been a child – just fourteen and he had taken advantage of her. But had he really? How often it was that he felt that it was he himself who had been seduced.

And now, all this time later, he had discovered that he had actually got her with child. Owen felt quite elated. Hadn't Katy accused him many times of not being capable of getting her pregnant? Well, what he had done once could be done again. There was no need for him to feel so guilty and degraded. No, now he had to pluck up the courage to tell Katy that he could no longer live with her. He could do that but could he live with Tinsel? Could he live with that delicate passionate child? Why, even the prospect of it frightened him. Perhaps it would be better if he left women alone.

His head swimming with these gloomy thoughts, Owen, wandered the dimly lit streets until dawn when he hailed a cab and went back to his lodgings to sleep. He was utterly exhausted.

'Well, you're a decent sort of fellow,' Forest commented sarcastically when Owen called in at the office next day. 'You left me hanging about in that damned bar. It's a wonder I was neither clobbered nor robbed.'

'I'm sorry,' apologised Owen, 'but it's settled. It's all laid on for tonight.' For a moment all thought of his own problems was submerged as he wondered again at the injustice of what had happened to Tom. Surely Tinsel's evidence would help, he thought vehemently.

This time Georgina was prepared for him. The light of battle flashed in her eyes. 'Who's he?' she asked abruptly when she saw Forest.

'A newspaperman, and a good friend of mine,' said Owen, introducing them.

'Umph,' Georgina said, pursing her lips in disapproval. 'Looking for dirt. I've met his kind before.'

Forest winked at Owen and set about charming the group. In no time he had softened up Georgina, chatting with Fred in the wings, and larking with the show children.

While Forest made himself popular, Owen helped Georgina tidy up the dressing room. It was in a mess. A mirror was broken, and make-up and candles had been trampled into the floor.

'Oh dear,' sighed Georgina, 'Tinsel is in a very bad mood tonight. I think seeing you again has really distrubed her, Owen.'

Owen picked up the débris from the floor, as Georgina anxiously hung up the costumes strewn about the place.

'She is muffing her show out there,' said Georgina. 'I've had to get the children behind the scenery to prompt her.'

'But why do this kind of show, Georgi?' asked Owen. 'I'm sure Tinsel is capable of something better.'

'How many times do I have to explain to you?' Georgina said aggressively. 'It's because I cannot get a resident permit to run a straight show. For this rubbish you don't need one.'

'All right, Georgi, calm down,' Owen reproached her. 'I'll see if I can help you get a resident permit.'

Suddenly the small dressing room became full of people all shouting and talking at once as they changed for the next act. Georgina walked out to the step-ladder which led to the stage and she sank down wearily.

Owen sat beside her.

'You see, Owen,' she confided, 'I love this life but it's not an easy one. I was the fool who persuaded them to stay in one place and not one of them is as happy as they were on the road. Sometimes I feel so damned responsible for them.' She took off her odd little spectacles which left a red mark on the bridge of her nose, and rumpled her short brown curls with both hands.

Owen felt pleasantly peaceful. He and Georgina seemed to have drawn closer, as they had in the old days. 'What exactly does it require to get this permit?' he asked. 'Money or influence?'

'A great deal of both,' Georgina replied. 'I have the local parson on my tail, as well as a host of do-gooders. And then there are the bigwigs on the bench, all with itchy palms. And all I want to do is entertain.'

'I might be able to help you financially,' Owen said.

'I might even let you,' Georgina replied with a grin.

Thus their friendship began to blossom once more. Moments later, Tinsel dashed in from the stage, having avoided a shower of pennies. 'Oh, Owen!' she cried, flinging herself at him and weeping madly.

Georgina went up on stage and, in a stentorian voice, restored order.

'Oh, don't cry,' Owen whispered, holding Tinsel close. His heart fluttered as he smelt her perfume wafting over him. He buried his face in her shining hair, and they did not move until she had calmed down.

Fred had invited Forest to supper at the house after the show, and so when Owen arrived with Tinsel and Georgina, the newspaperman was already installed at the big square kitchen table.

Rosita presided in a snow-white apron, ladling out a steaming broth. 'God in heaven!' she cried. 'I must get some bigger pots. This table gets more people around it every night.'

Georgina had collected some cheeky talented kids from the back streets. They helped on the show and often ended up at the supper table. They were bright and half-starved but very stage-struck, and Georgina loved them. They loved her too, and no task was too menial for them to do for her. They would hustle each other to collect her favours.

Tonight the big kitchen was indeed full. The oil lamp shed a mellow glow and the coal fire burned bright. Fried chicken and spuds in jackets followed the soup.

Rosita rarely attended the theatre nowadays. She was happy simply to supervise the cooking and to do the chores with the help of some of the children. She was most content.

Forest had sent the young lads out to fetch wine and beer, so tonight the atmosphere was particularly jovial and cheerful.

'Georgina and Tinsel have stopped squabbling since this Owen fellow came on the scene,' remarked Moira mischievously.

'Now, Moira,' warned her husband.

'He's such an odd-looking blighter,' giggled his wife.

After supper the usual antics were performed by the show children. Fred drew a chalk line across the room so they could play a game whereby a penny had to be picked up by putting the left arm over the right knee and not let it touch the ground. They all laughed a lot, especially when Moira, red-faced and full of gin, pulled up her skirt, exposed her large frilly drawers, and managed to get that elusive penny.

'Oh, they are great company,' said Forest on the way home. 'And I don't know what that pretty girl Tinsel sees in you, skinny swine,' he added enviously. Owen did not argue but a charming slow smile lit up his gloomy face.

'Funny chap, that George,' continued Forest. 'You say he's a woman?'

'I know her very well,' said Owen defensively. 'It doesn't surprise me that she chose her own way of life.'

'Well, I must say that I had a good time,' admitted Forest. 'It's a rotten show but really amusing.'

'Is there any chance of George getting a permit to run a good show?' asked Owen.

'Not an earthly,' replied Forest, 'not in that dog's kennel. It's a fire hazard to start with,' he added.

'Well explain then, what does it need?' urged Owen.

'One, a good building, two, a good character, and three, plenty of influence in the right quarters.'

'Well, I think I'll have a good try,' said Owen optimistically.

'And the best of British luck,' said Forest. 'Good-night.'

Out of loyalty and genuine friendship for Owen, Forest did a good write-up in his daily paper, extolling the virtues and hilarity of this down-town show. His review brought in a new kind of audience – the arty types, literary gentlemen on a night out, a better-paying, more exclusive and less noisy audience.

During this time, Owen did little else but hang around the variety show, establishing his new acquaintance with Georgina and Tinsel on a purely platonic basis.

Then one day, out of the blue, the newspapers suddenly announced the arrest of Slimy Jack as he stepped ashore in Liverpool.

'I don't want Tinsel mixed up in this court case,' insisted Georgina. 'I was never that keen on my cousin Tom,' she retorted.

'But Slimy Jack is a villain of the lowest type. It's your duty as a citizen to help.'

Georgina looked worried. It was unlike Owen to be so dogmatic.

'Oh, all right,' she said at last, 'but I want my name kept out of it or I'll get very annoyed.'

'I promise, on my honour, you will never be mentioned,' he said.

'Well, that's it, then,' Georgina said. 'I'll instruct Tinsel. I'm sure she will play her part to perfection. She can't read a damned word but once something is drummed into her head, her memory is excellent.'

It was a dull desolate evening as they stood chatting outside the Variety. Owen shivered. 'This is certainly a dreary spot,' he commented.

'Yes, I know it needs livening up,' said Georgina. 'I often dream of a big theatre with a green dome and fairy lights, and a long and orderly queue waiting to go in. Not rushing in as they do now, nearly breaking down the doors every night. But that can only be a pipe dream, Owen,' she grinned ruefully.

They stood side by side looking around at the grim row of cottages and over to the gin palace whence the sound of raucous drinking still came.

'You see that derelict land over there, next to the pub?' Georgina pointed. 'If I had enough money, I'd buy it. It's two empty shops and a skittle alley. It's just about the size I need to build a good bricks and mortar theatre.'

'Is it for sale?' asked Owen.

'Could be, but so far it would be way above anything I could afford.'

'I've got some money,' Owen said.

'You're joking, Owen,' Georgina said in genuine amazement. 'I thought you boozed all your earnings away.'

He shook his head. 'No, the money I get from my illustrations goes into the bank. And I still get a regular wage from the business as well as a yearly annuity.'

'Well, well, you are a man of means,' scoffed Georgina.

'I expect there must be quite an amount in the bank now,' said Owen thoughtfully.

'You amaze me, Owen,' exclaimed Georgina. 'You mean to say you don't know how much?'

'It has never really bothered me,' said Owen. 'I let Katy spend what she wants. Otherwise, I have no need for money. But the amount must be almost enough to buy that land for you, and it's yours, if you want it,' he said obstinately. 'Just tell me the amount you need.'

Georgina's astute mind ticked over, 'Well, and what would you want from me?' she asked, 'Tinsel?'

Owen blushed and frowned. 'No, Georgi, you're wrong to surmise that. I'll not want Tinsel until I am able to marry and protect her.'

'Katy will never let you go,' warned Georgina.

'Well, I can but try. In the meantime, Georgi, you apply for the land and I'll provide the capital.'

'Oh, how can I take from you?' she cried, softening up a little.

'I'd be a happy man if you did Georgi. It would recompense me, relieve me of some of the guilt I feel with regard to Tinsel.'

Georgina put a friendly arm through his. 'Come on, Owen, let's go home and discuss it with the families.'

That was the very first night that Owen stayed at the house on the corner. He did not need any more encouragement. He stayed the next night and the next. And after a few days, he sent Fred's boys to fetch his bag and pay his hotel bill.

He spent his days sketching the children at play or practice, or touring the slum streets with a group of hangers-on following him. He enjoyed their company and treated them all to hot chestnuts from a lively old Italian who had a stand near to the Variety, with a glowing bucket of coke perched precariously on a coaster barrow. The golden-brown nuts were bursting with heat as they roasted on top. Owen sketched the little children with their red noses as they warmed their cold hands on the hot bag of nuts. He drew the Italian with his straw hat and black curls tinged with grey.

Owen was lost to all else. He never shaved, and seldom washed. He just prowled about this depressed neighbourhood in ecstasy, revelling in all the exciting new material and keeping comparatively sober.

Tinsel felt neglected and often rubbed her soft face against his whiskers. 'Don't you love me any more, Owen?' she questioned him.

'Oh, I do, darling, but you must behave for a while, and then we will be together always.'

Those deep-set blue eyes regarded him seriously.

'For ever and ever?' she queried, 'to death do us part?'

'That is so, my love,' Owen replied gently.

Tinsel seemed satisfied with that and after a long lingering kiss, she went back to rehearse her new part in the show.

Another wandering family had recently joined the group. They had appeared at the stage door one rainy day in search of work. There was a small, middle-aged dapper man, his big good-looking son, and his daughter-in-law, a petite but obviously pregnant woman holding a tiny toddler by the hand. They were all cold, wet and hungry, having been with a travelling show that had gone bust. They bore the strange name of Moncaur and had a clever act called Monkey Tricks. This consisted of feats of magic, mind-reading, clever sleights of hand – tricks developed by the father and improved on by the son.

Meeting them and hearing of their plight, Fred immediately invited the Moncaur family home to supper. The communal kitchen with its big fire and Rosita's savoury soup were welcome. Georgina booked their act for two weeks, and they were bedded down in the attic. Once they had recovered, the Monkeys, as the rest of the household called them, were good fun and great show folk. But it was quite obvious to all that Nell, the young wife, could not be sawn in half by her father-in-law for much longer. And Tinsel stepped easily into her place.

Seeing how talented Tinsel was, Bill Moncaur was quite pleased to train her for his act.

'You'd better stay here, Nell, until the baby is born,' said the practical Georgina. 'I know we can only give you the attic but it's a roof over your head.'

The Monkeys were immensely grateful for the work and hospitality. They worked like Trojans for little money and quickly trained Tinsel for the various magic acts. For her part, Tinsel was delighted to dress herself in sequins and tights and fold herself in a ball to disappear every night.

Owen was astonished by the ease with which the Moncaurs were absorbed into the household. 'It's amazing; this house must have expanding walls,' he remarked.

'We show-business folk don't need much room, just a bed and food, and plenty of work,' replied Georgina. 'By the way, Owen,' she added, 'it's time you stopped lazing about so much and did some real work.' Owen's untidy, indolent nature was beginning to annoy her.

The house was a rather forlorn dwelling which had known better days. It had long dark passages and a big basement, with two floors below the large rambling attics. Sam and Rosita with their brood occupied the basement floor including the warm communal kitchen, in the back room. On the ground floor, Fred and Moira kept their lively family. The large front room with its high ceiling and folding doors was known as the rehearsal room and only used as such. This contained a faded carpet and an ancient piano. The walls were hung with bill-heads. Upstairs was a large bedroom shared by Tinsel and Georgina, and in the back room on this floor most of the young lads slept, the sons of both families, in a room that was nothing more than a dormitory, full of beds. Next door to this was Owen's room, a small airless chamber overlooking a forest of chimney pots. It was bare apart from a camp bed and a broken chair. There were noisy hazards, like the boys next door who played cards and larked about, but here Owen found peace and happiness. He was able to be left alone to do just as he pleased, to stay in bed all night or to prowl about, whichever mood he was in. Above him in the attics the Monkeys were now installed.

This large overcrowded house was seldom tidy and cleaning was done spasmodically. There were no immediate lights to hand, just a row of candles in saucers on the hall table. If anyone needed to find their way about the house at night, they had to light up a candle and carry it around with them. Overall the atmosphere in the house was happy and genial, with the sound of children playing, dancing and singing, the thump of the old piano, and the clatter of pots and pans from the basement.

Quite often quarrels broke out however, and Georgina would hold a kind of amateur tribunal to settle whatever difference of opinions had arisen. Most of Owen's life had been lonely until he had married. Then he was severly dominated until he moved to this amicable set-up. He felt released. The free and easy life here suited him to perfection.

Each day that passed Georgina did more to establish herself in the theatrical profession. She encouraged local talent and launched many ambitious young singers, musicians and writers. They certainly all gathered about her, anxious to take the public eye. And soon many of them were moving on, leaving the East End Palace of Variety for the more profitable West End shows. All were immensely grateful to Georgina.

Forest continued to review the shows and brought with him managers and talent scouts. Even Owen began to take a more active part, having been made to feel guilty by Georgina's comments. He painted scenery and collected tickets and generally made himself useful. He seemed to have submerged himself in this theatre world so much that he had almost forgotten Katy and his other life.

Tinsel's behaviour was proving to be a bit of a problem. He would often find her asleep in his camp bed when he came in late. When this happened, he would carry her back to her own room, where Georgina would be very angry and slap Tinsel spitefully, causing Tinsel to sulk for days. Owen did his best to stay out of her way but she would find him and come creeping up close to him.

'Why don't you make love to me now?' she would question him.

'Oh, darling little Tinsel,' Owen said, shaking his head, 'I wish I was free to love you.'

'But who will know?' she would tempt him.

'No, darling, not until we are married,' he replied.

'Let's leave here and take to the road,' Tinsel said one evening. 'I love you Owen' She pushed her slight body into his arms. 'Let's make love under the stairs, you and I,' she coaxed.

They were standing in the wings. She pressed closer to him, clad in her short sequin dress and flesh-coloured tights, and he responded, fondling her warm body and kissing her full on the lips.

'Go now,' he whispered, pushing her away suddenly. 'You're due on stage.'

After Tinsel had gone, all self-respect drained from Owen. Holding his hands to his burning forehead, he dashed out of the theatre, over to the bar, and went on a real bender. He visited every establishment that sold alcoholic liquor from Stratford to Mile End and ended up in a park full of tramps and pickpockets. He was instantly relieved of his wallet, his sketchbook and his boots, and he arrived back at the house two days later looking very much the worse for wear.

'Crikey!' yelled Georgina when she saw him come in.

'Naughty boy!' said Rosita. 'Stay outside while I prepare a bath. I'll have no lice in here.'

With a pair of tongs, Rosita collected Owen's dirty clothes as he took them off, then put them in a bag for disposal. Looking deeply ashamed, he then had to take a bath in a large wooden tub out in the back yard. He self-consciously sluiced the hot water over his body, his nostrils curling at the smell of carbolic. He knew he was being stared at from the surrounding windows.

The sound of a dry cough told him that Tinsel was also watching him from an upstairs window, and glancing up, he caught a glimpse of her silvery gold hair. He furtively wrapped himself in a towel and slunk off to bed.

As he stretched out and closed his eyes, he felt exhausted. Then the door opened and closed and a warm little body climbed in beside him.

'Hush,' Tinsel murmured, 'no one will know. Georgina has gone out. Love me, Owen.'

Owen's arms tightened about her, and his body reacted as he felt her naked skin next to his.

And so began the passionate affair which Owen had never intended to happen. He and Tinsel met secretly every afternoon to make love in the narrow bed.

This clandestine affair went on for weeks until one day Georgina returned early from her afternoon auditions and came looking for Tinsel. She pushed open the door to Owen's room and saw the two of them there, fast asleep on the bed.

Her reaction was very strange. She closed the door quietly and, with a dry sob rapping her throat, she fled to her room and did not appear again until the evening show.

'Something is up with George,' Moira remarked, but no one knew what was wrong.

Owen guessed that Georgina knew about him and Tinsel from the way that Georgina had begun to ignore him and was being extremely catty and spiteful to Tinsel.

This state of affairs lasted for a few weeks. Finally, matters came to a head one evening after a hazardous show. Tinsel argued with Georgina and then fled to her room. Georgina went up the stairs and locked her in.

Owen was in his own room lazing by the fire when he heard the key turn in the lock. Sadly, his thoughts turned to the day so many years ago when he had first found Tinsel. Since that day she had been a virtual prisoner, bound to the overbearing Georgina. It had to end, he had to do something to free her. But he could not decide on any definite plan to rescue his love.

Downstairs Georgina sullenly declined her supper. She had recently taken to smoking long black Russian cigarettes and drinking whisky after supper. Tonight she sprawled on the chair, cross-legged, a surly expression on her face, smoking and drinking incessantly. The others, sensing trouble, ate their supper quickly and went their different ways, leaving Owen alone with Georgina.

Georgina jerked her thumb in the direction of the bottle for Owen to pour a drink for himself. This he did with shaky hands. He could feel the tension; he knew a storm was brewing.

'Some things have to be settled,' Georgina said suddenly.

Owen looked at her in silence.

'Don't stand there like a silly fool!' she cried irritably. 'You know what I mean.'

He nodded. 'Tinsel,' he said quietly.

'Well, seeing as you broke your word of honour to me, am I not entitled to some explanation?' Georgina demanded.

'What is there to explain?' Owen shrugged. 'We both knew it was inevitable.' A tense silence followed, to be broken by Owen.

'All right, Georgi, I'll leave here tomorrow, if that's what you want.'

'Don't be such a bloody coward!' Georgina yelled viciously, stamping on the cigarette butt. 'You and I know that will break Tinsel's heart and I'll never get any work out of her.'

Owen looked astounded. 'Is that all she means to you?'

'No, for God's sake, it isn't,' cried Georgina, shaking her head mournfully.

Owen reached out a gentle hand to touch her but she pulled away violently. 'Why are you such an idiot?' she raved. 'Why did you ever find us? I knew I would never be able to control her once you came back on the scene.'

'Georgi,' Owen protested, 'Tinsel is another human being with a will of her own.'

'It's for her own sake that I protect her,' said Georgina, ignoring Owen's remark. 'Have you forgotten what you did to her?'

Miserably, Owen shook his head.

'Well, it remains very clear in my mind,' Georgina said brutally, 'because it was I who took care of her. It was I who saw that little stillborn baby buried so unceremoniously in a wood.' The condemnation in her voice was unmistakable.

Owen let out a wail of anguish. 'Oh, cease, Georgi,' he begged. 'This is all more than I can bear. If there is friendship between us, then let us try to understand each other's problems.'

'If that's the case, Owen, then it is for you to put things right,' Georgina replied bitterly.

'Tinsel and I belong together,' he said. 'I know now that it has always been that way.'

'Well, then why did you marry Katy?' Georgina demanded spitefully.

'You and I both know how that came about,' he reproached her sadly.

'Oh!' she sneered contemptuously. 'Why were you such a weak fool?'

'I now regret my weakness more than I can tell,' he replied.

She walked about rapidly for a while and then suddenly stopped and shouted: 'Well, bloody well do something about it! You can ask Katy to release you but don't make me party to your infidelity.'

Owen knew that she was right, so he made no answer.

At last, Georgina calmed down. 'Look here, Owen, it wasn't my intention to bawl you out, because no one knows better than I that Tinsel loves you dearly. I would give my life for her to love me that way,' she added sadly.

Owen stared awkwardly at her.

'Go on,' she jeered, 'say what you are thinking, that I was still born a woman even if I pretend to be a man.'

He held up a protesting hand. 'Hush, Georgi,' he begged, 'please don't.'

'Well, what of it? We all know I'm a crank and I have no place anywhere.' A wail of despair had entered her voice. 'Go on, ask me!' she insisted. 'Ask me! Have I got an unnatural love for Tinsel? The answer is, yes, it's true! And the sorrow of it is that Tinsel detests me because she is so essentially feminine and I repel her.'

Now Georgina's face was white, her eyes blazed. Owen had never seen her so worked up before. 'Georgi, please,' he begged. 'Don't crucify yourself. Let's sit down and talk like friends, as we used to do.'

Gratefully, she acknowledged the truce and they sat by the fire close together.

'If I thought that it would solve anything I would go tonight and never cross either of your paths again,' he said gloomily.

'No, Owen,' she said quietly. 'This must be faced. Take Tinsel under your protection and I'll live my own life. But promise me that you will settle fairly with Katy.'

'I swear by all that is holy, Georgi, that I will,' promised Owen, 'but I can't return until the trial of Slimy Jack is over. I swore I would help to free Tom.'

Georgina shrugged. 'Well, I suppose one feels bound in honour to a good friend.'

'If you recall,' he reminded her, 'Tinsel is a crown witness.'

'Oh, dear, I had forgotten,' she admitted.

'I promise to put my affairs in order as far as Katy is concerned. It will be no heartache for her or for me now. But also, as I promised, I will make the money over to you to start your new project.'

For a moment Georgina's hazel eyes gleamed. 'Conscience money, Owen?' she quizzed.

'Well, you can call it that if you want,' he replied dryly.

George smiled grimly at him. 'One thing is certain, you treat Tinsel right, or it will be me on trial for murder.'

'Georgi, Georgi,' he muttered, gently smiling at her.

CHAPTER FIFTEEN

The Trial of Slimy Jack

Triumphantly Tinsel moved in with Owen, bringing with her another camp bed which was seldom used, and a selection of candy boxes filled with her favourite ribbons, pins, and dried flowers.

'I'm yours now,' she said with childlike satisfaction.

'Hush,' Owen covered her lips with his hand. 'You must not say such things, darling.'

'Why?' she demanded.

But Owen could not find the right answer.

Tinsel held up a grubby doll with yellow wool for hair. 'She is also very pleased,' she announced holding up this monstrosity and cuddling it with affection. 'We once had a little dolly baby like this, Owen,' she said pathetically. 'Shall we have another one? She was so pretty.'

'Oh! my God, be quiet, Tinsel!' Owen cried in anguish, disturbed by her childishness. But amid Owen's own jumble of books and pencils, Tinsel settled into his room contentedly.

The rest of the house was amused by this sudden change of partners upstairs.

'Funny lot of blighters,' remarked Sam.

'What odd fellas,' giggled Moira.

'Mind your own business,' warned Fred. 'Tinsel knows what she wants.'

Tinsel's skimpy wardrobe amazed Owen. It consisted of a couple of ragged skirts and two blouses. 'One on and one off,' as she put it. In that long uneven skirt and familiar old plaid shawl, when off-stage, Tinsel would stroll down the street to the hot chestnut stand and munch the hot nuts in the street.

'How-do, Titch?' the local boys would call, and she would respond with a friendly wave. Her life revolved around the theatre or the house and she never bothered to go anywhere else or dress up for any occasion except on the stage.

One day Owen decided to buy Tinsel some decent clothes and he took her down to the market. When they returned to the house, all the residents gathered to see Tinsel in her new attire – a glorious emerald green dress with a medium stiff skirt, a matching fringed shawl and a straw bonnet trimmed with scarlet cherries which dangled against her pink cheek.

'Well, bless my soul!' cried Sam. 'Tinsel looks good enough to eat.'

'Like a blooming leprechaun,' joked Moira.

Everyone loved Tinsel, and they all admired her now. Then Fred gave her instructions on how to behave when she made her début at Bow Court.

'Don't let 'em worry you, Tinsel. Stand up and say your piece. Stand up, speak up, and shut up. You look just fine in that outfit.' For this was to be Tinsel's first real public appearance in her life.

There was no denying that Tinsel was the star of the show at Slimy Jack's trial. She played her part to perfection. The trial caused a sensation. People fought to get places in the public gallery. The prisoner stood in the dock looking evil. Throughout the case, he sneered and blasphemed and was as aggressive as one of his own fighting cocks. There was a long line of witnesses for the Crown, for during his years of crime, Slimy Jack had made many enemies. His deeds included larceny, murder, rape and even bigamy. The court was filled with pious men and religious fanatics all with a sudden avid interest in the welfare of the lost generation of children.

Before Tinsel was called, Sophie had given evidence in a loud clear voice. She was now a big, clean, country woman and respectable. She was very convincing as she described to the court how in her teens she had charge of the slave children at Polly's. She told them of Jack's peculiar kink for small boys, how he procured them and then sold them on to a sea skipper with the same sexual preference. Then she spoke of her thirteen-year-old brother who had disappeared overnight, and gave lurid details of the goings-on at Polly's home, which was well-known as a bawdy house for shore-leave sailors. The court was shocked by the details.

At last Tinsel was called. Her head only just appeared over the witness box. When she gave her evidence they could have heard as pin drop. She told how she saw Jack throttle Sophie's brother, slit his throat and bury him. She had seen it all, spying through a hole in the wood work.

She also stood up to cross-examination well. The defense declared acidly: 'One can tell that you are an actress. You play your part exceedingly well.'

'It's all true,' Tinsel cried.

'But you were not more than ten years old. How can you remember so correctly?'

'I remember, sir, and so would you if you had lived at Polly's.'

'You say a man rescued you,' the lawyer persisted.

'Yes, my Owen took me away from that place,' she announced proudly.

'This gentleman, is he now your protector?' the lawyer inquired sarcastically.

'I belong to him,' she said artlessly, and there was a titter of laughter all over the court.

The prisoner denied all the accusations and insisted that he had lived abroad and had not been in England for many years.

'But you *were* here, you were in the country on Christmas Eve of last year, and that can be proved,' declared the lawyer Owen had retained for Tom.

Several well-paid inhabitants of Rat's Castle gave evidence of having seen Slimy Jack. One had actually gambled with him that night.

Then big Tom was brought from prison. He had lost a lot of weight and there were silver flecks of grey in his hair. He looked honestly and conscientiously at the judge and told him he had helped to get the child Tinsel from the den of iniquity run by Polly and Slimy Jack. And he told of meeting Jack that night at Rat's Castle when Lord Buckley was murdered.

Jack had begun to look sick. He blustered and argued under pressure. And slowly the net tightened.

'All right,' he yelled on the last day of the trial, 'you're going to top me, so I done it, every bloody thing. I done it. And I copped that bleeding lord while he was lying in the ditch and I ain't sorry either, and books to the lot of yer!'

A great shout went up in the courtroom. Everyone was talking and whispering until the judge told them all to be quiet. People were astounded to see Slimy Jack confess. They had been convinced that he would deny it to the very end.

And so, after weeks of anguish, Tom was released with a pardon next day. Owen shook hands with him outside the prison gates.

'Thanks for everything, mate,' Tom said hoarsely.

'Great!' cried Owen. 'Come, pal, let's go and enjoy a celebration drink.'

'No, thanks,' said Tom quietly. 'I'm on the wagon. It's me and Old Dawg and Ma now. I've certainly learned the error of my ways in there.'

As his huge shape lumbered off down the road, Owen felt intensely sad at the loss of his good drinking friend. Although he knew he should be elated by the outcome of Tom's trial, he realised, with sorrow, that the episode had changed his big friend for ever. Feeling let down and dejected, he went along to the *Daily News* where they were busy running lurid accounts of the court scene.

At the office there were several letters for him, including long tear-stained epistles from Katy who claimed that unless Owen sent her some money soon she would eventually end up in the debtors' prison. She was, she wrote, being overwhelmed by creditors. She had also enclosed a letter addressed to Owen personally. This was from her father, Captain Browne, stating that it was his intention to start negotiations with an American steamship line with regard to amalgamation with the Sun Line. He planned to be home in the New Year. He was currently on a Pacific voyage but would be back in time to instruct the lawyers. He hoped that Owen would agree to this venture as it would bring good profits to all concerned.

Owen sent off a swift note to Katy, claiming that the pressure of work had detained him. He enclosed a blank cheque for her to settle her affairs.

Another letter he opened contained two complimentary tickets for a charity show. Deakins had requested his presence at some amateur theatricals in which Deakins and his friends and family were involved. Deakins wanted Owen to be there to do his clever lightning sketches. For a moment, Owen thought it would be nice to take Tinsel, but then he dismissed the thought. Deakins' show was on a Saturday night and he could not put the Variety at risk by removing its star performer.

When he returned home for supper everyone at the house seemed depressed. Tinsel was red-eyed from weeping, and Georgina kept sighing.

'It's been a bad night, Owen,' explained Georgina. 'We had a full house but a bad audience. Some were trying to break up the show, and others were there just to look at Tinsel. She's famous now, after Slimy Jack's trial. A lot of flowers and a disgusting depraved note were sent to her back stage. At one point during the act, a lout had called out to her and put Bill Moncaur off in the middle of an intricate feat of magic.'

Quite unused to fame and the muck it brings with it, poor little Tinsel had collapsed. The final straw had been the presence of the loud-mouthed women at the stage door who shouted out: 'Whore!' and 'Slut!' to her.

When Tinsel saw Owen she dashed at him, sobbing wildly. Georgina cast a malevolent glance at him. 'It's not done us any good, this fuss,' she complained. 'Those do-gooders are more than likely to try to get the show closed down now.'

It was obvious that Tinsel needed a break from the show. To Owen's surprise, Georgina agreed to give her the night off. 'We can get little Maisie Dillon to stand in for her for one evening,' she said. Owen was delighted. He took Tinsel in to town and bought her a real evening dress, and then took her to the amateur theatricals in Dean Street. It was a very social evening and on the way home Tinsel clung possessively to Owen's arm, chattering all the while about how those real ladies had made such a fuss of her back at the party after the show.

Owen was silent. He had almost gone mad with jealousy as his friends had fawned over Tinsel and she so naïvely encouraged them. Tinsel had been a great success with Owen's friends. They all appreciated her expressive, deep-set blue eyes, her small trim shape and those shining rolls of hair which Moira had dressed so well.

As they left the cab at the corner, Owen noticed that the lights were still on at the Variety.

'Georgi's working late,' he remarked. 'Come on, Tinsel, let's see if she has got any problems.'

As they approached, they heard Fred's voice talking in a very subdued tone. This was followed by a high pitched screechy voice.

'I don't care if I wait here all night. You go out and find them!'

'But, madam,' pleaded Fred, 'the lady has left the show and the gentleman is out, up in town. I don't know when he will come back.'

Owen drew a deep breath and stopped in the doorway. In the dimly lit foyer were two over-dressed women – Katy and her mother. Mrs Browne was dressed all in black with a beaded cape and high bonnet. With her beaky nose, she stood over Fred like a great vulture.

On the seat by the wall was Katy's large form. Owen looked at his wife in shocked silence. Her face was white and puffy and her red-rimmed eyes had sunk deep into their sockets from constant crying. She looked most unattractive.

'Ah!' cried Mrs Browne in warlike tones when she spied him. She ran forward waving her umbrella. 'So you *are* here and who is this strumpet? Your mistress, I presume.' She didn't seem to recognise Tinsel and waved her umbrella menacingly at her.

Tinsel crept up close behind Owen. 'Take Tinsel with you, Fred,' he muttered.

'No, you don't,' shouted Mrs Browne. 'I've got plenty to say to her. Where's my lovely daughter, Georgina? Five years gone and not a word. She was in your company when she left home. I demand an explanation!'

Tinsel crept into a dim corner, coughing and shivering as she did in times of stress.

From the shadows stepped Georgina. 'It's all right, Mama, don't panic, I'm here.'

Mrs Browne gave a wild scream. She threw her hands above her head, and her umbrella crashed to the floor. 'Oh, my lovely Georgina!' she cried, throwing her arms about her. Georgina held her and comforted her.

In stunned and embarrassed silence, Owen stood looking at his wife. In a melancholy manner, she sat looking back at him while Tinsel continued to press herself into the dark corner and cough.

Once Mrs Browne had calmed down, she stood back and

surveyed her long-lost daughter. 'Dear God, Georgina, you're dressed as a man!' she exclaimed.

'Stage props,' muttered Georgina uneasily.

'Oh, why didn't you write?' wailed her mother. 'Your poor papa was at his wit's end.'

Georgina turned to her sister. 'How are you, Katy?' she asked. Katy promptly burst out howling.

'Gosh!' cried Georgina, rumpling her locks. 'Look here, can't we all discuss these affairs in the morning? It's getting very late,' she said. 'Where are you both staying, Katy?'

'In the hotel on the Strand,' said Katy tearfully.

'Owen will take you home,' said Georgina. 'I'll come up in the morning and we can have a good talk,' she cajoled them.

'As you wish,' snivelled her mother. 'I must say, it has been a most disturbing day.'

With a resigned sigh, Owen went to call a cab. He brushed past Tinsel in the corner but he was so worried and pre-occupied that he ignored her presence.

Once inside the cab, his mother-in-law showered him with a tirade of insults. 'I knew what you were from the beginning. You never fooled me. You're just a fortune hunter. You went after her legacy, and then you left her to live like a pauper.'

She glared at him but Owen made no comment. 'Now, to add insult to injury,' continued Mrs Browne, 'you have flouted your mistress in public. You then had the audacity to get mixed up in that sordid murder case and to get it all published in the local paper.'

So *that* was how they had traced him, he thought.

'I tell you,' continued Mrs Browne, 'it has got to end. My husband will be home soon and he will settle with you,' she threatened.

Owen did not argue. He just stared morosely out into the night. Leaving the women at the hotel entrance, he turned to go. Katy looked up at him and said pathetically: 'I must speak with you alone, Owen.'

A wave of guilt welled up inside him, and he put a gentle arm about her. 'Don't keep crying, Katy, I'll come and see you tomorrow.'

She smiled weakly. His remark seemed to satisfy her, so he left very quickly.

He did not go home but went on down to Fleet Street where

the wine cellar was still open, and then on to a newspapermen's club, to complete his alcoholic round.

A porter roused him at dawn when he staggered round the corner to the office of the *Daily News*. There he lay on a couch till midday when an office boy poked him in the back.

'Do you want tea or coffee,' he asked.

'What's the time?' Owen slurred.

'Quarter past twelve, sir,' replied the boy.

Owen got up and stuck his head under the cold water tap. Thus refreshed, he made his way to his rendezvous with Katy. He was unwashed, unshaven and his head felt like a pumpkin.

Georgina was already at the hotel. He could hear her voice raised as she argued with her mother.

'I am twenty-five years old, Mama, and I will live my life how I please.'

'But, Georgina, in the Bible it is forbidden for women to ape men.'

Katy's voice broke in, to say something. It sounded very prim and proper.

'Shut up, Katy!' yelled Georgina. 'You make me sick.'

'I do not object to the theatre, Georgina,' declared her mother. 'Nowadays, some very nice people are connected with entertainment. In fact, they approve of it and support it. But going around like a crank dressed in shirt and breeches is just too much!'

'Oh, Mama!' sighed Georgina in exasperation, 'you will never understand me, so why should we bother to argue?' She stopped suddenly when she saw Owen. 'Look at what the wind's blown in,' she said.

Owen crept through the door, acutely conscious of his unkempt appearance. He wished the floor would open and swallow him up.

Katy folded her hands angrily on her lap. 'I've a letter for you, Owen,' she said coldly. 'It came by special messenger.'

She handed him a much-stamped envelope. He opened it nervously. It was another letter from Captain Browne:

Dear Owen,

Since our last correspondence, I have been unfortunate enough to contract yellow fever. I have not yet told my wife or daughters. I did not want to alarm them. But the fact is, my health is badly impaired. I trust that God will be willing to let me make the long hazardous journey home but you must go ahead and complete the deal with the American line as every penny I have is wrapped up in this venture. I trust you will take good care of the family. And if Georgina ever returns, she must share my estate equally with her sisters . . . if I do not get well . . .

Owen's face turned pale. He carefully folded the pages and put the letter in his pocket. The women in the room gazed questioningly at him.

'It's to do with the business,' he said shortly.

'Business?' snorted Mrs Browne. "There's very little left of the business. That fool Bertie has made a fine mess of everything.'

'It's true, Owen,' confirmed Katy. 'No bills have been paid and the boy has run off. I am sure he has interfered with the books. I cannot make head or tail of them.'

Owen felt as if a dead weight were on his shoulders. He nodded sympathetically and made no direct conversation.

'You will come back home with me, won't you?' pleaded Katy tearfully. 'I'll forgive everything if you come back now.'

Owen looked at her ruefully. 'It's hopeless, Katy. You know that you and I can no longer live together.'

Immediately Katy burst out into frantic hails of weeping. Owen grimaced, leaving Georgina to go over to comfort her.

'Go home with them, Owen,' Georgina urged. 'Settle their affairs for them, that's the least you could do.'

Owen's lips moved to form the word 'Tinsel' but Georgina raised her hand to hush him.

'Look here, Mama,' she said, 'I'm very busy working here. Owen will go back home with you and restore order. I will come and see you in a few weeks, after this show has come off.'

'We'll go now, this very minute,' declared Katy, her composure fully recovered.

Owen travelled home with his wife and mother-in-law in a first-class compartment on a brand new train.

The ladies were very nervous and Katy clutched at Owen's arm each time the train rounded a bend or entered a tunnel.

Owen was not bothered. He just lolled back in his seat, looking as disreputable as ever and very far away in thought. But Katy was extremely happy, having got back her man.

Arriving home filled Owen with nostalgia. Passing the Blue

Boar, and the Bull Hotel, he recalled the many happy times he had enjoyed in the company of big Tom and all those evenings riding home on the cabbage cart. As their carriage rattled up the hill, Owen looked back down on the town from that great height, a fresh wind blowing in his face. Yes, he thought ruefully, he was still fond of this rural city but he knew that his heart was now in smoky London.

Katy's parlour was more overheated and crowded than ever, with stuffed birds in glass cages, vases with crystal dingle dangles, and photos in velvet frames lined up like soldiers on a fringed and be-draped mantelshelf. Within minutes of arriving back, Owen felt irritable and full of a desire to sweep the whole lot to the floor. Mercifully, he controlled the impulse. As Katy discussed dinner with the cook, Owen began to search frantically for the brandy decanter. But it was nowhere to be found. Mrs Browne saw what he was doing and seemed to smirk before retiring to her own chambers.

At dinner Katy looked sweet and coy, dressed in a low-cut pink dress and a velvet choker about her plump neck. Owen still felt stifled. He could barely eat and was dying for a drink.

'Where is the smoking cabinet?' he asked, knowing full well that was where the whisky and brandy were kept.

'I disposed of it,' replied Katy calmly. 'We no longer have strong drink in the house, not since I became a member of the Temperance Society.'

Owen gulped but made no comment. When Katy went to supervise the serving of her special dessert, Owen dashed out of the French windows, leaped over the front gate and was soon off down town, heading for his own haunts.

The next morning dawned wet and windy. Owen rose long before Katy and although he had a terrific hang-over, he went down to the office to sort out cousin Bertie.

At the office, Bertie had not yet arrived but as Owen entered the room, the odour of snuff, stale tobacco and alcohol was overpowering. And the place was filthy; there were cobwebs and dust all over the place. Owen immediately tried to restore order, sorting out some of the files and disposing of the rubbish until Bertie eventually rolled in.

Bertie had become as round as a ball, and his little short legs in maroon gaiters seemed to bend under the weight of his body. 'Ho ho, you've come back, then,' he laughed mischievously.

'It's been very hard work,' he complained as he slowly stripped off his tight jacket.

Owen thought that Bertie looked like a fat caterpillar wriggling out of its skin. 'That bleeding boy ran off, he did, the thieving little cow's son.'

Quietly checking up log sheets, Owen did not reply.

Bertie wheezed down into his office chair, just as old Dobbs used to. 'Came here ragged-arsed, he did, and went orf like Lord Ponsonby.'

Owen did not respond but he found himself thinking that Bertie had probably done a little fiddling of the books himself and was now trying to place the blame on the boy.

'Better get someone to clean up this place.'

'What for?' asked Bertie. 'It's clean enough.'

'Because the auditors will be coming in,' Owen informed him. 'And the bailiffs too, no doubt,' he added dryly.

'What yer mean?' cried Bertie. 'We ain't going broke, are we?'

'More than likely,' Owen said. 'You had better stay at home and take a rest. I'll be here all this week.'

Bertie almost bounced out of the chair, and stuck out his fat belly aggressively.

'Ho no, you don't, Captain Browne gave me this position and here I stays. I hain't taking no more orders from you, not from an houtsider, I hain't.'

'All right, Bertie,' retorted Owen irritably. 'Stay if you wish but shut up, I'm busy.'

But Bertie continued to mutter. 'We all know about you, mister, you and your licentious, wicked ways.'

Owen ignored him and made no comment.

At mid-day, Owen took the book to the bank to beg the services of an honest accountant. Then he sent two local women down with buckets and mops to clean out the office. After a good lunch at the Bull, he idled the rest of the day away down by the river.

At dinner he had a cool reception from both his wife and mother-in-law. They spoke to each other as though he did not exist, excluding him from their conversation. After dinner, he retired to the library and pulled out the long pipe which had always offended Katy. As he lit up, he vowed that he would return to Tinsel the next morning. He had begun to miss her very much.

Suddenly, he heard the loud clanging of the front doorbell and the soft pad of the lackey's footsteps. Then he heard a muffled voice and a high-pitched scream. Owen peered out into the hall to see Katy and her mother sobbing and screaming and throwing themselves around hysterically. An elderly stranger stood by the front door looking on very bewildered and distressed.

'Oh, it's Papa!' screeched Katy when she saw Owen. Owen looked away. He remembered the letter in his pocket. Perhaps he should have warned them. He held Katy in his arms and soothed her.

The gentleman courier who brought the sad news of the captain's death had ridden all the way from Liverpool. The ship had docked there two days before, bringing home the captain's body. For Captain Browne had not wished to be buried at sea but wanted to lie in his own home town.

After a while, the women calmed down a little and refreshments were provided for the weary traveller who had known the illustrious captain since he was a cabin boy. And while discussions were going on about arrangements for the good captain's funeral, Owen's mind was in a whirl. Now he was trapped. He had to stay here. Even he could not desert his wife at a time like this.

CHAPTER SIXTEEN

An Empty Cage

Owen had not returned to the house on the corner and after a few days Tinsel had begun to look very forlorn. The others fussed her and comforted her, and bought her her favourite candy, but that small pale face assumed a melancholy line.

'Why has Owen not returned?' she would ask mournfully.

Georgina was always impatient with her. 'Oh, for God's sake, Tinsel, stop mooning around. I told you, he has many urgent matters to settle. It will all take time.'

'That Katy will not let him come back,' Tinsel muttered sulkily.

'Oh, what nonsense! You have his word of honour, and that should be good enough for you. It is for me. Now, settle down to some work. Let Wally teach you to read – that would be an asset.'

Wally was Sam's second son, and the only one who had attended school regularly. If anyone wished to have a letter transcribed or a tricky problem solved, Wally was the boy to ask. But Tinsel just chose to mope around.

Georgina was running auditions for the Christmas show. This year she had decided to put on an artistically disguised Cinderella. In her usual way, she wrote the script, designed the costumes, and basically did the whole show. This Monday in her office sat a long-nosed boy of indiscriminate age. He looked young but his quick beady eyes told of experience. He told her that his name was Solomon Finkelstein and that he lived in the East End. 'D'yer na a place called the Black Lion Yard? Yer na, dhan the ghetto?' He had a strange accent, she thought.

'Well, what can you do?' Georgina was rather amused at his attitude. Solomon gave an expressive shrug.

'Me, oi tickles de ivories.'

'You mean you are a pianist?' she asked.

With slow ease, he strolled over to the piano. 'Vat yer vant?' he asked. 'Classics or modern stuff?'

'Do you mean you can play both?' Georgina asked, rather surprised.

'Me?' he cried boastfully. 'Oi can do it all. Listen, my dear.'

Georgina was enthralled as she listened to the young man polish off concertos and German folk songs. He was magnificent. What a find!

'Well, Solly, is that what I call you?' she said.

'Please, yourself. I want to learn to act.' He said flippantly.

'Well, I must say, you are very good,' Georgina told him.

'What I want is to learn to act up there on the stage. I don't mind playing the piano.' He seemed suddenly to have lost that harsh accent, as if he had already mastered the art and that was just his entrance speech.

Georgina looked at him in amazement. She felt quite excited. 'Yes, I feel I could use you on the show but I can't pay a lot of money.'

'I don't want any money, just the training,' he replied.

'We'll discuss that later,' said Georgina. 'Let's say you got a job.' So that long thin lad with his big dark eyes joined the cast at the Variety.

Where Solly came from and where he went when off-stage, no one knew. His background was a mystery and even his strange London accent seemed to come and go, but he was quick, clever and hard working. He was also very funny but seemed completely unaware of it.

Fred and Sam used him as a stooge to liven up their act. Georgina rehearsed him for an ugly sister and in between he played the piano, thrilling the audience during the intervals with renderings of beautiful classics and popular ballads. Solly also loved to make up songs himself and set them to music. He would often be found curled up under the piano in the morning, having worked on a score all night and been too tired to go home. Yes, he fitted in perfectly with this *pot pourri* of show folk.

At the end of the exciting week she discovered Solly, Georgina received a black-edged card informing her of her father's death and requesting her presence at home for the funeral. She was very shocked and distressed at the death of her father. She had loved him and been so proud of him. He was such a brave, good-looking man, and not even so old. It seemed such a waste of life. But now he was dead and she was not keen to go to his funeral. She did not want to see her mother in widow's weeds.

'How can I go?' she asked, looking for excuses.

'You must go home, George,' said Rosita, quite shocked.

'I can't leave the show at the moment,' insisted Georgina.

'You've got to show respect, George,' said Sam.

'But I can't bring him back, whatever I do.'

'You mustn't worry about the show, George, we're quite capable of managing,' Fred assured her.

'We need the capital for the Christmas panto. We've got to keep a full house, Fred.'

'It'll be done, George, so go on your way,' he informed her.

Tinsel had tears in her eyes as she pleaded with Georgina. 'Can I go with you?'

'Don't be a fool,' retorted Georgina impatiently.

'But I want to see my Owen,' Tinsel wept.

'Now grow up, Tinsel,' growled Fred.

Moira came forward and cuddled her. 'Now come on, Tinsel, you'll be all right with me.'

And so Georgina set off for her father's funeral, looking extremely awkward in a long black skirt, a badly fitting blouse and a battered straw hat from the props room. She was furious at having to appear like a respectable female once more, and she simply dreaded returning to Chatham and the stodgy environment of her birthplace.

At the family home, Georgina was greeted by Katy wearing a wide crinoline that seemed to swamp the narrow hall. Her eyes were red and puffy and Georgina was struck by how quickly she had lost her looks.

Their mother was lying in a darkened room amid the odour of moth balls. She was crying hysterically but she looked up when they came in and said: 'It's nice to see you respectably dressed, Georgina, even if you are a trifle shabby.'

The longer Georgina stayed, the more depressed she

became. Owen was little comfort to her either. He just strolled about the house like a miserable caged animal, blundering into Katy's plant pots and whatnots on spindly-legged tables.

Now there was only one more day to pass while they waited for the body of the illustrious captain to arrive from Liverpool. To Georgina it seemed like the longest day of her life. Sitting in that stuffy parlour hour after hour was almost unbearable. Occasionally she smiled at the nervous antics of Owen, and once she laughed out aloud, much to the disapproval of the other mourners who had begun to gather.

Once her father had been laid to rest in the church grounds with great ceremony, Georgina made a hasty exit, giving Owen a comforting squeeze. He stared back at her, perfectly sober – for Katy had not allowed a glass of wine even at the funeral.

It was almost midnight when Georgina arrived home. She went straight to bed without announcing her arrival.

In the early morning, she arose and without any breakfast went down to the Variety. Solly was asleep under the piano, scraps of paper with unfinished scores on them scattered everywhere around him.

Georgina gave him a nudge with her foot. 'Get up and go home, Solly, or you won't be fit for work tonight.'

On a small oil stove she brewed some coffee and placed a hot mug into Solly's trembling hands. 'Idiot,' she said. 'You'll catch your death of cold, kipping down here so often in this weather.'

Solly grinned. He drank the coffee and then shook himself like a great dog and loped out.

Georgina laughed; Solly was so unconsciously comical.

Soon the young boys from the back streets had arrived and had set about their individual chores, cleaning up and servicing the stage props.

By midday Georgina was getting annoyed. So far not one person had arrived from the house. She was just about to send a boy to wake them up, when Fred arrived, looking very timid and white with anxiety.

Georgina eyed him intently. 'Hello, what's up, Fred?' she demanded.

'It's Tinsel,' Fred said hoarsely. 'She didn't come home last night, and no one can find her.'

'Come home? From where?' yelled Georgina.

'She went with Moira up town after the show,' Fred ventured. 'I gave my consent. I thought it would cheer her up.'

'Well, what has Moira got to say?' asked Georgina abruptly.

Fred fiddled with his hat. 'She has only just come home herself. I beat her, George, I was so angry.' His voice broke pathetically.

'I'll come home and sort it out,' Georgina said, ramming on her woolly cap.

Moira was in the kitchen looking very much the worse for wear. A white cloth containing a piece of bloody meat was bound over one eye. Her blouse was ripped and her lovely hair was very bedraggled.

'Good God!' cried Georgina. 'What happened to you?'

'Go on, tell her, you strumpet,' roared Fred.

'Now go out and cool down, Fred,' begged Rosita from the direction of the stove. 'Let George settle it.'

Fred went out, banging the door and Georgina sat on the table.

'Well, now, what's all the mystery?' she demanded.

'Tinsel's gone off,' howled Moira. 'I'm sorry, George, 'tis all me own fault entoirly. I had too much to drink, as always.'

'But where were you? She might be lost looking for you now?' quizzed Georgina.

'Sam and the boys are still up there searching for her, but she's gorn off with that fella.'

'What fella?' demanded Georgina, getting worried.

'We were invited to a party after the show, in a posh hotel, it was. I got boozed up and don't even know what happened to Tinsel,' confessed Moira miserably.

'Why, you drunken cow!' yelled Georgina.

Moira wept copiously. 'Poor, poor little baby. Oh dear, what will become of her? What will be her end?'

'Go and pull yourself together, Moira,' ordered Georgina. 'You're coming with me!'

'Can't go like this,' wailed Moira. 'Fred punched me in the eye.'

'Get going!' shouted Georgina. 'Call a cab, someone, we must find her before the show opens tonight.'

A tour of all the seedy hotels in Bloomsbury brought no results, and a visit to the police station brought little joy either. Tinsel had disappeared without trace. She had last been seen getting into a carriage at about three in the morning. But that was all the information they received apart from the fact that she had been accompanied by two men, one of whom looked foreign and wore a long black opera coat. No, the gentleman in question was not an hotel resident. Rooms had been especially hired for a private party.

In the evening, Georgina and Moira returned home still unrewarded. The show went on just the same. But Georgina was grim-faced and almost silent. Fred and Moira did not speak to each other and the boys were worn out from walking about London in search of their much loved little Tinsel.

It was an unhappy little group which sat round the supper table that night.

'To be sure, she has been brutally murdered,' wept the dramatic Moira.

'Shut your stupid big mouth!' warned Fred.

Georgina went to their room and surveyed the litter. It was a mess, with the two narrow beds and a jumble of ribbons, pens and pencils all mixed up together. Oh, dear, how was Georgina to explain Tinsel's disappearance to Owen? Oh what a foolish child Tinsel was! She was so immature and did not have enough brains to protect herself. Like a golden canary she had fled the cage to be eaten by the wild birds. On the wall in front of her was written in straggly letters by a tiny finger dipped into the rouge pot, 'I luv Owen.'

Tears did not come easily to Georgina's eyes, but they did now.

CHAPTER SEVENTEEN

The Assassin

Every day Katy and her mother made it increasingly difficult for Owen to leave. Each time Owen announced that he was needed urgently in London, Katy collapsed into hysterical weeping. Then her mother sallied forth into battle with her vicious tongue, and *her* waspish attacks usually defeated him.

In order to keep sane, Owen threw himself into the business, trying to save it from the chaos he had found it in.

Captain Browne had died in the middle of his most ambitious business venture and now Owen was left to complete the deal. Lawyers and agents had to be consulted, books had to be brought up-to-date, company meetings attended to. Gently but firmly Owen pushed out cousin Bertie and began to tie up all those loose ends. His decision had been made. He would sign over his part of the business to Katy. Then he could be finished with it for good and leave the Medway.

The weather was getting cold and the office was draughty. He spent as many hours as possible away from the house, going back and forth to the Sun Inn for refreshment. He kept thinking about old Dobbs. He had this depressing vision of himself getting old and obese, tied to Medway and surrounded by nagging women, just as old Dobbs had been.

At last the deal was wound up and the office closed its doors after a hundred and fifty years of business. The Browne family company became part of a smart new shipping line, incorporating three old companies.

After much debate and squabbling with Katy and her

mother, Owen managed to persuade them to accept his part of the business in return for his being allowed to come and go as he pleased. A sensible lawyer brought them to an affable agreement on the business. But Owen got a flat rejection from Katy when he raised the possibility of a divorce.

A divorce was too much to expect but Owen was still relieved to be released from the business. He was now a poor man again. He did have some money in the bank but that was all promised to Georgina to enable her to purchase the land she wanted so badly. He was not in the least bothered about his financial state. He could still work and had many good contacts. At last he was free to return to Tinsel.

How cold and empty the world was without Owen! Those weeks after he had returned home with Katy and her mother were long and dreary. Tinsel felt desperately sad and inflicted her gloom on the rest of the house. The others tried to cheer her up without much success. Moira had recently acquired a rather ardent admirer who hung around the stage door. Moira was delighted and when he suggested taking her out to supper up in town, it was eagerly accepted. And, to cheer the girl up, Moira asked Tinsel to come with her.

Fred and Moira had been married twelve years and their relationship was a very stable one. They had produced four talented children and worked well together on and off stage. And they got on well, in spite of the fact that Moira was inclined to drink too much and flirt with admiring members of the opposite sex. The easy-going Fred Dillon saw no harm in his wife having a mild flirtation with this loud-mouthed stage-door Johnny who had made his pile at the gaming tables. To him, there was little to worry about.

'Get ready straight after the show,' Moira told Tinsel, 'and oi'll come and fix yer hair for you.'

In the classic white silk evening dress which Owen had bought for her, Tinsel looked radiant. The low neckline was relieved by a jet choker and long jet earrings to match. The jewels were presents from Rosita. With her golden hair bunched and curled and tied back with a white velvet ribbon, Tinsel was as sweet and enchanting as a china doll.

The supper party was held at a large private hotel. Tinsel was almost overwhelmed by elegant ladies escorted by over-

dressed beaux, the flowers and the candles, the long table laden
with food. Young men kissed her hand, murmured sweet nothings in her ear and then passed on.

One man who was much older but immaculately dressed,
lingered by Tinsel's side. He took her hand and whispered: 'So
this is our famous lady. I have been most anxious to meet you,
my dear. I did see that dreadful show. You must not allow your
beauty to be exploited in that way.'

All this conversation was quite unintelligible to Tinsel. She
stared solemnly at the man's thin face and those penetrating
eyes. His long white fingers held on to hers.

'Excellent,' he murmured. 'A woman of beauty with little to
say. Such an accomplishment in this age of female chatterers.'
He turned for appreciation for his witty remarks from a young
man standing beside him. This youth was dressed like everyone
else in dress suit. His hair was swept back off his handsome
dark face. He seemed to be suddenly struck dumb but then he
burst out: 'It's you! Tiny Tinsel! I would have known you
anywhere.'

'Why, it is you, Jan,' Tinsel said quietly. She offered a sweet
smile of welcome for her old lover as he came forward. They
clasped hands.

'So! I see you are already acquainted with the young lady,'
said the older man, a trifle bitterly. He drifted off gracefully.

'Come on, Tinsel, let's sit outside,' whispered Jan.

Tinsel giggled. 'Oh, you have grown very handsome, Jan.'

'I've been living in France for a number of years. I've
changed my name for a French one. I even carry French
papers, so don't let me down,' he whispered.

She snuggled close to him. To find a familiar face amid all
these strangers was wonderful.

'How well I remember when we played Romeo and Juliet!'
he said.

'Oh, yes,' Tinsel sighed. 'That was up north, when I had my
little baby.'

'Never look back, Tinsel, life is too short,' Jan warned her. 'I
went to see your show but I didn't dare come too near,' he told her.

'Your parents would have been so pleased to see you,' she
reproached him.

'Yes, I expect so, but you still have Uncle George, I noticed,'
he said sarcastically.

'Yes, Georgi runs the show now.'

'I wanted my master to see you,' he said.

She looked at him questioningly.

'Your master?'

'Yes, the gentleman who spoke to you. He's a mesmerist. We make up a travelling show and are just off to tour the United States.'

'How lovely!' Tinsel cried impulsively.

Piece by piece the jigsaw of the lost years was thus completed. 'Owen has gone away now but I know he will come back for me,' she said childishly, 'because rightfully I belong to him.'

Jan's expression changed. His eyes looked hard. 'Is that the fellow who illustrates the newspapers and magazines?'

Tinsel nodded proudly. Jan looked down at her in wonder. How simple she still was! And that damned fellow had abused her all her young life! A knot of rage burned within him as Tinsel chattered on about everyone back home and all the kids who were now growing up.

'It's time you moved on,' Jan said gloomily. 'It's time you made a career for yourself.' He brought her fizzy champagne to drink, and little trifles from the buffet table. They sat close together reminiscing about their youth, when they used to chase each other through the heather-covered moors.

The large ornate room was gradually emptying, then quite suddenly, Tinsel remembered Moira.

'The red-hatted lady left quite a while ago,' the waiter informed her.

'Oh, my goodness!' cried Tinsel. 'I don't know how to get back home.'

'Don't worry, you're quite safe with me,' Jan assured her. He brought his cape and put it about her, then accompanied by his master they drove off in a carriage. In no time, Tinsel was sleeping with her head on Jan's shoulder, like a very tired child.

When Tinsel awoke the next day she found herself at the rural lodgings of Jan's travelling show. They were warm and comfortable and there were many young women there as well. They all seemed to play cards and gossip in several languages.

Tinsel stared out of the window at the misty green fields and wept for Owen and the house on the corner, knowing she would never be able to find her way home now.

Jan was very suave and most patient. 'Don't worry, little one, Owen Oliver only used you. I will make you happy. With me you will become a famous actress with lots of clothes and plenty of money,' he cajoled her.

'But Georgi needs me,' Tinsel protested.

'To hell with Georgi!' Jan replied angrily. 'What is she to you? Half-man, half-woman? Your destiny lies with me. I left my parent's home because I loved you so much. I cannot let you go again.'

He held her close and kissed her passionately. To the simple loving Tinsel there was no way of turning back.

'A new beauty for our show, Jan?' asked Monsieur Henri, the master.

'*Oui, oui,*' replied Jan abruptly.

'*Bon,* we move on today. Next stop, Dublin,' the master said.

'Please, Jan,' pleaded Tinsel. 'I must try and find Georgi to tell her where I'm going.'

But Jan held her with quick passion, the veins in his forehead protruding with temper. 'Forget that damned place. Forget that damned Owen. None of them exist for you.'

Big tears rolled down Tinsel's pink cheeks. 'I would still like to say farewell,' she wept.

'Write a letter then, for God's sake,' Jan snarled.

'I can't write,' she sobbed.

Jan softened at the sight of her. 'All right, darling.' His conscience pricked him. 'I'll help you to write a note and I'll even deliver it myself. I might even get a word with the old folk,' he muttered thoughtfully. 'Promise on all that's holy that you will never leave me.'

He took Tinsel's hand and looked deep into her eyes. She sniffed and nodded, not strong enough to defy Jan.

Then Jan scribbled out a note and read it out to her. She seemed satisfied enough, but didn't know that Jan had secretly substituted her requests to tell Owen that she still loved him, for the words: 'tell Owen that I am finished with him'.

The coach was outside and all the boxes on board.

'Come, Tinsel,' called the showgirls.

'Go with them, Tinsel,' said Jan. 'Don't delay. I'll soon catch up with you.'

Monsieur Henri slipped his arm gently through hers and

helped her inside the coach. 'Come, little one,' he whispered. 'I'll take good care of you.'

Against her true wishes but unable to do otherwise, Tinsel obediently climbed into the coach and Jan rode off on horseback in the other direction.

Young Jan Silver, alias Jean Sillette, was destined never to meet the love of his life again. The next night at Fishguard, the passenger ship sailed from the harbour. The lights from the shore twinkled farther and farther away in the distance. Tinsel watched them from the ship's rail. She felt quite dazed.

Dressed in a large hat and flowing cape, Henri stood beside her and placed a comforting arm about her. 'Do not worry, little one, Jean will catch up with us,' he assured her.

Her blue eyes looked up childishly at him. 'Oh, thank you for being so kind, but how can I live without Owen?'

Henri looked puzzled. 'Owen? I thought Jean was your lover?'

She shook her head but still clung tightly to his hand. 'No problems, *ma chérie*,' he told her. 'I'll take good care of you.'

On his return to the house, Owen immediately sensed that there was something different about it. An odd sort of gloom pervaded the hall. Rosita was busy in the kitchen. Owen thought that her shoulders seemed to have drooped a little more. Perhaps all this domestic work was too much for her. Dropping his bag on the floor, he went straight on down to the Variety. There, he was sure, he would see Tinsel.

He found Georgina in her office surrounded by bills as usual. Her face had a hard expression, her eyes were dark and sombre.

'Hello, Owen,' she greeted him.

'I'm back at last,' he said. 'Where's Tinsel?'

Georgina grimaced and shook her head. 'It seems we have both lost out, Owen,' she said quietly.

'What are you talking about?' he asked with a perplexed expression.

'Tinsel has gone missing. She's been absent for these last three weeks. So far there's been not one trace of her. I thought she might have turned up in Chatham.'

'Oh, my God!' Owen cried. 'What happened to her?'

'No one knows. Moira was the last one to see her.'

'Have you informed the police?'

'I have done everything possible to find her but she has just disappeared. She was very unhappy when you went away. She kept saying that Katy would not let you come back to her.'

Owen put his hands over his eyes.

'It's no good crying,' Georgina said harshly. 'God knows we have all shed enough tears over her.'

'I'll go and see Forest. Perhaps he'll help,' Owen said pathetically.

'I've tried that already. It's no good,' she said.

'Is there nothing we can do?'

'Not much,' she shrugged. 'I just hope that she will come back. My immediate problem is finding someone to take her place as Cindy in my Christmas show. We open in a few weeks.'

Owen stared at her dumbly. How could she think this way when his whole world had come to an end?

From the doorway an urchin's head appeared. 'Well, what's wrong with me?' she called cheekily. 'Why can't I play Cindy?'

Georgina laughed. 'Hear that? That's show biz. It goes on whatever happens.'

Owen had heard enough. He got up and drifted outside.

In the dimly lit foyer lurked a young man with dark sideburns and a tanned skin. He wore a choker around his neck, gypsy fashion. Owen decided that he must be a new member of the cast but as he walked past, those dark eyes followed him menacingly. Or was it just his imagination? Owen turned and looked directly at the fellow. The look of dark bitter hatred which met his gaze shocked Owen. Feeling quite shaken, he set off into town to have a drink.

He visited various clubs and bars and ended up in Forest's rooms at Gray's Inn where the great novelist Deakins, on a fleeting visit from Italy, read aloud from his current novel. No one was bothered that Owen Oliver slept boozily through it all.

That evening there was another charity show in Dean Street. Owen found himself drifting along with the rest of the crowd to see the show but as he stared out from the cab, he was sure he saw that same gypsy face staring at him. Then it was gone. Owen shook his head in puzzlement. Was he going mad? His eyes scanned the West End streets all the time, always hoping for a glimpse of Tinsel's flaxen head.

The show was over and the lights of the entertainment
houses winked warm welcomes. The streets were filled with
people – and men and women in immaculate evening dress,
wide skirts swishing, jewellery glittering as they enjoyed a night
out on the town. Dressed still in his travelling clothes and
rather woozy, Owen stood looking about him forlornly.
Suddenly he saw that gypsy face again. It was seized with
hatred and seemed to fly towards him. He also saw a flash of
steel aimed right at his heart. Owen raised his arm to protect
himself. The knife slashed through his wrist. A second vicious
jab severed his lip. Warm blood flowed into his mouth as he
crashed to the ground. Within seconds, other men were on to
the gypsy fellow and beating him with canes. The women
screamed hysterically as the Peelers came running. Someone
propped Owen up against a wall and tried to staunch the flow
of blood.

'Who did it?' someone asked.

'A foreigner,' another replied.

'The police have taken him in.'

'Was it meant for Deakins, do you think?'

'Could be! This was a brave fellow to try to get the knife
from the assassin.'

'Why, that's Owen Oliver, the illustrator. He's a boozy cuss
by all accounts.'

A red mist hovered before his eyes. Fragmented voices
seeped through to Owen's brain. His arm was limp and heavy,
and he could not move his lips. So this was death. He felt calm
and peaceful. He was slipping away. Had this not been what he
had always wished for?

The ship tossed and turned in the stormy Irish sea. That night
Tinsel lay in her bunk bed, too sick to care any more and
unaware that her old lover Jan was now locked up in a London
jail. Now he lay on a hard plank bed with his hands pressed to
his battered face. An angry crowd had beaten him up first and
the Peelers had finished the job. The police had decided that
Jan was some audacious foreigner who had come to our land
with his bloodthirsty revolutionary ideas. Yes, they said, he was
definitely an anarchist trying to kill one of our leading writers.
It was only the bravery of Deakins' illustrator that had saved
the great writer's life.

The newspapers were full of it, and the public was up in arms. So far the prisoner had only jabbered threats and curses in several languages, and refused to co-operate with the police. It was decided to keep him in custody until someone charged him with attempted murder.

The secret of Jan's identity might never have been revealed but for the curiosity of his younger brother, Wally. Wally was a good deal younger than Jan but he still remembered his older brother very well.

Wally was a bright lad and now had a job in the city as a messenger for a solicitor. On an errand to Bow Court for his boss, he waited at the back of the court to catch a glimpse of this terrible anarchist he had read about. Jan was being brought up for his second hearing. With his foreign accent he may have confused the law but he did not fool Wally. Wally was immediately convinced that this man was his brother Jan, and hurried home to inform the family.

'He's the living image of our Jan,' he repeated as supper was being served.

Rosita placed the heavy stewing pot back on the stove and sank wearily into her chair.

'Get on with your supper, Wally,' growled Fred.

Wally was breathless and excited as Georgina came in carrying a bundle of scripts in her arms. 'What the hell's wrong with Wally?' she asked.

Rosita's voice was heard through twisted lips as if in pain. 'If the boy is right, then it was our Jan who injured Owen.'

A deep silence shocked the room. Then Wally's squeaky voice piped up: 'I told yer it was our Jan.'

Rosita began to weep as if her heart were broken. Her husband and small daughter ran to her side to comfort her.

'Well,' said Georgina, sitting on the edge of the table, 'perhaps someone had better explain.'

'I saw him,' garbled Wally, 'pretending to be French, he was.'

'Hold yer wisht, Wally,' declared Moira, pouring out hot coffee for the distressed Rosita.

There had been so many crises in this tight community and many of them had been settled by Georgina. 'Let's all calm down and we will listen to Rosita,' she now told them.

'Yes, Jan was here,' said Rosita tearfully, 'but I did not tell a

soul. He had a letter for Owen. He said that Tinsel was going
away with him and they were never coming back. Then Owen
came back to the house, left his bag and went off to the
Variety. Jan hid behind the door and I never saw the going of
him. Oh, my God, it has worried me so,' she wailed. 'For after
all, he *is* our son,' she appealed to Sam.

Sam put an arm about her. 'Hush now, missus, don't cry
any more.'

It was as if a bomb had hit these happy families. Moira was
now weeping almost as loudly as the two little girls.

Fred strolled up and down, his hands deep in his trouser
pockets. And now Georgina sprang into action.

'Come on, Wally,' she said. 'Let's go and find Dill.'

Dill was Fred's eldest boy, stage manager and loyal helper,
placid and sensible as his father had always been. Soon
the three of them were rattling their way up to town in a
hansom cab to the nursing home where Owen's friends had
taken him.

Owen looked battered and very self-conscious as he sat up in
bed and was fed from a spoon by one of the efficient male
attendants. One of his arms was heavily bandaged and the
bottom half of his face was plastered where his lip was stitched.
He seemed pleased to have a visit from Georgina and the boys
and smiled crookedly at them.

'I hope you're well enough to receive a shock,' said Georgina
in her forthright manner.

Owen nodded.

'Well, it seems that it was our own young Jan who knifed
you. And he's also responsible for Tinsel's disappearance.'

Once the meaning of her words had sunk in, he asked
huskily: 'Where is she? And why, in God's name? What did I
ever do to him?'

'Jan is in love with Tinsel. He always was,' explained
Georgina. 'It's an old score he settled. I don't know where she
is, I must confirm some facts first.'

'Surely there is some mistake. I was told I was attacked by
some lunatic Frenchman.'

'No, Owen,' Georgina shook her head. 'Wally has seen him
and his mother told us he was behind the kitchen door when
you came in back to the house. Rosita's word is good enough
for me.'

'The police are waiting for me to charge him,' said Owen glumly.

'What will you do, Owen?'

'I want to know where Tinsel is,' he said slowly and painfully. 'I'll not charge him if he tells me.'

'Good boy,' said Georgina, giving him such a thump on the back that he winced. 'I'll go and settle with the law.'

In spite of repeated attempts to see the prisoner, Georgina failed. The police were suspicious of everyone and every thing connected with the case. The victim refused to press charges, the prisoner refused to see anyone and would not co-operate, and the French authorities insisted that they had never heard of him. Tinsel's pathetic little note had been blown about the narrow alleys of the district, torn, trampled and blood-stained, having been torn from Jan's pocket when the crowd attacked him.

In the house on the corner there was a great deal of tension. The usually strong Rosita seemed to have crumpled. Nowadays she just sat sadly looking into the fire. Suppers were no longer hot and tasty. Potatoes got burned. The soup was oversalted.

'The heart has gone out of the old lady,' Sam commented sadly. He was still virile and active, and with his great sense of humour, he was an asset to the show.

Georgina was still up to her neck in work, determined to launch a Christmas pantomime. A new government act had been passed which had broken the monopoly on small booth theatres. Now Georgina's variety show was licensed and allowed singing and a certain amount of spoken drama. Thanks to the versatile Solly, she had plenty of new songs and had engaged several professional artists for this Christmas show. For her the troubles in the house were secondary to the show. She dismissed Rosita's depression and Owen's condition from her mind. Her work came before everything, as always.

Katy and Mrs Browne returned to town and whisked the protesting Owen back home too. Meanwhile, the police relieved their consciences and deported Jan back to France where he was immediately arrested for possessing forged papers. He was then sent off to a drab prison in Marseilles.

A few weeks before Christmas, Georgina launched her new

show. As always, most members of the two families took part in it; the small girls were Christmas fairies, the boys played instruments in the orchestra pit, the stage sets were designed and built by the stalwart Dill, and Maisie was the star of the show as Cindy. Between acts, Sam entertained and sang his most popular song *Hot Codlins*, inviting the audience to join in the chorus.

The house was packed every night. The double-tiered boxes at the sides were fully booked and accommodated the better class of audience, the wealthy, well-fed families. The rougher lot of men and women pushed and shoved to squeeze on to the long wooden benches which made up the stalls. Babies yelled, children shouted, and fights broke out. Vendors packed the foyer, calling for people to buy their wares – hot meat pies, jars of stout, baked spuds and cockles, mussels and a whole variety of other shell fish. These sellers always left behind a dreadful amount of litter which had to be cleaned up by the company after the show, regardless of how tired the actors were.

So far the show had been a great success and they had received some good notices in the press. On Christmas Eve, to celebrate, they had a party after the show. It was held in the rehearsal room where lamps gleamed and music drifted out in that poor slum street, spreading a glow of warmth and light. Shabbily dressed women in shawls stared in at the windows, while ragged children gathered on the front doorstep to take in the smells wafting from the house. It was rare for such feasts to be seen in this depressed area. The table groaned with delicious food and was decorated with holly, mistletoe, and candles.

Georgina was dressed in male clothes as usual – a gleaming white shirt front, tailored black suit, and paste cuff-links which glittered like diamonds. She was enjoying herself, and laughed and joked with the other members of the two families as they all tucked in to their Christmas fare.

At midnight Georgina went out on the doorstep to talk to the crowd of little urchins waiting there expectantly. She gave each one a small parcel containing an orange and an apple, a small present and a few sweets. Such a treat was much appreciated by the barefooted children who had known little but hunger all their young lives.

'Merry Christmas, George!' called the adults.

'Happy Christmas to our George!' chanted the children.

Georgina was ecstatic. She called out to the children 'Come on, give us a song!'

As *The Holly and the Ivy,* and other popular carols wafted out into the night air, Georgina's spirits felt higher than they had ever been before. Even though Tinsel had gone, she was so happy that night that she wanted to embrace the whole world. For she had that very day received a letter from Owen and with it a banker's draft for five hundred pounds. It was the money Owen had promised to give her to buy the land for the theatre of her dreams.

CHAPTER EIGHTEEN

The End of the Old Variety

January and February were cold and bleak months. Very little of importance had happened at the house on the corner. After a few weeks of shut down, Georgina reopened the theatre with the old burlesque and an occasional blood-and-thunder drama. There had been no news of Tinsel for months. Maisie Dillon was well established in Tinsel's place.

The vivacious Maisie had recently become rather secretive and she had started to make mysterious trips up town on her time off. She offered no information about where she went, and she made it clear that she did not want to be asked.

Solly was still proving to be a great success. His own compositions and parodies of other musical arrangements went down well every time. The arrangements were humorous and topical and extremely popular with those who liked to join in the singing. When he was not working, Solly spent most of his free time having fun at the piano or lounging about in Georgina's office.

Georgina was a little concerned about Maisie's odd behaviour and decided to see what Solly thought.

'You know, Solly,' she remarked one day. 'I think something's going on . . .'

Solly squinted his beady eyes furtively and rubbed his nose.

'All right, don't get nervous,' Georgina assured him. 'I didn't mean with you. It was young Maisie I was thinking of.'

'She's got a fella,' blurted out Solly, with a snigger.

'Oh! Has she, and does Fred know?'

Solly shook his head. 'No, she's scared of her pa. This bloke's an actor up at Covent Garden.'

'What, the Madame Vestry Show?' asked Georgina with amazement.

'Yup. He's trying to get her a part in a singing and dancing piece.'

Georgina was stunned. It had never occurred to her before that Fred and Moira's lovely children, whose whole life had been spent back stage, would not be content forever in this tinpot show. For Georgina was concerned for the future of her own show. After all, no one had ever bothered with contracts, or anything; it was a family show. But if Maisie left suddenly, they would find themselves in trouble.

Georgina's fears were realised a few days later when a row broke out among the family one night after supper. In a raging temper, Maisie shouted and screamed that she was quitting the show because she had got herself a better job.

Fred gave a great roar and slapped her into silence until her big brother Dill rushed forward with his fists raised to stop Fred attacking Maisie.

Now it was Georgina's turn to wade in. She knew how to deal with this excitable family

'Maisie! Come over to me. Fred, Dill, sit down. Now we'll all talk it over reasonably.' She barked out her orders like a sergeant major. And it worked. The others all took their hands off each other and separated.

But Dill was quite worked up. 'We're not slaves to this tuppenny booth,' he said. 'Maisie's right to go for what she wants. Things are happening in this profession. It's no longer a low-class thing. In fact, being an actor is quite well thought of.'

'Shut your mouth, boy,' shouted Fred. 'My daughter is not going to work up in town. She belongs with the family.'

'Clown! Silly fool! Old ass,' stormed Maisie. 'Look where it got you!'

'Leave the room, you sassy piece!' screamed Moira. Maisie played her part of haughty defiance and stood her ground.

'May I ask where you intend to go, Maisie?' Georgina asked mildly.

'I've been offered a part at Covent Garden,' replied Maisie. 'I'd give my all to get up there. Oh, George,' she pleaded, 'don't let them stop me!' Almost on her knees, she threw herself at Georgina's feet in a melodramatic manner, weeping madly.

Georgina cuddled the girl's curly head. 'I can't stop you,' she replied. 'We have no contract.' She spoke in a kindly way.

'Oh, thank you, George,' cried Maisie, knowing that with Georgina's support the battle was almost won.

'But I must go with you to see Madame Vestry,' continued Georgina. 'I can't let you be exploited. I've taken care of you for too long to allow that.'

'Oh, George, darling, I'd be so grateful,' cried Maisie.

So sulkily, Fred had to give in and allow his daughter to have her way.

Dill was very grateful. 'I knew you wouldn't stand in the way of ambition, George,' he said.

Georgina smiled but inside she felt sad. This was the same old problem. All her show life the West End shows had milked her company of young talent. This was an obstacle she would never be able to surmount.

That spring Maisie went out into the wide world, and a few weeks later, Dill followed her.

Rosita had lost all interest in life and was slowly fading. Help had to be arranged in the kitchen every evening, and it was sad now to watch Rosita sitting by the fire staring pathetically into the flames.

'I am really worried, George,' Sam confided in her. 'The old lady seems to have lost heart since the boy got into trouble.'

Georgina nodded sadly. She felt there was little she could do.

She was also preoccupied with other problems. The state of her theatre worried her a lot. Since Dill had left, it had fallen into a state of disrepair, with broken window panes and rotting front doors. Dill had done all that sort of work before he left. 'I do miss Dill,' she said to Solly. 'Who else is going to do jobs like that?'

Solly had his head down over a score. He sniffed and snuffled. 'Then why bother? I thought you were after a new place, George?'

'It's not that easy,' she replied. 'I've still got Owen's money but I can't find out who owns the land I want. That old devil over at the tavern won't tell me and that damned old parson has begun a campaign to prevent me building another place of entertainment. All I ever get is opposition,' she complained.

'Well, well,' said Solly, 'if it's the old skittle alley you want, it belongs to old Mo.'

'Who the hell is that?' she asked.

'He is my grandfather's brother,' said Solly slowly, 'so I fink it makes him me great uncle.'

'Why! You know the owner? You are *related* to him? Oh! Solly, you lovely darling!' Georgina cried impulsively.

Solly grinned with pleasure. He liked to please Georgina.

'Come on,' she cajoled, 'put me in the picture. What is the secret of your background?'

'Nuffink to boast abaht,' mumbled Solly. 'I'm a bastard. Me muvver's family only just managed to accept me. You see, me father was Jew Douglas.'

'The actor?' Georgina was amazed. 'But Jew Douglas was not a real Jew, was he? He just mimicked them. Didn't he come to a sad end?'

Solly nodded. 'Yup. Booze killed him. The family wouldn't let me muvver marry 'im, so she ran off wiv 'im. I was born in a prop basket. Then she died when she was only ei'een. The rough life on the road was jus' too much for 'er.'

Sadness filled Georgina's heart as she suddenly thought of Tinsel, another theatre orphan.

'Funny though,' continued Solly, 'my grandfather took me from the workhouse when I was ten and educated me. It was probably his guilty conscience.'

'This doesn't really surprise me,' said Georgina. 'There was always something very secretive about you. For instance, I often wondered how you got that classical musical education.'

'That's the only bloody thing that did sink in from all the posh schools,' said Solly. 'Then he left me his fortune, the old rogue, but I can't touch a penny till I am twenty-one.'

'Oh, Solly! You mean to tell me that you have an inheritance? How extraordinary!'

'Yes, but I'm not ready to be rich yet. I've got to write songs at the moment.' He quickly diverted the conversation. 'You need a new building, George,' he said, 'before this one collapses about our ears.'

Georgina grinned. 'Well, will you take me to see this relative who owns the skittle alley?'

'I'd be glad to,' said Solly, with a nonchalant shrug.

The next day Georgina went with Solly to a place in the East End to an area of long narrow alleys full of dark little shops, all of which had the star of David over the door. The air was heavy with the smell of garlic. At the end of one of these dark alleys, Solly's great uncle Mo was tracked down. His habitat was a shop which sold and repaired musical instruments. In the small grimy window were exquisitely crafted old violins, penny whistles, flutes and oboes, all jammed tight. Inside the shop it was even more crammed, with a piano, a base fiddle, a set of drums and all the odds and ends of the musical profession.

Old Mo was a hunched little man with a long beard and a little skull cap. He and his great nephew argued in Yiddish for a while. Georgina listened but couldn't understand anything. She wasn't sure if he was friendly or not. At last the men stopped talking and Mo beckoned them into a small back room which was full of dust and cobwebs and some overstuffed old-fashioned furniture.

Now Mo switched to English, but he had a heavy Yiddish accent. 'Yer vant ter see me abaht da shop?'

Georgina was puzzled. She had not come to buy a shop.

Solly immediately realised what she was thinking.

'It's all right, George,' he assured her. 'He means the shop next to the skittle alley. It's all one property. It used to be a Kosher butcher where all the family were brought up. He says he won't sell it. He wants to lease it.' As always, Solly's accent improved dramatically, now that he was confident.

'Nice property,' muttered the old man, '... the shop, the pub and what-yer-me-call it.' He rummaged in a desk full of papers that were yellow with age.

'Ask him what he wants for the freehold, I don't particularly want to lease,' she informed Solly.

The men began to argue once more in Yiddish, hands waving, heads nodding. The dust and the smell were beginning to make even Georgina feel faint. She began to regret having come. Gradually they reverted to English again.

'For a thousand pounds you can have the lot,' Solly told her, 'but only on a long lease.'

'For how long?' she asked.

'Thirty years.'

'But why?' Georgina was puzzled.

'He wants to keep the land in the family. That's the way with Jewish folks.' He handed her a piece of paper. It was a copy of the deeds, with the whole area outlined.

'But I only wanted the skittle alley,' said Georgina. 'There's a shop and the tavern outlined here as well.'

The old man sat in a chair nodding and smiling.

'He won't split it up,' Solly informed her.

'But I've only got five hundred pounds,' she told them.

'You may borrow the rest from him and pay him back with interest,' Solly informed her with a grin.

'No, no decidedly not,' she said firmly. 'I can't afford to get into debt.'

Once more the debate went on in Yiddish, with much gesticulation, shouting and protesting. Then with an even bigger grin, Solly finally said: 'It's all right, George, now. You got me for a partner, if you want me.'

'Now explain it to me in English,' Georgina said rather crossly.

'Get some wine, Uncle Mo, we will make a deal,' said Solly.

The old man shuffled off with his carpet slippers flopping up and down.

'Look here, George,' said Solly, 'he won't split up that property, even if we argue all night. That's why I'm willing to put up the other five and we can be partners.'

'Where will you get that much money?' she asked.

'From my inheritance. Old Mo is the executor of the will. He will give me a loan and then draw it back from the estate with interest.'

The old man had returned with a bottle of wine and three glasses. 'Noice property,' he kept muttering. 'Don't never lose on land. Yer can't split it up but you can lease it a nice long time.'

Solly poured the wine. 'Here's to us, George, and the new theatre,' he toasted.

'Goot, goot,' said the old man. 'Vat, you vant to build an entertainment place? Plenty money in show biz these days.' He nodded approvingly as he sipped the wine. He looked very pleased with his deal.

Georgina was still feeling a little confused by the time they had returned home. She was not at all sure that she needed the entire side of the street facing the Variety but she seemed to have acquired it with considerable ease. Good old Solly.

The acquisition of this land made Georgina's business life considerably more complicated, whereas it had been relatively straightforward before. Previously there had been an unwritten agreement between herself and the two families. She had always handled the business end of the Variety, and kept the books in order with the help of young Wally who worked in the city all week and on the show at the week-ends. Between the two of them they kept accounts, paid out wages and the rest went into a kitty. Now she had several more commitments – money from Owen, and from Solly, as a business partner. And a problem with the tavern she did not yet know about.

The show had flopped since the New Year. Times were bad for everyone except the rich. And they were particularly bad for the theatre world. Recently there had been a series of accidents at other theatres, with several fires and once, a child killed in a rush for seats. For Georgina trouble was coming from *The Stratford Express*, an old enemy, which had begun a series of articles criticising the derelict state of the Variety's building. The bad publicity caused her audience to dwindle. Georgina went around with a worried look as she waited for the final details of her new land deal to be legalised.

The brightly lit gin palace over the road worried her the most. The tavern was inhabited by low-class women thieves and hooligans from the slum streets. They had a tendency to fill up with alcohol at the tavern and then cross the street to the Variety where they would kick up merry hell. Although Georgina had grown used to the regular Saturday night fracas, the thought of actually owning this bar scared her stiff. 'What the devil am I going to do with it?' she asked everyone one night at supper.

Solly was the only one with any bright ideas. 'Chuck him out,' he suggested.

'Chuck who out?'

'The landlord. He owes a year's rent.'

Georgina looked interested. 'Are you sure of that, Solly?'

'Of course I am. He's had notice to quit often enough, but he won't go. That's why old Mo was so anxious to let it.'

'Well, who collects the rent now?' she asked.

'You, if you can get it,' grinned Solly.

'Well, here's a pretty kettle of fish,' she declared. 'Now I'm loaded with old Mo's problems.' She paused for a moment. 'Solly, tell me. What would I do with the gin palace, even if I did manage to chuck the landlord out?'

'Turn it into a music hall,' replied Solly. 'You'd make plenty of money that way, and you could then use the profits to build a good new theatre.'

'Well, I must say, Solly, you are a mine of information,' returned Georgina sarcastically. 'What on earth is a music hall?'

Sarcasm was lost on the eager Solly. He got to his feet and began to describe this new kind of entertainment, waving his large hands as he did so. 'You put on a continuous show while at the same time serving a good supper. No females are allowed in unless accompanied by a gent. That way, you keep out the whores, who cause a lot of trouble. You ban children and you get a big bouncer on the door to keep out the toughs. And you charge plenty money. It's going to be big business.' Solly seemed to be beyond himself with excitement, strutting about up and down as he outlined his plans, and his ideas.

'Calm down!' yelled Georgina. 'Where are these places and who runs them?'

'I know a fella who started with practically nothing, making pots of money,' cried Solly. 'God's truth, I know the geezer.'

'All right, sit down, Solly, and we'll talk about it,' she said kindly.

'It's over the river in Southwark. He's a kind of second cousin to me. He used to own a West End gambling cellar and then he bought this old mission hall dirt cheap. It's also getting very fashionable for the nobs to go to these music halls.'

Georgina was getting interested. She was not going to dismiss his ideas, having already learned that there was more to Solly than met the eye. She asked Fred if he knew anything about this modern form of entertainment. Fred nodded. 'Yes, I've heard of it. They got them all over now, I hear. One fella told me how he earned big money doing one-night stands.'

After that evening, Georgina began to study this new form of show business. First, she paid a visit to Solly's cousin, south of the town. His establishment was a very large restaurant which offered continuous entertainment from singers, jugglers and wrestlers, and comedians with quick lively patter. The place seemed to attract a new kind of audience, particularly well-dressed clerks and young middle-class husbands and their wives out dining with their colleagues. Humour and wine flowed freely and the atmosphere was warm and congenial. A large uniformed man stood at the entrance and only allowed in those who he had vetted. There were no screaming babies, and no blousy hags, and ladies only when accompanied by gentlemen. Georgina was very impressed. She was hooked.

Getting rid of the unpleasant tenant of the tavern was easier than she had imagined. After a little discussion, and a discreet but firm lawyer's letter obtained by Wally from his boss, the negotiations were over.

'Take the flaming place!' the landlord of the tavern snarled. 'It's losing money all the time, and you're welcome to it.'

When the tavern was vacated, it was left in a filthy condition but there was no shortage of volunteers to help clean it up. For a few coins, all the back street children waded in to help Georgina. The bar's former customers complained nastily but then moved up the road to another bar.

Inside the building, the small bars were knocked down and a stage erected. Solly used his contacts and relatives to pull all sorts of strings with caterers, barmen and doormen. After a good coat of paint, the Tiger Tavern was ready in July. It was then that the old Variety closed its doors.

Fred and Moira readily agreed to stay with Georgina.

'I don't mind being in the box office,' said Moira, who was drinking much less lately but had put on a lot of weight. 'I've had my fill of the boards. It's time I took a back seat.'

Sam and Rosita begged to be released. 'I'll take the old lady out to Italy to visit her family,' said Sam. 'That might buck her up.'

Georgina knew it was young Jan that Sam and Rosita were seeking. The rest of their big family had already left them, and gone out into the world, all, that is, except their youngest girl, Winkie. Winkie was very attached to Moira's youngest girl Bubbles and refused to leave with her parents. She and Bubbles planned to go to stage school together and become famous actresses.

After much argument, Sam and Rosita agreed to let Winkie stay in London while they set off.

After so many years of working together, it was painful for everyone when they finally said good-bye. Georgina knew she would miss them terribly.

The Tiger Tavern was an immediate success. A large and talented number of artists, carefully picked by Georgina, performed there and passed through, spreading the tavern's fame world wide. With its ornate red plush seats and checked tablecloths, it became the favourite place of all sorts of people. They loved the singing and entertainment as much as they liked the delicious food – roast beef and fruit pies.

Dressed in immaculate white tie and tails, Georgina was master of ceremonies. She loved it and for the first time since she had entered the profession, money flowed in freely. This she ploughed back into the show, or stowed away for that dream theatre that would one day rise up out of the waste land.

CHAPTER NINETEEN

The Wanderer

Travellers on their way to the coast had to pass over the medieval bridge that crossed the Medway river, in that ancient cathedral town. It is a peaceful place and anyone looking down at the flat muddy banks and the isolated little boats waiting for the strong tide to carry them seaward might have spied a solitary figure sitting beside the river come rain or shine.

The cavalcade of traffic passed over the bridge. The gulls swooped down over his head. The man sat with his easel in front of him, his palette strapped to his wrist. With steady concentration he recreated the busy river scene, often incorporating the beautiful sunset which is so common on the Medway shore.

His face was screwed up at one side, pulled up by a long scar that ran from ear to upper lip but most of the disfigurement was disguised by long curly brown side whiskers. The right hand, to which the palette was strapped, was limp and useless. But with painstaking care, the man applied the paint to the canvas with his left hand to recreate scenes of breathtaking beauty.

From early spring to late autumn Owen Oliver spent his days this way, out in the sweet fresh air and away from the stuffy over-furnished house inhabited by his wife and mother-in-law. When the evening drew in and a chill wind blew up from the river, he slowly packed his equipment. His tall shape was painfully thin, and his shoulders now drooped a little as if the cares of the world rested on them. Then he walked down to the local, where he would spend some time drinking or joining in with the other customers and consuming liquor until he was in a kind of drunken stupor.

At ten o'clock a carriage rattled down the hill. A hefty servant got out, picked up the painting equipment and then hustled Owen into the carriage. Taking him back up the hill, he then helped him into bed.

'Pity about old Owen,' remarked the locals. 'He ain't going to last much longer what with the booze he puts away.'

But Owen was neither old nor incapable. He was just overcome by this addiction which dimmed his fine mind with strong drink.

Katy did not know what to do. She knew that nothing she did would keep him away from the drink. So to ease her conscience, she employed a servant to collect Owen and put him to bed each night. This saved her the embarrassment of having the police knock her up late at night having found her husband asleep half-way up the hill.

This loyal servant was a large, surly man and a member of the newly formed Temperance Society which Katy was now so involved in. Owen was indeed an embarrassment to her. Repeatedly she rebuked her errant husband when he came home smelling so heavily of the evil drink.

She herself was now fatter and fussier than ever. She was also a woman of considerable means since the steamship line had prospered. Her shares in the business had increased threefold with the coming and going of these new ships. And the big office downtown now employed many local people. Yes, these days Katy was an important and affluent figure.

She lived ostentatiously, driving about in a fine carriage and now often accompanied by her cousin Bertie. Katy tried her best to ignore her disreputable husband. She thought that if she took no notice of him, with a bit of luck he might just disappear.

It was strange that Owen stayed on in the house. He had mostly recovered from Jan's attack on him but the sinews in his right wrist had been severed and he was still unable to draw those striking little figures which had made him so famous. So he whiled away the days painting in oils, using his left hand. The paintings were exceedingly well done, but once he had finished one, he simply gave it away or set it aside, having no more interest in it at all.

He seemed to have lost his commissions from Deakins after an unfortunate visit from the great novelist. Deakins arrived at the house on the hill and said, in a rather patronising manner, 'Ah, you must get well, old chap. I've got plenty of work waiting for you.' As he had presented Owen with a copy of his latest novel, Katy bustled into the room and cornered the writer, engaging him in a long conversation about Owen's unacceptable mode of living.

Deakins had been very embarrassed and irritated. He hurried away to return no more.

So, now, in this backwater, Owen remained, stagnating with grief and disappointment and watching with disdain the antics of his rich wife and dragon of a mother-in-law. Mrs Browne still insisted on mourning her late husband, even after three years. Every day she would sweep through the house with long black widow's weeds sailing behind her, an abject look of misery upon her face. Owen could not bear the sight of her.

The one bright spot in his life was Georgina's correspondence. She had kept writing to him all through his illness and the letters still came, full of gossip and excited descriptions of life in the company. She confided in him, and often asked his advice about her new venture, the Tiger Tavern. When her letter arrived each day, he would take it to his room and read it slowly, enjoying every word. Now, Georgina often opened out her heart to him, and they had become as close as they used to be in the old days. She told him of her struggles to keep the families together, of her failure with the younger members of the group, her dislike for this profitable music hall, and her burning desire to build a big new real theatre.

She still had problems. 'I have recently made a new enemy,' she wrote one day. 'The new young editor of the *Express*, is himself a lecherous young devil but he's still determined to close me down. He published supposedly humorous quips regarding my mode of dress and tasteless jokes about whistling women and crowing hens. Goodness knows, I have lived like a holy being all my life. All I care about is my show.'

Owen's heart ached for Georgina. He alone was the one who understood her; he had even shared Tinsel with her.

But Georgina's letters were not always sad. As time went by and the Tiger Tavern progressed, she would relate humorous stories about the colourful characters and the adventures of running the place. Her letters became a mental comfort to him, a stimulant in those long dreary days.

Sometimes he imagined himself escaping this existence, leaving that appalling house, slipping away one night and sailing far away over the sea, as Tom had done.

But it had been a long while since Tom had departed. Tom had found Owen down by the river one day. He was ready to leave, his pack on his shoulder. His brown eyes were full of warmth and friendship. He was no longer the rogue he used to be.

'I've come to say good-bye, Owen,' he said. 'I'm off to the deep sea. There's nothing to keep me here now that Ma has passed on. She died peacefully in her sleep at the beginning of the year, and not so long ago Old Dawg went off to his happy hunting ground.'

The two men shook hands silently. Their friendship was special to both of them. Owen's eyes were filled with tears as he watched Tom's tall figure boarding the small cargo vessel tied up at Sun Pier. He waited until it pulled up anchor and was riding high on the waves. He waved to Tom, who stood on deck, until he could see him no more. It was a sad day for Owen.

Winter came. Snow settled on the hills and ice floated down the river. Owen persisted with his painting. Every day he went down to the bridge to paint the winter scene. When it got dark he would go off to spend the rest of the day and evening in the bar of the Blue Boar. He went there so often, that the locals said he was almost part of the fittings.

One night Owen developed a severe chill which infected his lungs. The rest of that severe winter was spent confined to bed, and he was unable to get any alcohol. Pathetic attempts to make his surly servant bring in a drink failed, so slowly his addiction waned and eventually he dried out. His condition improved.

When spring began to creep over the meadows, Owen was still weak but he was up. He spent many hours staring out of the window and longing to be free. In this time, his wrist had strengthened and slowly he began to draw again – small carica-tures of Katy in a voluminous crinoline, or her mother in black with her beaked nose and trailing gowns.

His mouth was twisted into a grim smile as he worked studiously, filling his sketch-book with images of the people he came across – the fat, fussy little doctor who took snuff, the prim old lawyer, the red-nosed skivvy. Slowly but surely, the great cartoonist was coming back to life.

During that last cold winter the old family lawyer had passed on and his practice had been taken over by his son, an astute, well-educated young man who had inherited a terrific muddle of family affairs. One day with polite decorum he came to visit Owen. Katy and her mother had gone out visiting their friends.

'Pardon me calling on you like this,' the lawyer said, 'but I must have a little confidential talk with you.'

Owen raised a wan face and looked at him coldly. He had little time for this polished young man. 'My wife handles all business affairs,' he said sharply. 'I can't see what you want with me.'

'But I have some personal property belonging to you sir,' he said. 'My father should have returned it, but as you know he was in bad health and his papers got into great disorder.'

Owen suddenly looked interested.

The lawyer handed him a pile of letters. 'These are personal letters but I took the liberty of perusing them. There is one that interested me very much.'

He unfolded a sheet of paper and Owen recognised a copy of the captain's last letter to him.

'As you can see it was the late captain's last letter. In it he mentions a daughter I was not aware of.'

Owen scanned the letter with puzzled brow. At the bottom of the page the captain had written: 'If Georgina should ever return she must share my estate equally with her two sisters.'

Owen nodded. 'Yes, I remember, but why raise the matter now?'

'My father was inclined to be slack, especially since there was very little money at stake then. Captain Browne's estate went to his wife and two remaining daughters – Mary and Katy. But now that the captain's investments have trebled, there is a good amount to be divided and this matter is left in my unexperienced hands. I shall be contacting Mary in Canada but this other daughter, Georgina, is surrounded by secrecy. Your wife and Mrs Browne refuse to discuss her. I wondered if she were dead, or perhaps in an asylum. I'd be grateful if you would put me in the picture.'

'Georgi?' exclaimed Owen. 'Why, she's very much alive,' grinned Owen.

'Can you give me her address?' The lawyer looked excited.

'I would be very pleased to,' grinned Owen. Why, Katy must have pretended that Georgina was dead when Captain Browne's will was settled. He felt most indignant.

After the lawyer had left, he began to chuckle. He walked over to the mirror to examine the scar on his face.

'You'll be all right now, Georgi,' he muttered to his image in the glass. 'As for you, you unsightly mess, it's time you moved on.'

At dawn he stood on the end of Sun Pier dressed in old clothes and carrying a sailor bag over his shoulder. After a few words with the skipper and a quick exchange of money, Owen was welcomed aboard the small boat.

'We sail within minutes,' the captain said.

The wind ruffled his hair as Owen stood on deck and watched the shore slowly disappear. Where he was bound for he did not know, but go he must.

His feelings as he stood there were mixed. He was not yet thirty years old but he felt old and jaded. He was now physically deformed by a long scar which travelled across his mouth to the side of his ear. It gave his face a sneering expression. And when he smiled, his was a sad smile which twisted his face lopsidedly with a look of ironic humour. His sketch-book and pencils and a few sovereigns in his pocket were all he possessed in the world. He had no regrets. He could not have endured one more minute in the company of the patronising Katy and her vitriolic mother. What lay ahead for him he did not know or even care.

The captain put Owen ashore just outside the port of Rotterdam, directing him across miles of waste land lined with dykes where herds of Friesian cows grazed in flat meadows. It was a peaceful and picturesque scene. He dawdled as he walked, watching the large multi-coloured dragonflies darting in and out of the dykes, and the windmills turning their wheels gently in the breeze. At nightfall he slept in a barn and was chased out at daybreak by the farmers' dogs. He walked along wide paths bordered by tulip fields, with their lines and lines of red flowers. Such beauty he had rarely seen. He wandered slowly, making the occasional sketch of a windmill, or a dutch maid carrying two buckets of milk. This one, dressed in a stiff white cap and wooden shoes, had a very friendly smile on her rosy face as she rewarded him with a cool drink.

Early evening he had his first meal in an inn and then moved on through tiny, tidy villages, clusters of houses by canals. Along these waterways were many small boats. Owen sat down to sketch a boat full of children which seemed in danger of sinking. The children seemed quite unconcerned. With their little blonde heads and bright caps, they sat placidly as the boat was steered to the shore by a boy of about eight years. They had no fear of the water, having spent most of their lives on it.

At nightfall, Owen slept under a hedge and awoke in the morning feeling slightly stiff but wonderful and mentally restored. In good spirits, he plodded on. He bought delicious black bread from a village baker and drank water from the pump.

By the end of that day he had reached a small town. He sat down by the quayside to watch the ample barges unload and reload. The men worked at a furious pace in their wide trousers, little peaked caps perched on their heads. He sketched a thick-set hard working *hausfrau* and her blond children on the barge and then made the acquaintance of the skipper who offered to transport him down the river.

All that day Owen lay half-asleep on the sun-baked deck as the long flat barge nosed its way down the wide river. All his cares and worries had left him. It was as if he had been reborn.

At the next large port, in the lovely city of Rheims, the barge anchored once more. Owen said good-bye to the friendly Dutch family and went on his way to explore the beautiful cathedral city with its grand clocks and stained glass windows.

Two days later he had left Rheims and begun the long trek down the main route to Paris. He was unshaven and looked very dishevelled but he pressed on. The pangs of hunger seemed to satisfy his empty soul. His shoes had worn out, his jacket was grubby and his shirt was torn. He was no pretty picture when he finally arrived in the great city of Paris.

All night Owen wandered along the wide boulevards, mingling with the merry throng, Parisians at leisure. At dawn he wandered down to the flower market where the stallholders were busy arranging their colourful blooms. Outside private residences, servants with buckets and brooms hustled him out of their way. He paused outside a large building with posters displayed on the walls. It looked like a place of entertainment. What grabbed Owen's attention was the sight of a cripple, a man with a leg which was just a mutilated stump. He wore threadbare pants held up by a big safety pin. The upper part of this man's body was strong and active as he moved about backwards and forwards over the ground, quickly drawing large pictures on the pavement in coloured chalks. A clumsy wooden crutch was propped up against the wall nearby.

In spite of his weariness, Owen was captivated. He stood silently and watched this man's quick movements and the comical way with which he would rub the chalk into the ground with the ragged stump of his leg. His pictures were of overweight ladies, buxom angels in frothy white clouds, and naked cupids in luscious landscapes.

Suddenly the artist sensed that he was being watched. He paused in his work and, as he squatted on the ground, he looked up at Owen in amusement.

'Christ!' he ejaculated. 'You don't arf look bleeding rough!'

Owen was astounded to hear his own language being spoken. He was so taken aback that he could not force a word through his cracked dry lips.

'Sit dahn afor yer fall dahn,' said the artist, thumping the paving stones with that grotesque stump of a leg.

Weakly, Owen sat down, his back against the warm brick wall, while the artist continued to put the finishing touches to his work. 'Don't look the type to be dahn and out round 'ere,' the cripple muttered.

Owen indicated his sketch-book.

The man smiled wryly. 'Oh, a wandering artist, eh? There's no money in that, there ain't.'

Owen sat staring at his own dirty toes sticking out of his broken shoes.

The other man placed a large floppy cap in front of his work. 'Bet you could do with some grub,' he said. 'I'm just orf to the café. I'll bring back something for you, too. You stay 'ere.' He grabbed his crutch and hobbled off.

Owen was too tired to argue. So in the early morning sun he sat and dozed beside the voluptuous chalk ladies while a trickle of people came forth from the tall surrounding houses on their way to the market. As they passed, they dropped coins into the floppy cap and gazed sympathetically at the ragged figure asleep on the pavement.

The one-legged artist returned half an hour later. He was grinning cheerfully and hopping along with the crutch tucked under his arm. He carried a long loaf of bread and a bottle of wine. He laughed as he grabbed up the coins in the cap. 'Did well,' he said. 'I thought you would, looking in such a shocking state. Tuck in, mate,' he urged Owen, breaking off some bread and thrusting it at him.

The bread and wine tasted delicious to the starved Owen.

Once refreshed, Owen found he could converse with Hoppy Bill, his new friend, as he was called.

'I can't go home,' Hoppy Bill informed Owen, 'I did a bunk from the army. I got fixed up with some French biddy but me leg got infected, so they took it orf. It's no trouble now.' He waved the offending stump under Owen's nose.

'Wounded in battle?' asked Owen.

'No, mate. Bloody sergeant took a pot shot at me as I did a bunk.'

Owen grinned. He liked this man's sense of humour.

'Seeing as you are one of me own countrymen, so to speak,' continued Hoppy Bill, 'and I don't see many poor Englishmen out 'ere, mate, you can muck in with me, if you want to.'

'That's kind of you,' murmured Owen with uncertainty.

'It will be nice to be with me own kind,' said Hoppy Bill. 'Froggies is all ri', but it ain't the same. You sound like a toff, but I don't mind that as long as you pulls your weight.'

It did not take Owen long to decide to join forces with his new friend. There was nothing else he felt like doing. So, in the heat of the afternoon they left the pitch for Hoppy Bill's lodgings to have a siesta. They travelled down a long dark alley to a rough wooden building. The doorway was filled with gossiping women and squabbling children, and sinister-looking men dressed in large checked caps, red chokers and bright shirts.

'Right lots of geezers dahn here,' commented Hoppy Bill, 'but they don't interfere with me, they knows be'er.'

Hoppy Bill's lodgings consisted of one room containing a muddle of artists' brushes, paints and unused canvases. 'I used to share this place with a bloke what painted. But he got his throat slashed one night, poor sod.'

Very tired and rather nervous, Owen collapsed onto the offered couch and slept the sleep of the dead.

He was woken in the evening by Hoppy Bill who now looked very spruce and clean. His hair was brushed flat and he was wearing a red shirt and velvet pants. What astounded Owen was that the unsightly crutch had been discarded and he now limped along on a wooden leg which was covered by his rather natty pants.

'Ah! surprised yer!' exclaimed Hoppy Bill. 'How do I look?'

'Very dandy,' replied Owen.

'Got to look a bit tidy because I go' a nice little fiddle going at night, selling dirty pictures to those damned stupid foreign travellers. I work along the boulevards and the dives along the Left Bank, depends where the business is. Come on, mate, get up,' said Hoppy Bill. 'I've got some togs for you, too.' He produced a cotton shirt and some faded trousers. 'These should fit yer. Yer ain't much bigger than me.'

But Owen was definitely much taller than Hoppy Bill, for the trousers only reached his ankles, though that was the least of his troubles. He washed and ate and felt ready to face the world once more.

Hoppy Bill proved to be the most invigorating company, and all night the two men prowled the boulevards dodging in and out of cafés to avoid the *gendarmes*, and selling their artistic nude pictures, sketched and painted by Bill.

They breakfasted at dawn in a café and then moved on to the pavement pitch outside the theatre to doze again amid the chalk ladies.

CHAPTER TWENTY

A Kept Man

The spring breeze carried the scent of blossoms from the flower market to the theatre pitch where Owen was dutifully sitting. This hand-to-mouth existence had become a way of life for him and he could not now imagine living otherwise. It had been a big night at the café and Hoppy Bill had still not arrived home from his rendezvous with a certain lady.

Dreamily Owen closed his eyes and huddled against the warm brick wall. A carriage drove up and a woman swathed in silk got out and pattered past. The smell of perfume under his nose increased. In his daze, Owen caught a hazy glimpse of high heels and yellow stockings. He heard the chink of a heavy silver coin being dropped into the cap. He smiled nonchalantly, closed his eyes and drifted back to sleep.

Half an hour later, swearing and cursing, Hoppy Bill arrived. He snatched up the silver coin from the cap and spat on it for luck.

'She's back!' he exclaimed. 'I always get a bit of silver when she's in town.' He sank down beside Owen who slurred sleepily.

'Who?'

'You mean to tell me you don't know Madame Sylvia, the singing canary? She's so beautiful she takes your breath away.' Hoppy Bill kissed his fingers with an exaggerated gesture.

'No, I don't,' mumbled Owen.

'She's been out of town to visit her sick husband. He's got consumption, so they say. But Sylvia, she is always the toast of

Paris. And she's one of us,' he added. 'She's English.'

Owen was unconcerned and had already gone back to sleep.

Several days later, that same perfume came wafting by. Owen was a little more alert and he opened one eye to see once again a neat ankle in yellow stockings. As the coin fell into the cap, he looked directly up into the deep-set blue eyes of Tinsel.

She dropped her parasol. 'Owen! My dear!' It was almost as if they had never been parted. Without a moment's hesitation, she threw herself on to him, her tiny shape shrouded in frills and stiffened petticoats.

Passers-by stopped and stared at the astonishing sight of this beautiful little lady cuddling a dirty old beggar on the cold hard ground.

'Come now, love,' Owen whispered. 'Get up, everyone's looking at you.'

Reluctantly, Tinsel released her hold.

Owen got to his feet and placed a gentle arm about her. 'Let's go to the café,' he said.

At a table in a remote corner of the café, Tinsel placed a finger on the angry red scar on Owen's face. 'Oh, darling,' she cried, 'what have they done to you?'

Owen smiled inwardly. She was just the same, his Tinsel, so childish and over-emotional.

'How are you, my love?' he asked quietly. He thought that her small face, so heavily rouged and painted, looked quite tragic.

'I'm married, Owen,' she said. 'I thought you no longer loved me.'

'Oh,' Owen gasped, 'I did, darling, I searched everywhere for you. Wherever did you go?'

'To America, with Monsieur Henri. We had a mesmerist show and he was the master. The show came to grief out there, so he married me to protect me. He's much older than me but so kind and so generous. I owe everything to him.' In that breathless, excitable way, the words poured from her carmined lips.

'I'm so pleased for you, darling,' Owen said kindly but sadly. 'I often worried about how you would fare, out in the cold hard world.'

'Yes, I was lost without you,' she said. 'And no one ever replaced you in my heart.'

'You must not say things like that, love,' urged Owen. 'I'm nothing but a beggar now and you're famous, I hear. You have a grand career ahead of you.'

Tinsel snuggled closer. 'But my darling, Owen, I still belong to you.'

'No, dear, we must not meet again,' he told her patiently. 'Tomorrow I will return to England.'

Tinsel twined her tiny fingers into his and squeezed. 'Tomorrow,' she said coyly, 'you and I will make love just as we used to in our little old camp bed in the house on the corner.'

'No, no, darling, I can't stay,' Owen said, shaking his head. 'I'll destroy the life that you have made such a success of.'

But feelings of passion overwhelmed him as she fixed him with those blue eyes.

'Just one more time, Owen, and I will part from you content.' She looked at him plaintively.

So Owen took that fatal bite of the apple. In the evening he waited for Tinsel after the show. He felt powerless to resist her. He allowed her to take him over entirely. He could not face parting from her again.

And so once more Owen became Tinsel's lover and lazily he accepted his fate. He moved out of Hoppy Bill's room to an apartment rented and paid for by Tinsel.

'Madame Sylvia?' exclaimed Hoppy Bill, when he learned of Owen's plans. 'Why, you lucky tyke! Wish it was me, and her old man with pots of money on 'is way out, too.' He roared with laughter.

Owen shivered. What he was doing seemed so cheap and mercenary.

Before long it was well known that the melancholy Englishman was escorting the petite singer. It was known that the popular entertainer had an ailing husband and it was felt that she was perfectly within her rights to take a lover.

Their love nest was beside the river, an immense and fabulously furnished apartment in an old house. Tiny Tinsel lived according to her husband's income. She enjoyed exotic gowns, expensive meals and now kept a lover. She was much loved in the city and notably generous. Thus Owen became a kept man.

He was not sure if he liked the situation or not. Every month Tinsel disappeared to visit her sick husband in a Swiss clinic. She always returned looking very sad and needing Owen's support more than ever.

Owen could not stand this. 'For God's sake, let's give up this pretence and go home,' he would beg of her.

'No, I will not desert Henri when he needs me most,' Tinsel would retort sharply.

'What will happen if he recovers?' Owen would ask lamely.

'Oh, we'll find a way,' Tinsel would reply confidently.

But Owen was not happy. Weighed down with jealousy, he watched Tinsel's performance in the theatre, night after night, drinking continuously. His disreputable reputation grew.

'Whatever does the canary see in that unmannerly swine?' people would ask. But Owen was still Tinsel's. All the sad love songs were always focused in his direction.

Viciously, Owen hoped that her husband would soon die. But, alas, it seemed with the care and money lavished on him, he was likely to get better.

Owen would often watch Tinsel's little wan face in the mornings, pale, without its make-up, and listen to that dry nervous cough. As always, he worried about her health. But she would never rest.

They lived together for more than a year in this atmosphere of high tension. Then suddenly Owen began to get very bored with it all. As always, when he felt like this, he started to wander the back alleys with his sketchbook, making small live sketches which he gave to Hoppy Bill to sell. Tinsel did not mind at all. She fondled him and said: 'I'm pleased that you are back working, darling. You're so clever. Some day I might let you take care of me again.'

Matters were slowly coming to a head. Owen was back to his old form – careless of his appearance and drinking heavily. Tinsel was very emotional, over-possessive but also flirtatious. Owen got sick of having to push his way through that ring of toffs clamouring for her attention each evening and he began to avoid the theatre and sit by the Seine commiserating with himself instead, pondering on the reason why he never really got much happiness from his love life.

It was here one night that Hoppy Bill found him.

'Blimey, I ain't harf glad I found yer,' he cried. Owen smiled but said nothing.

'Those sketches you gave me,' continued Hoppy Bill, 'they went like hot cakes. I had only one left and along comes this fella ... "Who drew that?" he asked, pointing at the sketch. I pretended not to understand, like, you never can be sure with people, but he gives me a poke with his stick – quite nasty he was.

"You're no Frenchman," he says. "Explain who drew that." Then, cor blimey, he held out a bunch of bank notes. "Find 'im and bring 'im to me," he says. So, mate, what could I do?' said Hoppy Bill apologetically.

Owen looked concerned.

'If it's trouble, mate,' said Hoppy Bill, 'I'll ward him off while you make a bolt for it.'

'What did he look like?' asked Owen quietly.

'Thick-set, flashily dressed. Loud voice.'

Owen sighed. 'It's Forest, a newspaperman. Yes, I'll come and meet him.'

Forest was so glad to see Owen that he almost overwhelmed him. He pumped his arm up and down. 'Why, you old devil!' he shouted. 'Where have you been? Everyone has been searching for you.'

Owen smiled but said nothing.

'Still the same cagey old cuss,' roared Forest. 'When are you coming back? I've got plenty of work for you.'

'Not any more,' said Owen very quietly.

'Get away!' shouted Forest. 'A smart chap like you can't drop out, I won't let you!' He explained that he was in Paris with Deakins, having been on a tour of Italy.

'We'll be in Paris for two months. Now, don't let me lose you again.'

After a few cognacs with his old friend, Owen left the bar and went down to the pavement pitch where Hoppy Bill was putting the finishing touches to his pictures, rubbing in the chalk with his stump of a leg.

Hoppy Bill looked at Owen and said: 'If you're not happy with the canary bird, mate, why don't you come back and live with me?'

Owen stood silent and sad.

'Money ain't everything,' commented Hoppy Bill, 'but once they got the bit in their teeth, like 'orses, they need a lot of handling.' He wiped a smudge of blue chalk from his nose with the back of his hand.

Homesick and very forlorn, Owen listened to Hoppy Bill's

philosophising. 'One bleeding bird now and again is enough for
me,' declared Hoppy Bill, sitting back to admire his latest work
of art.

When Owen went home to the apartment, he discovered
that Tinsel had gone away again to visit her sick husband who
was now in hospital just outside Paris.

'I may bring him home,' she had said earlier. 'He's very ill
and he wants to die at home. I shall stop work and nurse him.
He's so very tired of those blood-sucking doctors.'

Owen had looked at her in dismay. The more he thought
about the situation the sicker he became at this sordid business
of waiting for the other man to die. He loved Tinsel and could
not live without her, but slowly she was destroying him, even
as Katy had done.

Within weeks, Tinsel had kept to her word. She left the
stage and retired to her own home, a large château on the other
side of town, arriving now and then at the apartment ready and
eager for love, but looking wan and tired.

With Tinsel's good nursing, her husband made a miraculous
recovery, and they even appeared in public together. He was a
thin elderly gentleman who walked with the aid of a stick.

This event was more than Owen could bear. Immediately,
he began to make plans to return to England. But first he spent
a night on the town with Forest and his former literary pals.
They went to the opera where Deakins appeared with his very
young mistress.

Then, drunk and bedraggled, Owen went home to the apartment where he prowled around like a caged tiger, haunted by
Tinsel's elusive perfume. Although he had begun to avoid
seeing her, preparing for his departure, everything about the
place reminded him of her. She was everywhere, in every dark
corner. He could hear her high-pitched giggle, see the glint of
her golden hair. He could take it no more. At dawn he went
down to the railway station to await the first train out to take
him to Calais. As he waited he stood idly in the shadows
watching, and taking in the general excitement of the
travellers, the nursemaids with the long string of children, the
pet pug dogs that were so popular, red-faced matrons arguing
with porters, and the wide-skirted damsels with their boxes and
baggages.

To his surprise, he saw Deakins and Forest climb aboard the

train but he kept well out of sight. He did not want to converse
with them. Then almost as the train pulled out, Owen jumped
aboard, travelling in a windowless compartment full of large
Parisian women with wide wicker baskets of bread, sausages
and cheese – the noisy French all off to the coast.

The Channel crossing was very stormy and unpleasant with
passengers in all classes retching and vomiting. It was such a
relief to reach Dover and to step on dry land again.

When he reached Dover, Owen climbed on to the London
train and sat slumped in a first-class compartment. The train
pulled out and was just beginning to get up steam and move
when Owen suddenly smelled a perfume which penetrated his
brain with nostalgic sorrows, How he longed for the touch of
Tinsel!

Then, astonishingly, there she was beside him, breathless
and excited, and wrapped in black fox fur. Her fair hair was
uncovered and very untidy.

'Oh, Owen!' she gasped. 'I thought I'd never catch you up.
On the boat I felt too ill to look for you so I knew that my only
chance was on the train.'

As the train gathered speed they swept into a passionate
embrace.

'My husband is dead. I couldn't save him. Now I really
belong to you,' said Tinsel. 'I just couldn't believe it when
Hoppy Bill told me that you had left for England.'

Choked with emotion, Owen stared down at his hands. He
couldn't even explain.

'You're a very naughty boy.' Her tiny hand smoothed his
brow. 'Don't look so worried, darling,' she purred. 'You and I
will be together for a while now, and we will find great happiness.'

'No,' said Owen firmly, shaking his head. 'It must be
forever. I will make Katy divorce me,' he declared passionately.

Tinsel put her head on his shoulder. Her face had become
distraught. 'No, Owen. No rash decisions, please,' she begged.
'My life is not a long one, my lungs are also infected.'

Owen pulled her to him and held her tight as fear almost
distracted him.

'It seems,' Tinsel explained, 'that my lungs have never been
healthy. It's quite possible that it was I who transmitted that

infection to my own poor husband ...'

Owen held her close.

'Aren't you afraid of me, darling?' she asked.

'Oh, my God, don't say such things!' Owen cried. 'I'll get you well, my darling. We will build a house high up on the Medway where the air is fresh and clean. I'll work hard for you, my darling, and I'll give up the drinking.'

Tinsel sighed and snuggled close. 'Just let us be together, Owen, that's all I ask.' Two bright spots of colour had appeared on the cheeks of her unusually pale face.

As the fast express rattled its way through the Kentish hop fields and over the wide Weald towards London, it swayed from side to side. Tinsel clutched Owen's arm nervously.

He smiled warmly. 'There's nothing to worry about, darling,' he reassured her. 'We're just crossing the ...'

He never finished the sentence. Suddenly there was a horrible grinding screech as the wheels of the train left the track. As the carriage mounted high in the air and crashed down again, Owen held Tinsel tight. They tumbled around together, her shrill screams piercing his ears as the débris from the wreck pinned them down tight in each other's arms ...

As the sun went down over the Weald of Kent, its blood-red rays lit up the early train disaster. Human bodies lay all along the rail tracks, ignored, as the rescuers tried desperately to release those who were still alive and trapped in the wreckage.

The famous novelist Deakins and his stocky friend Forest were among the unscathed survivors who were doing their best to give comfort and aid to the wounded and shocked people. Forest was just wiping his hands when the rescue squad brought out from the wreckage two bodies tightly wrapped around each other. He recognised the long thin man immediately. It was Owen Oliver, with a tiny little lady whose golden hair hung down in a long mane as they were carried out and laid on the blood-stained ground.

'Good God!' cried Forest hoarsely.

'Why, it's my old illustrator,' declared Deakins.

'Poor devil. I wonder who the lady is?'

'She's dead,' said the doctor. 'But the man lives. We'll get him to hospital.'

Three weeks later, with his head still bandaged, Owen stood beside a newly covered grave in the old church yard at

Halstow in the shadow of the ruined Norman Castle. The only other mourner there was Georgina, looking a little stouter and mature. The two of them stood in silence looking down at the grave of their lost love – the tiny, sweet-singing Tinsel.

After a while Georgina made a weak attempt to console Owen. 'I know how you loved her,' she said, 'and so did I in a different way.' She placed her hand softly on his.

Owen lifted his lined face and looked directly into her eyes. 'How strange, Georgi, I suddenly feel at peace, as though she's living within me.'

Georgina closed her hand over his. 'Will you come back with me or return to Katy? It's for you to decide.'

'With you, Georgi,' Owen replied without any hesitation. 'There's nothing left for me here except Tinsel's grave.'

Together they walked slowly from the churchyard. As they walked under the old yew tree by the gate, Owen imagined the headstone he wanted for his love. All it would say was: 'To Tinsel of this parish, who gave only happiness in her short life.'

CHAPTER TWENTY-ONE

The Finale

After Tinsel's death, Owen's personality changed completely. Gone was his desire to drown his sorrows in alcoholic liquor. From drinking to excess, he began only to drink occasionally. Georgina was his constant companion and he her right-hand man.

There were no more drunken days or weeks when he was incapable of any sort of work. Now his creative efforts turned more in the direction of the theatre. He painted scenery and did lightning sketches of the members of the audience at the Tiger Tavern, a much more affluent gathering, which proved most profitable.

Georgina was still always busy and unable to relax. She worked hard at the music hall, of course, but her main interest and ambition were centred on that brand new building being erected on the land she had leased from old Mo. For the last few years, Georgina had poured all her resources (including her inheritance, which she had finally received) into the building of her dreams. In spite of the set-backs and opposition, the project was now well under way. The building, with its green dome and ornate facade, was gradually becoming a reality.

More than five years had passed since the tragic railway accident and now, installed in that rural churchyard in Kent, was a large memorial, a white marble angel with outstretched wings in memory of Tinsel, Owen's lost love.

Owen still cut a tall figure with his mop of now prematurely

229

snow-white hair at most first nights in London. Sometimes he was accompanied by Georgina, always dressed in a dress suit, white tie, and top hat. She still wore men's clothes, regardless with the passing years. It was as if she had forgotten she had ever been born a female.

She and Owen still lived in the house on the corner in Stratford. There the attics were still a refuge for out-of-work or homeless professionals. Many people in the acting profession who had made it good always remembered that first hand-out and the lodgings at the top of the house on the corner.

Downstairs, their own apartments were now well furnished, the doorstep was white and the brass knocker shone.

Fred Dillon had passed on and Moira had returned to her home in Ireland. Their lovely family was now universally acclaimed in the world of entertainment. The talented red-haired Maisie was in a light operatic show – a new thing in America. She was star of the show which was directed by her big brother Dill and she sang the popular songs written by that new genius, Solly Finklestein.

Solly had now reached his majority, and received the capital from his legacy. It was not long before they heard that Maisie had married him.

The dancing stage sisters, Bubbles Dillon and Winkie Silver, now toured the world with their clever act of dancing and impersonations.

Only Wally had not conformed. He married his boss's daughter and now had a flourishing practice as a solicitor, handling the majority of the family affairs.

So all the young Dillons and the young Silvers had made it good – those grubby little children who had worked since they could walk in the backstage wooden booth theatre.

Sam and Rosita were still together, working hard in their little restaurant on the Italian–French border. In the evenings, when Georgina sat browsing through her correspondence, her mind would revert to the old days, driving the old wagon as the sun shone down on the children on the tailboard singing their heads off. Yes, she would agree with Owen, they were good old days.

Puffing on his pipe, Owen would smile dreamily as he recalled Tinsel's golden head resting on his shoulder. He could almost hear her sweet voice demanding some favour from him that he would not refuse. Now he felt he really had peace at last. Never before had he felt so secure. Katy had finally stopped persecuting him for, after her mother died, she had gone off to live with her sister Mary in Canada. So now there was just Georgina and himself, and their interest in the theatre. He was indeed very happy and content, something that had always eluded him in his youth.

Every day they went together to inspect the progress of the new building. Its progress seemed to have slowed down again and Georgina was in constant battle with the builders.

'You know, Owen,' Georgina remarked one evening, while puffing thoughtfully on a long black cigar, 'I sometimes get the feeling that I'm never going to get this new theatre finished.'

'Goodness gracious!' cried Owen, amazed at her unusual despondency. 'Why not, Georgi?'

'Because we're certainly not getting any younger and my capital is running out. When the theatre is finally completed, I doubt if I'll have enough money left to float a decent show.'

'Well, we'll just have to fish around for backers,' he told her.

Georgina shrugged. 'Don't forget that I have two powerful enemies – the local press and the church – and anyone I know with that kind of money seems to be of the opinion that a straight show will not be profitable in this run-down district.'

'Well they could be right,' replied Owen tactlessly.

Georgina frowned. 'I'm not quite beaten yet,' she said. 'There's still Solly. And now he's part of the family. I'll send Wally to America to talk with him in person.'

'Well, that's certainly an idea,' said Owen timidly.

'It's a bloody good idea!' cried Georgina. 'I'll make it a family affair. That's how it started, so that is how it will succeed, a combination, with all the Dillons and the Silvers ... and Solly's money.'

So that winter, the enterprising young Walter Silver and his young wife set off to America on a new fangled passenger liner, to meet up with his famous sister, Maisie, and her new husband. In his briefcase he carried a long letter from Georgina, stating her intentions. Meanwhile, Georgina and Owen waited in London for an answer.

One winter evening Owen sat waiting for Georgina to arrive home from the Tiger Tavern where she still compèred the show several times a week. He had cooked a tasty supper and polished the glasses. The whisky decanter was full and ready for her. But now it was almost midnight and there was still no sign of her. He looked anxiously out of the window at the yellow fog that was now swirling about outside and obscuring his view of the tavern. At one o'clock, feeling extremely worried, he walked down to the tavern. It was closed and in darkness. Not a soul in sight. Where was Georgi?

'Georgi!' he called. 'Are you there?'

Suddenly over from the building site a stentorian voice replied: 'Here I am, Owen! A plank has fallen on me and trapped my leg.'

Owen ran over the road to find Georgina all muddy and very subdued, lying under the building rubble. A heap of bricks and some long planks had collapsed on top of her.

'Lie still. I'll get help,' cried Owen, dashing off to the doctor who lived further down the street.

Soon Georgina was in splints at the local hospital. Her leg was broken and her back dislocated.

'Walking around the site at night was a damned silly thing to do,' said Owen.

'Oh, be quiet!' snapped Georgina. 'It could have been worse.'

After a few weeks Georgina was back in action, stumping about the stage on her stiff leg and making jokes about it. She was not easily defeated. But the broken bones did not knit easily or the muscles in her back heal quickly. Owen felt sad every time he saw the tough Georgina wince in pain.

It was the beginning of the end of Georgina's active life. No longer could she leap up on the stage and do the splits or turn cartwheels to distract a restless audience. It was sad. Soon a new manager was hired for the shows at the tavern and Georgina now spent all her evenings sitting by the fire with Owen.

Then one spring day the house on the corner was tense with excitement. The steps were whitened and the knocker highly polished. The curtains were renewed and an army of workers laid the tables in the rehearsal room for the evening celebration supper. All the Dillons and Silvers were coming back, back to the house on the corner to discuss the opening of the new theatre. For at last, Georgina's dream had come true. The theatre was finished.

It was a grand do in the rehearsal room that night. There was the affluent Maisie – rather plump but still lovely – her rich clever husband, Solly, who had changed very little. He still sniffed and squinted and gazed out at the world with a look of sardonic humour. The biggest surprise for Owen and Georgina had been the marriage between Dill and tiny little Winkie Silver. This ceremony on the liner coming over had now united the two families.

Georgina was overjoyed. These were the only real family she knew. There was happy, laughing Bubbles with her friend, a sexy American actor. And Wally with his posh wife and brood of children and, best of all, Moira, very large and rather blowsy but still good to look at. Her rich Irish voice was sheer music to Georgina's ear. Later in the evening the orchestra boys arrived after their West End show – Charlie, Bobby and Sonny, those enterprising musicians. For Georgina, it felt like her greatest night. All those years of effort had paid off.

'Tonight,' she said, 'we will celebrate and tomorrow we will get down to business.'

And celebrate they did until the early hours. Show business tales were swapped, they danced, and Maisie and her mother sang duets in fine strong tones. Yes, when the Dillons and Silvers returned to the house on the corner it was a night to remember.

The next morning, they were all back at work. Maisie toured agents, and Solly went down to the East End to settle finances with his host of relatives. Solly's intention was to buy up the various rundown places of entertainment and give them a new face lift. This he did very successfully, and within weeks a kind of theatrical syndicate had been formed.

Owen and Georgina were now only part of the family company and both rather glad to be able to relax as the younger generation went on with their careers.

Of late Owen had begun to paint holy pictures. And in each one, every madonna, every angel, had a face just like Tinsel's. This hobby was a source of amusement to the youngsters but proved extremely worrying to Georgina who was a strict nonbeliever.

'Why don't you get back to your pen and pencil sketches, Owen?' she said. 'You could still make a good living for the newspapers.'

Soberly Owen shook his head. 'No, I'm quite content, Georgi, I don't need the money. In any case, you can't take it with you,' he added quietly.

'Why? Where on earth are you going now?' asked Georgina, with some irritation. It seemed to the still-energetic Georgina that Owen had slowed down well before nature intended. But he only smiled and continued painting. After the physical and mental hardships he had suffered in early life he now seemed to radiate a resigned peace. He had come to terms with his fate at last.

The next few weeks Georgina saw little of him as he was very busy with the last minute details for the grand new theatre opening. At last, the council had passed the building as correct to all specifications and she had secured a new play called *The Cardinal* to perform. She also had a great cast. Thrilled and excited, she pottered about here and there on her silver-knobbed cane. It was not long now before the first night, when all the town would be there.

Georgina lay awake one night, unable to sleep. There was so much on her mind. Then, going out to get a glass of water, she noticed the light still on in Owen's studio.

'Pack up working and get to bed, Owen,' she yelled.

There was no reply.

Impatiently, she pushed open the door of the same little room where she had first discovered Tinsel in bed with Owen all those years ago. Owen was sitting with his back towards her, leaning back as if to admire the portrait of a lovely white angel which he had just completed.

'Whatever is that, Owen?' she demanded as she stepped forward to examine the picture.

But there was still no answer. The hand that still held the brush was stiff and cold. Owen had departed this world, gone to join his lovely angel, Tinsel. He had gone peacefully, without any pain or farewell.

Georgina sank to her knees and sobbed loudly for the loss of her friend. Owen had been a man of such talent, talent which was recognised but which he never fully put to use. Although his final years had been fairly productive, Georgina had always felt that Owen failed to fulfil his early promise. Something inside him had prevented him, had pulled him back, had made him self-destructive with his drinking and depression.

But he had in his time done some very fine sketches and his illustrations to Deakins' books would survive him as monuments to his brilliance.

Georgina sniffed and let the tears of sorrow slip down her cheeks. Owen had always been an outsider and had recognised the same characteristics in her. He had been a good and loyal friend to her for many years. She was going to miss him terribly but she felt united with him in their everlasting love for the golden child Tinsel.

Life would go on. Her theatre would open with the new play. Owen would not be there beside her but she knew, nonbeliever though she was, that he would be there beside her in spirit.